HOUSEWIFE ON TOP

ALISON PENTON HARPER lives in rural Northampton-shire with her husband and two daughters. In 2004, watching *Richard & Judy* while in bed with the flu, she learned about the 'How to Get Published' competition that Amanda Ross, Cactus TV's Executive Producer, was running with Pan Macmillan. Inspired to write, Alison's debut, *Housewife Down*, became one of the five finalists and was published in 2005. Her second novel, *Housewife Up*, was published a year later. This is her third book in the *Housewife . . .* series.

Also by Alison Penton Harper

HOUSEWIFE DOWN

HOUSEWIFE UP

ALISON PENTON HARPER

HOUSEWIFE ON TOP

PAN BOOKS

First published 2007 by Pan Books

This edition published 2013 by Pan Books
an imprint of Pan Macmillan, a division of Macmillan Publishers Limited
Pan Macmillan, 20 New Wharf Road, London N1 9RR
Basingstoke and Oxford
Associated companies throughout the world
www.panmacmillan.com

ISBN 978-1-4472-6182-7

A CIP catalogue record for this book is available from
the British Library.

Typeset by SetSystems Ltd, Saffron Walden, Essex

Visit www.panmacmillan.com to read more about all our books
and to buy them. You will also find features, author interviews and
news of any author events, and you can sign up for e-newsletters
so that you're always first to hear about our new releases.

For Violet and Scarlet,
the colours of my world

THE CAST

If you've just tuned in, here's a quick Who's Who
to help you navigate my strange world.

Me (the Merry Widow)
Helen Robbins, professional housewife,
not quite over the hill.

Julia
My big sister, married to the delectable David.
Wildly successful, long overdue for a breakdown.

Sara
Julia's rottweiler protégée and all-round super-friend.
Currently trying to adjust to married life.
She has a law degree, you know.

Leoni
Best friend, shackled to three kids, married to Marcus.
Killing him slowly on a high cholesterol diet.

Rick
My boss. Much married.
Incapable of looking after himself.
Good for unexpected pay rises.

Helga
Rick's cleaning lady. Russian.
Barking mad. Possibly dangerous.

Sally and Paul
My upstairs neighbours. Highly decorative.
Camp as a row of Cath Kidston tents.

Christmas is coming,
The goose is getting nervous.

Chapter One

ONLY 2,638 SHOPPING HOURS TO GO

'THANK GOD YOU'RE IN.' Leoni barged past me into the flat, almost knocking me to the carpet. 'I'm having the most hideous morning ever and I need somewhere to sit down and calm my tattered nerves.' She shook her head savagely and ploughed through to my kitchen, blindly stepping over the two bulging grocery bags I hadn't yet unpacked, and reached for the kettle. 'Un-bloody-believable. And you know what?' She tapped her foot angrily on the floor. 'I blame the government.' I returned her knowing look, keen to join in with today's hot topic. 'I'm going to write to those tossers in Downing Street and tell them exactly what they can do with their child-friendly policies. It's no wonder kids turn out the way they do these days.' The kettle bubbled its agreement. 'It's all want, want, want.'

She paused for breath and threw me a withering stare. I spotted my chance to get a word in edgeways, although it isn't always a good idea. 'What's up?'

'Up? I'll bloody tell you what's up. It's the second week of September, you can't buy a school shirt any-where for love nor money and they've stuck all the Christmas stuff out in the shops.' Leoni hurled a couple of defenceless teabags into the pot. 'It's a bloody conspiracy, that's what it is. Just when you think you might finally get a bit of peace and quiet with the free-loaders back at school, every supermarket in the land starts issuing stern reminders that you are about to enter the Twiglet zone.' Leoni's sigh hung heavily on the air. 'I dunno. It's an utter disgrace. Shame on them. Got any biscuits?' I pointed to one of the bags on the floor. She up-ended it on the worktop sending the contents rolling across the granite surface, sifted through the provisions and settled on a double box of Jaffa Cakes. 'Just what the doctor ordered,' she pro-nounced with a bitter smile. Plonking herself down on one of the kitchen stools, she tore the packet open and tipped a whole sleeve of them next to her mug.

'It's outrageous,' I agreed. (Discretion is always the better part of valour with Leoni and only a fool would have said anything else.) 'But it's ages away,' I patted her hand and bravely snuck away a couple of her Jaffa Cakes, 'so you don't need to get yourself all het up about it just yet.'

'Too late,' she said, then started sniggering. 'I had a right old ding-dong with the manager in the big Tesco up the road from us. He gave me the usual guff about "early availability of seasonal goods for our customers", but I wasn't having any of it. I've had words with him before and the only way to get your point across to a senior grocery upstart is to brazen it out and go full volume.'

'Well, good for you.' I know I shouldn't encourage her, but the reserved part of me lived vicariously through Leoni's crusading vitriol. Gordon Ramsay's got nothing on that woman.

'I told him that I could hardly send my sons to school dressed in a giant pannetone, could I? And what bloody use is a flashing reindeer head when what his customers *really* need right now is a multi-pack of drip-dry Aertex PE tops?' Leoni half-closed her eyes against the steam rising from her tea and attempted a couple of noisy sips. 'You should've seen me,' she glanced up momentarily. 'Loads of people stopped to watch and I got the distinct feeling that I was speaking on behalf of every mother in the country. Cheeky little bastard said

that most of their customers buy all their school sup-
plies before the start of term, not after, so I left my
trolley right there in front of him and marched out.'
I made sure to look suitably impressed by her act
of rebellion. She put another (whole) Jaffa Cake in
her mouth and raised her mug towards me. 'So,' she
mumbled, 'what's new with you?'

'Nothing much,' I shrugged. 'There's a mouse in
here somewhere. I came in to put the kettle on yesterday morning and there it was, bold as brass, sitting in
the middle of the kitchen floor.'

'No!' She was aghast. I nodded, oh yes.

'We both did something of a double-take, then it
weighed up the odds and squashed itself under that
cupboard.' I pointed to the one that holds all the pots
and pans.

'That's bad news, Helen. I mean, really bad,' Leoni
said, pulling her feet up onto the crossbar on the stool
and nervously looking around the floor. 'The trouble
with thinking you've got a mouse is the distinct proba-
bility that you actually have an entire army of them
squatting in the corner behind the fixed units. I should
bloody know. The kids found one in our utility last
year and started feeding it picnic eggs. Turned out to
be a Trojan horse. By the time we realized and Marcus
put a load of traps down they were going off like
sodding popcorn. It was carnage.' She shuddered. 'If I
were you I'd call the council in.'

'No need,' I said, rummaging in the other shopping bag on the floor. 'I've got a humane trap.' I found the box and took it out of the bag to show her. 'You just pop it down, the mouse runs in and can't get out, then you take it outside and release it in the garden. No harm done.'

Leoni barely gave the contraption a glance. 'If it doesn't result in a corpse, forget it. You're wasting your time. You do realize they breed every six hours?'

'I don't like killing things.'

'And I expect you'll take it to the vet's for a once-over and send it for a Swedish massage before you set it free.' She rolled her eyes at me. 'Just sling a load of poison down and be done with it, you mad woman. I'd have brought some over with me if I'd known.'

'Leoni!' I gasped. 'You shouldn't have things like that in the house with the children around! One of them might get hold of it and, well, heaven only knows what could happen.'

'Not unless my luck changes.' She finished her tea with a noisy swallow and pulled out the second sheath of Jaffa Cakes. 'I feel a bit better now. Sorry to burst in on you like that. I think I might be a bit hormonal.'

'You're more than welcome.' I said. 'Any time.'

'December is the worst month of my life, every year, without fail,' she said. 'And I've just had an in-yer-face warning shot that it's less than three months away. It'll come round before I know it.' I smiled sympathetically and sat myself on the stool beside her. 'I'm not being horrible' – she was clearly about to say something deeply offensive so I braced myself – 'and I know it's not your fault that you haven't got any kids.'

'Or a husband,' I offered.

'Yeah, whatever, we all hated him anyway. But you have no idea what it's like to deal with a growing family at Christmas time. Honestly, Helen. You should count your blessings. It's a living hell. If everything's not perfect it's all your fault. Everyone thinks the whole thing happens as if by magic. I always end up having to do absolutely everything myself while Marcus lies around and limbers up with fifteen tons of mixed nuts. Fanny Cradock declared Christmas "slave labour for women" on national TV years ago. She was a woman ahead of her time, though I still reckon she was a man in drag.' Leoni crammed a tenth Jaffa Cake in her mouth and appeared to doze off for a moment before clearing her palate sufficiently to come back at me with a second wave of complaints. 'You know, I even have to anticipate who might or might not turn up on the bloody doorstep and have a few extra presents at the ready, just in case. Last year our old next-door neighbours from Fulham just bowled over without so much as a phone call. When they left empty-handed, I found out that I had been dubbed Scrooge by their kids.' Leoni tossed her head around in annoyance. 'How bloody unfair is that? I'm seriously thinking of crossing them off my card list and sending them a load of dog shit in the post instead.' She would as well.

'Why don't you get Marcus to give you a hand this time around?' Even as the words tumbled from my mouth I could see the ridiculous nature of my suggestion.

'Excuse me?' she said incredulously. 'Marcus? Help? Are we talking about the same man here?' She sighed and leaned her head on her hands. 'I fucking hate Christmas.'

And so it begins, the season of good grief to all women.

Stollen, Leoni Style

Cut pieces of shop-bought stollen
into bite-size chunks.

Steep in equal (huge) measures
of sloe gin and brandy.

Keep in an airtight Tupperware
container marked 'poison'.

Secretly pop into your mouth
at regular intervals.

Chapter Two

HE'S BEHIND YOU!
(OH NO, HE ISN'T)

IT'S BEEN A WHILE since I've been let loose on the roads. Although I have no intention of becoming a car owner again (heaven knows it's the quickest way to burn money, what with petrol costing slightly more than caviar these days), I do miss that sense of freedom. Just being able to jump behind the wheel and take off whenever you fancy, hitting the road at a heart-stopping fifty miles an hour. Moderate, yes, but I have always believed that I was a woman built for style rather than speed. My itchy feet demanded that I throw caution to the wind, so I dusted off my driver's licence and treated myself to a little weekend frivolity.

'Good morning!' I greeted the woman behind the service desk with my most insurable smile. She raised her eyes from the gossip magazine she was scrutinizing to reveal a faceful of vibrant make-up. Vivid blue eyeshadow clashed with not quite matching mascara. Her bright fuchsia lipstick had bled into little rivulets pointing upwards towards her pinched, powdered nose. Golly. Maintaining that lot must be a mini-career all of its own.

'Can I help you?' She weighed me up for a minute then returned my smile to flash a set of heavily tobacco-stained teeth.

'Yes. I rang yesterday to book a car for the weekend? The name's Robbins. Helen Robbins.'

She ran a lilac frosted acrylic up and down her list.

'Ah yes. Here you are,' she said. 'We've got a nice little jeepy number for you.' I felt a ripple of excitement. 'Would you mind just filling these in for me?' She set a couple of yellow forms on the counter and handed me a chewed biro. 'And if you could let me have your driver's licence please.' I was already tearing it from my handbag.

Formalities over, I was soon perched eagerly in the vehicle on the forecourt, nodding impatiently while the painted lady pointed out the controls and wondering how long it would take me to hit the nearest unclogged road. 'Yep, great, thanks,' I said, my eyes never leaving the keys hooked over her taloned index finger. At last, she placed them in my hand and got out of the car. I turned the ignition over sensibly, resisted the urge to rev the engine wildly, gave the lady a courteous wave and kangarooed to the exit without glancing back. That's the thing with driving an unknown vehicle. It's a very intimate relationship, you and your car. You get to know all its idiosyncrasies and both of you eventually learn to make allowances for each other like any generous couple would.

A mile or so down the road it all started to fall back into place. Smooth gear changes, not putting the windscreen wipers on full pelt when you actually meant to indicate left, managing to get the seat into a less dangerous position while waiting at the traffic lights. I had a close call a couple of hundred yards from the garage when I went to hit the brake at a zebra crossing and stamped on the accelerator instead. Thank God he wasn't a pensioner.

After crawling through a five-mile bottleneck (and the traffic was relatively good that day by London standards), I saw the sign I had been waiting for. A glorious round white circle with a diagonal black strip running through it. *National speed limit applies*, if my recollection of the Highway Code serves me correctly. In other words, step on it and keep your eyes peeled for speed cameras. I filled my lungs with a deep breath of air, turned Radio 2 up full blast, pressed the pedal to the metal and waited to be flung back in my seat. Bracing myself for the surge of power, I realized within three seconds that I had been fobbed off with a gutless Dinky toy. The engine whined like a clapped-out Singer sewing machine and I watched incredulously as the speedometer (yeah, right) groaned slowly from thirty-five to forty, then to fifty before begging to change down and finally lumbering towards a deafening sixty miles an hour. I can only liken the crushing disappointment to bagging the good-looking doctor off *ER* as your new boyfriend then discovering he has, well, let's just say an inadequate stethoscope.

I eased off the gas, stuck it in fifth and set aside my plans for a Stirling Moss re-enactment. Probably no bad thing. I'd rather turn up a little late than find myself wrapped around a tree next to a roadside burger van, so I trundled along quite happily after a while and bonded with my weekend escort. We forgave each other's shortcomings and by the time I rattled up Leoni's drive, I was well and truly smitten. Leoni's face appeared at the bay window. She opened her front door moments later and dashed out to greet me.

'Got a new car?' she squealed, running up and jumping in the passenger seat beside me.

'No,' I said. 'I just fancied having a drive so I rented one for the weekend. It's going back tomorrow. I expect I will have had enough of it by then.'

'Cor! It's really nice.' She ran her hands along the dashboard and started playing with the controls. 'I've been on at Marcus that I need a new car. I don't know how he expects me to keep driving around in that old banger. Bloody thing. It's stinks of old socks on the inside. I'd like to see him try and cope with it for a while, but oh no – ' she pulled a face and waggled her head from side to side – 'he's got to have a new car every two years because he goes to work, you know.'

She looked like she was just getting warmed up for another Why I Hate Marcus session, so I turned the engine off and stepped out of the car. 'Come on,' I urged her. 'Get your kettle on. I've got some good news for you.'

The kitchen smelled of the freshly laundered sheets she had draped over most of the available furniture, the tumble-dryer being on the blink. 'Today is your lucky day,' I announced, pulling up a seat at the messy table while Leoni poured the tea. 'I've been thinking about what you said about the run-up to Christmas being your worst nightmare.'

'Oh yes?' She set her cup down and reached for the biscuit tin again, fishing out a Jammie Dodger and nibbling her way around the edges.

'I was lying in the bath imagining all the things that you have to do and, frankly, my brain started to hurt.'

'Too right,' she mumbled. 'I might even have mine removed this year.'

'It sounds to me like what you could really do with is an extra pair of hands. You know, split the jobs up and recruit a bit of help.'

Leoni twisted the biscuit around, evenly creeping further towards the sticky red heart in the middle. 'Go on,' she mumbled.

'So I'm volunteering my services to do whatever you need between now and the big day.'

Leoni stopped eating. 'Really?' she asked quietly. 'Do you mean it?'

I nodded earnestly and pictured myself running around after my own little imaginary brood the way I had dreamed for three consecutive nights the week before. Helping them to write their cards. Queuing up outside Hamleys for that year's must-have toys. Making little mince pies and stocking the freezer with social niceties. Leoni interrupted my thoughts. 'I honestly don't think you know what you're letting yourself in for.'

'Then it's about time I found out, isn't it?' I said. 'So yes, really, I do mean it. This year I want you to be able to enjoy your Christmas instead of letting it push you to the brink of insanity. Just let me know what you need and I'm all yours.'

Leoni leapt from her chair and threw her arms around me. 'You're a real pal, Helen! I do love you, you know.' She offered me the middle of her Dodger. I raised my palm in polite refusal. She shrugged her shoulders, dropped it in her mouth, went to the kitchen drawer and took out a pad and pen.

'Shall we write a list?' she suggested, clearing her mouth and licking the crumbs from her fingers.

'Good idea,' I concurred, feeling all efficient.

'Then we can make bullet points and get Marcus to put it on a PowerPoint presentation.'

The list-writing exercise began with a lot of umming and ahhing from Leoni. She paced around the kitchen a lot, sat down now and again, drummed her fingers on the table and kept trying to change the subject. Attempting to keep her on track was simply hopeless and she finally confessed that she had stopped writing lists years ago because they would either induce terrible panic attacks or fill her with fury, depending on the time of the month.

'I can't do it,' she groaned, slumping across the table in defeat. 'If you write it all down it just looks like an insurmountable task. I think I'd rather just freefall the whole thing again and get extra rations in from Majestic.'

'Look.' I took the pad and pen from her. 'Let's just list all the names of the people you need to get presents for, then take it from there.'

Leoni didn't bother raising her head from her elbows. 'Oh, whatever,' she said. 'Just wake me up when it's all over.'

Just as we were finally managing to make some

headway we were both yanked rudely to attention by the most God-almighty crash outside, as though someone had dropped a grand piano from a great height and it had landed in spectacular fashion right by the front door. Leoni and I sprang from the table and rushed outside.

'It's Marcus!' she said. 'Oh my God!'

'Who the bloody hell put that there?' Marcus bellowed angrily, marching towards the front of his car. The children were all loaded in the back, the twins shouting enthusiastically out of the window at their mother.

'Dad crashed the car! Dad crashed the car!' William had already freed himself from his seat belt and was busily clambering out of the car while twin-brother Josh tried to kick him in the head. Little Millie was scared senseless and bawling her head off. Leoni immediately went to rescue her.

'Marcus!' she screamed. 'What on earth do you think you're doing?'

'What?' he shouted back at her. 'How am I supposed to know that some idiot was going to hide a bloody army truck behind the hedge? That's my space!'

Leoni bared her teeth at him. 'Well, maybe if you didn't drive through the gates at a hundred miles an hour you might have had a chance of spotting it, you maniac!' She pulled Millie from the car and settled her on her shoulder, even though she was getting a bit big for that sort of thing these days. Leoni is surprisingly slight for a woman with such a high biscuit intake and she struggled momentarily under the weight of her youngest.

'It's not my fault!' Marcus yelled at her. 'And whose bloody car is it anyway?'

I'M NOT GREAT with kids. I do try, honestly I do, and I think that for the most part I manage to mask my aversion quite well, but I have to say that the little blighters rather get on my nerves. I used to feel broody all the time and I remember that round about the age of thirty my biological clock wasn't so much ticking as going off like a top-of-the-range car alarm. It screamed for a very long time but my late husband wasn't keen. Not just on the children issue but on making them. With me, I mean. I had once longed for a family of my own, but now that my ovaries are marching towards shriveldom, the urges have waned somewhat. I felt my patience beginning to wear thin after an hour of being roared at by the twins and even little Millie (who is going through that endless questions and whining at her mother stage) lost something of her usual charming lustre.

Two hours later, I was standing on Julia's gravelled drive while her husband knelt down behind the injured car and inspected the damage with a series of tuts and teeth-sucking noises. 'Thank God he didn't hit it front on,' David said. 'I doubt it would have been driveable.' Julia hung her arm round my shoulder and led me into the house. It was a beautiful day, if a little cold, and she had set a big log fire in the blood-red sitting room to counteract the chill from the patio doors left wide open so she could enjoy an uninter-rupted view across their glorious garden. It was like a small park, well stocked with billowing shrubs and specimen trees all cleverly angled from the house to give an illusion of endless greenery. Whoever planted it all those years ago certainly knew what they were doing. I settled myself on one of the plush velvet sofas and watched a squirrel bounce along the lawn with an acorn in its mouth. Julia returned to the room with two enormous Burgundy balloons hanging from one hand and a bottle of something interesting from David's cellar in the other.

'I won't ask how your weekend's going,' she smiled, pouring two generous glasses. 'Try this.' She lifted hers towards me. I took a sip of the delicious wine at perfect temperature and nodded my approval.

'Mmm,' I said. 'That's good. You said there was something you wanted to talk about?'

Julia looked at me with pursed lips for a moment as if trying to find the right words to tell me I had six months to live. She toyed with the glass in her hands, had another sip then took a deep breath and squared up to me. 'David has been making noises about a holiday. Like I have the time.' She raised an eyebrow at me. 'I get the impression he wants to go away for Christmas this year.'

'That's a relief.' I smiled. 'I thought you were going to say something terrible for a moment. Where are you thinking of going?'

'Somewhere warm, I expect, away from the winter, but that's not the point.'

'Oh?'

'Mm. Well, it's Mum and Dad.' She twisted a long strand of dark hair in her elegant fingers. 'I think they're taking it as read that they'll be coming here as usual.'

I didn't really see what she was worried about. Mind you, that was all very well for me to say. With the way my life had gone, I had stopped seeing my parents for Christmas years ago. They soon realized that no amount of protest could persuade my venom-spitting spouse to include them in any way, so Julia drew the short straw and had seen to their turkey and cranberry arrangements ever since. 'That's OK, isn't it?' I said naively. 'They'll understand.'

'I wouldn't bank on it,' she grumbled, topping up her glass. 'I've dropped a couple of hints about the possibility of us not being here but Dad went selectively deaf and Mum started going on about the tradition of families being together on that one day of the year and how she would never have dreamed of being anywhere else. Christ, anyone would think that the whole world would come to an end the way she was harping on about it.' Julia stood up. 'Fancy a bit of cheese to go with that? There's a piece of Brie in the kitchen that should be at prime ectoplasm stage by now.' She disappeared out of the door and I let my thoughts become lost in the flickering flames of the open fire.

'How's Sara?' I asked when we were comfortably ensconced in Julia's boudoir later that evening, painting each other's nails. 'Tell her from me that I haven't seen her for far too long.'

Julia nodded. 'You and me both,' she said. 'She's practically running the company for me these days. Mind you, I'm not complaining,' she laughed, screwing the lid back on the varnish and picking up her hot chocolate. 'Talk about a chip off the old block.'

'And how's her fairytale marriage to Dudley going?' I leaned back on the pillows and inspected my perfect manicure.

'I tell you what,' she said. 'That girl's got him well and truly by the jolly green giants. I reckon she's seen the light since marrying a millionaire's wallet and decided she'd rather make a pile of her own.'

David appeared at the door with two glasses of brandy, set them down on the dressing table with a smile then left without a word. I sighed as the door closed behind him. 'God, you're lucky,' I said. Julia didn't answer. She had her back to me but I could see her unsmiling face in the soft reflection of the mirror.

THE DRIVE HOME the next morning was pleasantly empty. Michael Parkinson kept me company along the way with some sophisticated jazz and fine conversation. Then I struck gold and found a parking space virtually outside my shiny front door. I expect it was a grand household once, as were the identical, elegant white affairs that lined the streets around the communal garden square. When most were converted into flats I'm not sure. Probably about the time when you couldn't get the staff any more.

I had barely got my key in the latch when the door flew open. It was my upstairs neighbour, Paul, beaming from ear to pierced ear and practically grasping me by the shoulders. 'I don't believe it!' he squealed. 'You've got a new car!'

'No I haven't,' I said.

'Yes you have! Look! It's there! Let's go and tell Sally.'

'It's rented,' I tried to explain, but Paul was already dashing up the stairs taking them two at a time and shouting to his boyfriend, Salvatoré. They're a lovely pair. In the year or so that we've been neighbours I have to say that I've seen a lot less friction between those two than you might reasonably expect from your average hetero couple. Maybe same sex is more compatible than trying to mix the two together. Like oil and water, men and women are so fundamentally different that there's bound to be better empathy and a deeper level of understanding if you stick to your own kind. It's not something I'm planning on trying, but I suspect my life might have been a lot less complicated had I been born to holiday in Lesbos.

Paul reappeared trailing a sleepy-looking Sally behind him. 'She's got a new car!' Paul pointed at me then clapped his hands together excitedly. 'And if we ask her really nicely, I'll just bet we can borrow it on weekends!'

'Hi, Sally,' I said as he bent down lazily and kissed my head. Paul was already bounding across the road expecting us to follow. Sally looked down at his bare feet. 'The car's rented,' I told him. 'There's nothing to get excited about.'

Paul sprinted back to the pair of us waiting in the hall. 'Did you buy it like that?' He looked visibly shocked. 'Was it some kind of police auction where you get joy-ridden vehicles on the cheap? What on earth were you thinking of?'

Sally yawned and scratched his head. 'I'm going back to bed,' he drawled in his languid South American lilt. He has, without doubt, the most erotic voice I have ever heard.

'Wait for me!' Paul shouted, then gave me a giggling wave and ran back upstairs. Stopping for a moment at the top of the flight, he turned back towards me. 'Oh, your boss came round here looking for you yesterday. Has he lost weight?'

That was rather unusual, I thought, being as I am little more than a paid minion who picks up dry cleaning and runs errands for the big man, who can't even remember his kids' birthdays. Rick thinks nothing of phoning me at all times of the night or day for the most trivial of reasons, but to turn up on my doorstep at the weekend? I must admit that a frisson of concern crossed my mind. I've grown terribly fond of Rick and I wouldn't want anything bad to happen to him. What that man really needs is a wife.

'What did he want?'

'No idea,' Paul shrugged. 'I think he's afraid of Sally. Couldn't get away fast enough!' He skipped off up the second flight.

The light on the answerphone wasn't flashing, but I checked it anyway to be reminded that no, I didn't have anyone who cared enough to leave me a message. I dialled Rick's number. There was no reply.

Marzipan Fruits

Unleash your creative skills by fashioning little edible fruits or animals and painting them with food colouring.

Making your own marzipan is literally a piece of cake.

The strong taste of almonds is a wonderful, natural mask for any additional ingredients you may wish to include.

Like cyanide.

Chapter Three

A PIECE OF CAKE

THERE COMES A TIME of year when we must all reluctantly let go of the urge to walk out without a warm coat. I tend to string it out for as long as possible, sticking to something lightweight and rejecting the inconvenience of a scarf that I would be bound to lose on its first outing. It's the unbearable rush of hot air which hits you the minute you enter a shop that gets me. Either you stand by the door and struggle free of your outer layers before entering, or risk collapsing from heat exhaustion before you've made it as far as the cosmetics counter.

This was the first morning I had felt the chill of early winter nipping at my cheeks, so I reluctantly swapped my raincoat for the tweed and found to my delight that my favourite pair of pink gloves were still languishing in the pockets. I managed to bag a seat on the bus and made my way to the big old house behind Victoria. My place of work, although I use the term rather loosely. I let myself in and heard Rick shouting at somebody on the telephone in his study. Situation normal.

Popping my head round the door to make my presence known, I found the room chokingly thick with blue cigar smoke, so opened one of the windows to let it out before retreating to the kitchen to make our morning lattes. It used to be a very complicated affair on account of the humungous machine that we had laughingly nicknamed the Silver Beast. It had always been a hound, like an expensive new car that's never really been right, so Rick finally had it torn out while I was off work for a couple of weeks and he could stand the caffeine deprivation no longer. We've got one of those little coffee pod contraptions now. It's an absolute cinch. You just stick in a little mocha flying saucer, press a button and whaddya know. Perfect coffee. I took it through.

Rick was off the phone now, struggling with the open window. 'It's fucking freezing in here!' he complained.

'Well, I'm not staying in if you close it. It's against health and safety regulations, you know. I could have you arrested for attempted corporate murder.'

'Masochist.' He left the window as it was. 'Good weekend?'

I weighed it up. One smashed-up car. One medium-sized red-wine hangover. 'Not bad,' I said, placing the two hot mugs on a pair of coasters on the desk. Rick sat in his big leather chair, picked up the coffee and leaned back, taking a noisy slurp.

'I hear you dropped by my place on Saturday,' I said casually. 'Sorry I wasn't in. You should have called me on the mobile. Did you need something?' For a split second, Rick looked as though he hadn't a clue what I was talking about, then the fog lifted.

'Oh, yes, that.' He brushed it off. 'It was nothing.'

'Sure?'

He didn't seem convinced, knitted his brow, stared into his mug and let out a sigh. This is normally my cue to sit quietly with a sympathetic countenance and wait for him to get whatever it is off his chest. We're like a well-rehearsed double act.

'Hell?' he said. 'What kind of a bloke do you think I am?' I looked at him quizzically. 'I mean, do I come across to you as a right uncaring, selfish bastard?'

Blimey. That's a pretty probing question for a Monday morning. I wonder what's brought this on? I thought Rick prided himself in being an uncaring, selfish bastard.

'Of course not!' I sprang to his defence immediately. After all, this was the man who had once done me a favour so generous that I probably owed him everything (it's a long story). 'I think you're anything but,' I reassured him. 'And anyone who thinks otherwise obviously doesn't know you very well at all. Who on earth would say such a terrible thing?'

'My daughter.' He looked utterly dejected.

'Oh, Rick. That's awful. Which one?' Rick has five children, courtesy of assorted ex-wives and mistresses, ranging in age from fifteen to twenty-six (the children, although you could be forgiven for thinking otherwise).

'Lola, and it seems she's not the only one.'

Lola is nineteen and lives in Brazil with her impossibly beautiful mother, who receives a mind-boggling palimony cheque every month and is now married to a cosmetic surgeon. Mr Buttocks, Rick calls him. Not that you need to know any of this, but it gives you some idea of what I'm dealing with on a day-to-day basis here.

Rick finished his coffee. 'I had a bit of an argy-bargy with her on the phone the other night and she basically told me I could stick Christmas up my arse.'

I tutted and shook my head sympathetically. 'Do you want another one?' I asked, picking up his empty coffee cup. He nodded and followed me into the kitchen.

'I don't know what she expects me to do,' he moaned. 'Her mother's a complete fucking nightmare and does nothing but scream Portuguese abuse down the phone at me. I send her anything she wants, pay for their house, their holidays, their bloody everything, and all I get is an earful. No "How are you, Dad?" or "What's happening in your life?" – just send us more money or we'll set the lawyers on you.'

'Well, I think you're a great dad,' I said. 'In fact, I wish I could have had a dad exactly like you.' Rick's face dropped and he looked as though he'd been stabbed in the heart. 'You know what I mean,' I added gently. Between you and me, from the little I know of his offspring they're a bunch of utterly spoilt brats. And as for the mothers. Well, with the exception of ex-wife number two who strikes me as perfectly decent and rather nice actually, the rest of them are the kind of rapacious silicone-enhanced vultures who give women a bad name.

'Are you driving anywhere today?' I asked him.

'No. Why?'

I left the kitchen and came back a few moments later with the big decanter of Armagnac he keeps in his study. He watched me with a smile as I poured a generous slug into his mug and a small splash into mine just to keep him company.

'Let me tell you a few things,' I said to him, picking up my coffee and cradling its warmth in my palms. 'I've got to know you quite well, Rick Wilton, and while I would be the first to concede that your family-planning strategy has been rather haphazard' – he cracked a broad smile – 'I think that you are a thoroughly honourable man who has met your responsibilities with more patience and generosity than most absent fathers could claim in a lifetime.'

Rick nodded then looked a little emotional. 'Thanks, Hell. No one gets to me like the kids. I knew you'd be on my side.'

All part of the service, Rick. 'It's completely understandable,' I told him. 'Lola's at that awkward age where she wants to spread her wings and test her abilities as an adult. She's bound to take out some of her frustrations on you. Don't you remember what it was like to be nineteen?' I cast my mind back and confessed wryly, 'I certainly do.'

'Fuck, yeah,' he laughed.

'She'll come round,' I concluded knowledgeably, as though I were versed in such things. 'Just you wait and see. She's probably got boyfriend trouble or something.'

Rick shook his head and drained his coffee. 'It's nothing to do with that. It was about her Christmas present.' I lifted my eyebrows towards him. 'Yep,' he said with a sigh. 'She wants a new pair of baps, a set of porcelain crowns and a Porsche or she's never going to speak to me again.'

I rest my case.

*

'LEONI?'

She screamed her answer back into the telephone. 'Will you two stop fighting before I come in there and bang your heads together! Can't you see I'm on the phone?' I heard her fumbling. 'Hang on a minute – ' then the receiver clattered sharply to the table. I heard a mighty yell of 'Give that to me right now!' followed by some screaming from the children, a crash and a yelp of pain, then a door slamming. She breathed heavily into the mouthpiece. 'All yours.'

'Is this a bad time?'

'Nope. Perfect. What can I do for you, honeybun?'

'I think what you mean is what can *I* do for *you*,' I said proudly. 'I've written your foodie list and the first thing we can cross off it is your home-made Christmas cake. I'm starting it today.'

'What? But it's barely Halloween! I haven't even got my head around the pumpkins yet. The boys are driving me mental about trick-or-treating tonight and that little bastard William has only gone and brought home a can of fart spray he bought off that hideous ASBO school friend of his with his lunch money. He's squirted it all over Millie's favourite teddy bear and she's completely inconsolable. I've stuck him in the washing machine but it's not looking good. One of his eyes has come off and I'm not sure he's going to hang on to all his limbs either.'

'Oh, Leoni! I don't know how you do it, I really don't.'

'Yeah, well, I'll get them back when I'm an old hag. Just wait until they've got nice homes of their own and girlfriends they're trying to impress. I'm going to come round and piss all over their sofas.'

'Good plan,' I said. 'I'll come and help if you like.'

'So what's this about the dreaded list?'

'Don't worry about it.' I could see that she already had more than enough on her plate. 'Just calling to let you know that I've got everything under control.' Just then I heard a high-pitched scream from Leoni's end, followed by a sorrowful wail that could only have been Millie.

'He's blinded!' Millie sobbed woefully. 'Teddy's blinded! Get him out! Get him owwwwwwt!'

'I'll leave you to it,' I said quickly.

'Thanks a bunch,' Leoni muttered and hung up.

COOKING IS THE one thing I truly miss from my previous life. Through those miserable years of dom-estic drudgery, I had learned to vent my suppressed emotions through the art of cordon bleu. Self taught, I learned through a million mistakes and the careful tinkering of ingredients, until there was not a single dish anywhere in the world that I couldn't recreate with some degree of competence. You name it, I can cook it. But living alone, I soon discovered that there are some things you just can't make for a single person. To try to do so smacks of a certain tragedy.

Today, thanks to Leoni, I had been given the perfect excuse to toil deliciously over a raft of country kitchen ingredients. I don't understand what all the panic is about when it comes to making your own Christmas cakes and puddings. All you have to do is shove some stuff in a bowl and drown it in hooch, leave it over-night, then sling all the ingredients together the next day and bung it in the oven. Wrap it up well, leave it somewhere you won't forget about it, douse it in more brandy every now and then, job done. It's hardly rocket science. I've tried to explain this to Julia several times but she just glazes over and reminds me that if God had meant for her to fret over currants he wouldn't have created Marks & Spensive. Heathen.

I rummaged through to the back of the lower cupboards to retrieve my big mixing bowls and give them a good wash and brush-up. Pulling the large copper one from the corner of the lower shelf, some-thing caught my eye. There behind it, sitting very still, was the mouse. She fixed me with her beady eyes then darted off into a tiny crevice. I worried about it for a moment but decided I had far more exciting things to do this afternoon than to chase around after mini-vermin, and shut the cupboard door.

I gladly lost myself in the riveting play unfolding on

Radio 4 with lots of windswept sound effects. An old woman searching for fossils on a rocky coast some-where in craggy Cornwall became trapped by the incoming tide while trying to rescue a suicidal teenage girl in a woolly jumper. With mounting tension, I measured out great bowls of plump, luscious dried fruit and glistening whole candied peel to chop and mix with sinfully generous mugs of French brandy. The little schooner I took for myself was merely a cook's treat, you understand, to soothe the drama of the plucky women caught by the tempestuous sea.

Mulled Wine

Mulling over whether or not
it's too early to open a bottle.

Chapter Four

ROCKET MAN

'WHAT TIME SHALL we put the jacket potatoes in?' Leoni was holding a big, empty roasting tin and looking thoroughly overwhelmed. Dear Lord, if she can't get her head around baking a few spuds for a handful of friends, what chance does the poor woman have of surviving a week of extreme catering at the end of next month? Julia caught my eye and suppressed a smile. She was sitting at Leoni's kitchen table with Millie on her lap arranging mini sausage rolls on a non-stick oven tray. Millie kept putting them upside down deliberately so that Julia would tease her and call her a silly sausage, which she found hilariously funny. Millie worshipped her auntie Julia and never left her side whenever she visited. They were as thick as thieves those two.

The whole crew had piled over to Leoni's house for a Saturday-evening fireworks extravaganza. It's an annual event featuring the usual suspects and fraught with the crackling tension of omnipresent danger. No matter how many times we have tried to impress upon Marcus that properly organized displays are by far the better, cheaper (and safer) option, he completely takes leave of his senses when it comes to setting fire to things in his own back yard. Yes, Leoni's husband is that neighbour who many of us know so well and would dearly love to kill. The one who starts huge, stinking leaf fires every weekend and some autumnal evenings, ruining everyone's laundry and filling every house in the neighbourhood with bitter fumes.

Sara marched up to Leoni, stood right in front of her with hands on hips and said, 'How long have you owned an oven?'

Leoni looked at her sulkily. 'Stop asking me complicated questions,' she said. 'You know I've still got jet lag from the clocks going back last week.'

Sara took the roasting tin from her hands. 'Why don't you sort the drinks out instead?' she suggested.

Leoni's face lit up. 'Now that,' she declared, pointing a finger in the air, 'is one thing I definitely can do.' She pulled a big glass jug down from one of the kitchen shelves and reached for the fruit bowl.

'Are we making mulled wine?' I asked.

'Don't be stupid,' Leoni said sarcastically, slicing a pile of apples and oranges. 'If you heat it up all the alcohol burns off. We're having turbo Pimms. You'll love it. Where the bloody hell have those men got to?'

'Pub, I expect,' observed Julia, nodding her head at Millie. 'What do you think, Pooch?' Millie nodded back gravely. 'Naughty Daddy,' said Julia, 'sneaking off to the pub when they're supposed to be coming straight back with the fireworks.' Julia and Millie pulled their best cross faces at each other then giggled. 'I think I might have a packet of sparklers in my car. Do you want to come and help me find them?'

We all knew very well that some kind of beer-drinking diversion was bound to be involved the minute the three of them had insisted on fetching the remaining essentials together. Marcus couldn't get to the car keys fast enough, David didn't even take his coat off, and Sara virtually pushed Dudley out of the door and instructed him to go and do some male bonding. They've not yet been married six months and she goes to surprisingly extreme measures to get shot of him at every opportunity.

'He's doing my head in,' Sara grumbled the minute we heard the car leave the drive. It was still rattling like loose Meccano around the fanbelt area after Marcus's failed attempt to dock with the hire car, and we all took a sharp intake of breath and winced at the painful noise it made as he pulled away. 'He still expects me to be all lovey-dovey,' she said. 'But now that we're married, I just don't feel the same way any more.' She searched for a suitable simile. 'How can I explain it? I suppose it feels like incest. Like I'm sleeping with my brother.'

'Oh my God,' Leoni said. 'That is completely disgusting.'

'I know,' agreed Sara. 'I've never been with the same man for more than three months before. Sex is only any good when you're having it off with somebody new. Now it's just a bodily function. Like blowing your nose or something.' Was it only me who thought this was a worrying sign? 'Maybe I'm just not cut out for long-term relationships,' she mused.

'Isn't it a bit late to be making rash decisions like that?' I asked her.

'That's exactly the conclusion I came to myself,' said Leoni, hanging on Sara's every word. 'Only by the time I'd worked it out I was already nailed to the floor by the twins. Why somebody didn't slap me to my senses prior to fertilization I'll never know.' She shook her head ruefully. 'You could always start shagging complete strangers,' she suggested. 'I've heard it's all the rage in some circles.' Leoni put down the kitchen knife and pulled up a chair. 'There are these clubs where swingers go, all very posh and expensive apparently, and just do it with whoever they like.' She nodded to us that it was definitely true. 'I read all about it in a magazine but they'd changed all the names and didn't say where it was. And there's nothing in the Yellow Pages.'

By the time we heard Marcus's rattling chuggerbug rolling back up the drive, the potatoes were snugly in the oven and all the sausage rolls were the right way up. My contribution to the evening was an enormous vat of spiced butternut-squash soup for the adults and a smaller pot of home-made cream of tomato for the delinquents. Leoni tasted it straight from the Tupperware tub, seemed impressed, so I moved it quickly before she demolished the lot. She's an invisible eater, you see. I've witnessed whole dishes of food contributions mysteriously disappear before the first guests have arrived.

The men piled in through the front door, guffawing loudly and being all matey with each other in that manly way that betrays the extent of their lager intake. Marcus staggered through the kitchen with a couple of huge bags, one filled with bottles of barbecue lighter fuel (we weren't having a barbecue), and the other packed with various explosives. 'Everything all right, darling?' he asked Leoni cheerfully, then threw the rest of us a friendly wink and disappeared out of the back door. David came in carrying two more packages, the bigger of which was about the size of four shoeboxes strapped together. There was a single fuse hanging from the top of it. Leoni narrowed her eyes at him.

'Tell me that's not a firework,' she said.

David looked sheepish. 'OK. It's not a firework,' he replied, then took it outside.

Silence befell the kitchen and we all looked at Leoni and attempted to gauge what she might or might not be about to do. She said, 'Hmmph,' and went to the fridge for another bottle of the Cava she was using to top up the Pimms jug instead of lemonade. It was a deliriously heady mix and surprisingly warming for a November night. Dudley was trying to put his arm around Sara and give her a kiss, nothing serious, just a small marital one, but she pushed him off and told him to go outside and set fire to something with Marcus. He crept out of the back door obediently, as though it would win him some Brownie points.

A short while later, Marcus put his head around the back door. 'Everybody ready? How long before you want to start?'

Leoni glowered at him. 'Are you sure everything's safe out there?'

'Yes,' he said with a big affirmative nod.

'Have you got buckets of sand and water?'

'Yes, dear.'

'Have you made sure that nothing's pointing towards the Hibbles' conservatory this time?'

'Definitely. Everything will go straight up. Promise.'

'And you haven't bought anything stupid, have you?' she asked sternly. We heard a small, distant snigger from David and Dudley. Marcus made a very poor attempt at masking a guilty expression.

'No,' he said. If Leoni had had a rolling pin to slap onto her palm the picture would have been complete.

'All right then,' she said. 'Send the boys back in before you start the bonfire. I want to make sure the children are properly wrapped up before you blow us all to smithereens.'

The rest of us grown-ups convened outside on the patio. The warming mugfuls of hot soup lay neglected on the table, passed over in favour of Leoni's Molotov cocktails. The men amused themselves by pretending that they were whiter than white and making polite conversation with us as though we had all fallen out of a tree that morning.

'OK!' shouted Leoni from inside. 'We're ready!' She led the children out of the kitchen door.

Marcus looked around. The glass slid from his hands and fell silently to the lawn. 'What the . . .' For those few fleeting seconds we were all speechless. Each of the children was armed with a riot shield. Exactly like the ones you see on the news. The three of them shuffled out behind their mother like a little row of Roman centurions protected by a curtain of floor-to-ceiling Perspex. Leoni looked triumphant.

'You didn't seriously expect me to just take your word for it, did you? Thank God for eBay,' she said. Marcus was still dumbstruck. 'Well? What are you waiting for? Light the bloody thing then!'

Without further ado, Marcus moved towards the silver dustbin piled high with knobbly lumps of wood and bits of broken furniture. The boys had made a guy with some of their father's old clothes and a few bags of straw from the local pet shop. He had a paper plate for a face, to which they had stapled a photograph of their dad and topped him off with an old, moth-eaten bobble hat. When he had reached an unsafe distance, Marcus edged towards the heap with lighted taper in outstretched hand like a swordsman swashbuckling sideways. The match made contact with the half gallon of kerosene and there was a loud, muffled whoomph as the lighter fuel did its thing and the solvent burst into flames, sending an enormous fireball into the air. Fingers crossed there wasn't anything flying directly above it. I waited momentarily for the soft thud of chargrilled songbird.

Beaten back immediately by the searing heat, Marcus scurried away and we all cheered and clapped our hands and were instantly charmed by the orange, licking flames. Within seconds, Millie became agitated, then started screaming. 'He's on fire! He's on fire! Get him off! Get him offffffffff!"

Josh shouted, 'Oh shut up, Millie, you stupid idiot.

He's a guy. He's supposed to be on fire. Don't you know anything?' Leoni bent down and whispered in her ear. Little Millie soon settled, thumb in mouth, earlobe twiddled, and seemed satisfied that the ritual burning of an effigy of her father was perfectly normal family entertainment.

Marcus reappeared from the shadows in the shrubbery, draped in one of those foil safety sheets, shouting, 'Who wants some fireworks?!' The kids all squealed with delight from behind their barricade. Leoni sidled up.

'Fuck me,' she whispered. 'It's sodding Batman.' At which point there was a violent hiss and whistling screech as the first of a barrage of rockets flew high into the night sky and exploded over our heads in a shower of twinkling red and green stars.

We cheered and clapped and the children begged for more. Marcus made a brilliant job of it. Even the wind was going in the right direction for a change, carrying the smoke from the bonfire across to the neighbours' gardens rather than into our faces as it usually did. When the last Catherine wheel had petered out and the children's final sparkler trailed off with a fizzle, the boys complained that it wasn't fair and Leoni tried to rally some enthusiasm towards the soup and sausage rolls.

'Don't like soup,' snivelled William.

'Don't like sausage rolls,' scowled Josh.

Millie looked up. 'Don't like . . .' She thought for a moment then turned to her mother. 'What was the other thing, Mummy?'

Marcus clapped his hands loudly to demand our attention. We all turned to see him standing between us and the bonfire with an enormous grin on his face. 'Who wants just one more?' he shouted.

The children went berserk, jumping up and down and yelling. 'Yes, Daddy! Yes! We want another one!'

'OK!' he beamed. 'But this is a *very* special one!' He disappeared behind the bonfire to the distant end of the garden. We could no longer see him, but could just hear his voice as he called back his commentary. 'Just getting to it now! Everybody get ready!' About five seconds later Marcus came sprinting towards us from the shadows, silver cape trailing, eyes crazed with excitement. 'Any moment now!' he yelled, nodding wildly.

David was standing tall, Dudley beside him, beer in hand. David turned to the rest of us. 'Marcus said that this is the biggest firework money can buy without a professional pyrotechnic's licence.'

'What?' Leoni went pale.

David nodded. 'He ordered it off the internet from China. Weighs about half a ton.'

Leoni's eyes darted to Marcus, who was standing a couple of feet away, staring towards the heavens with arms wide open as if to welcome the Saharan rains.

None of us actually saw the firework. All I remember is a blinding white flash and an extinction-level explosion. Then everything went muffled except for a shrill, high-pitched ringing in my ears. I saw the children abandon their shields and scatter in all directions, Millie's eyes wide with terror as she ran towards Julia, both of them with mouths hanging open in a scream that none of our shattered eardrums could attune to. Dudley rushed to hold onto the boys, their faces deranged with fear. The force of the blast had flattened poor Marcus. He was lying face down on the lawn, stock still. For a moment I thought he was dead. My heart stopped but soon juddered back into action when Leoni rushed to his side and kicked him right in the spleen.

'You madman!' she screamed at him. Leoni has a strict rule about swearing in front of the children. How she sticks to it, I don't know, and *bloody* doesn't count. Marcus let out a low groan and rolled onto his side. Leoni bent down and started pummelling his head with her fists. 'What the bloody hell do you think you're doing? Are you insane? You could have killed us all!'

'Get off me!' he shouted at her and tried to pull himself to his feet while protecting himself with upturned elbows. He had a childish smile on his face and restrained Leoni easily by the wrists. Marcus looked across to David who was standing in the corner of the patio with a video camera in his hand. 'Did you get it?' he shouted.

David was laughing his head off and gave Marcus a cool thumbs-up.

Crafty Christmas Creations

Why rely on the shops for all those
expensive decorations?

Get busy with a few crafty creations
of your own.

Voodoo dolls are simple to make and will
reward you with hours of fun.

Chapter Five

COSTUME DRAMA

'YOU DID SAY that if there was anything I needed you'd come to my rescue,' pleaded Leoni with a guilty expression while I racked my inadequate brain. 'And I'm about as much use with a sewing machine as Wayne Sleep would be in a wrestling match. You can't leave me to cope on my own. I'll kill myself.'

'It's not that,' I said. 'Of course I'll help. I'm just wondering where on earth we're supposed to start. Haven't they got a pattern or something?'

'Nope.' Leoni shook her head. 'She's never got a bloody pattern for anything,' she snarled. 'I reckon she sits around for the whole of the summer holiday mulling over the most difficult costumes she can think of before dropping the bombshell on all the mothers with as little notice as possible.' She got up to free the head-mistress's letter home from beneath the Bart Simpson fridge magnet. 'Just look at this. We couldn't have something simple like a wise man with a dishcloth tied to his head or an angel with a tinsel halo. Oh no.' She began to read aloud in dramatic fashion. 'Dear Parents of, blah, blah, blah. Here we bloody well go, listen to this. The boys are to appear as dwarves.' She nodded at me hard. 'Yes, *dwarves*. And Millie is to bring a costume suitable for her role as the star of Bethlehem.' She slapped the sheet of paper on the table. 'Without a fucking pattern.'

'Don't you worry about it,' I said bravely. 'Leave it with me and I'll see what we can come up with.'

'Thanks, Helen. I knew I could count on you.' She flopped into the chair opposite me. 'I can feel my stress levels going through the roof already and I haven't even got off the starting blocks yet.'

'That's probably got something to do with it,' I smiled.

'You know what I really hate?' she sniped.

'What?'

'Those sickos who do all their Christmas shopping in the summer sales and have the whole lot wrapped and tagged by the end of August. How sad is that? Bloody smug bastards.'

I agreed with her wholeheartedly and hid my blushes behind my mug.

I THINK I MUST have cleaned out John Lewis's entire felt stocks. When I'd taken the last roll of green, the woman behind me in the queue shot me such a look of daggers that I thought she might lie in wait for me outside the exit with a taser gun. I trudged into the kitchen with the felt mountain and humane rodent trap version two. Baiting it with a few cornflakes and a nice little morsel of Port Salut, I popped it into the cupboard where I had last seen the fugitive. There was a sharp rap on the door.

'Paul!' What a nice surprise. Before I could kiss him hello, he leapt in and closed the door quietly behind himself.

'Have you heard the news?' he asked proudly. I looked at him blankly. 'The downstairs flat has been sold. We're getting a new neighbour!'

Well, well. The subject of the empty flat had given us much opportunity for wild speculation over the last month or two. The previous occupant had been completely invisible, having apparently moved out in the dead of night without any of us noticing until the For Sale sign went up. It had lain empty ever since and we had concluded that it must have become some kind of hideout for a terrorist cell.

'Any idea when?' I dropped myself on one of the cream sofas.

'Soon.' He plonked himself down beside me. 'There's a whisper that it could even be some time next week.'

This was interesting news indeed. Paul's pretty fickle when it comes to friendships. Sally once told me that he has a habit of completely falling in love with everyone he meets then dropping them like a stone within a fortnight. I consider myself honoured to have held his favour this long.

'How come you know all this?' I eyed him suspiciously.

'Don't ask,' he said with mock horror. 'I'm such a genius!'

'Does the genius need a glass of wine?'

Paul slapped my leg. 'Is it that time already?' He looked at his watch, got up and followed me to the kitchen. 'I got all the details from the estate agent. Everybody knows he's as bent as a bottle of chips. All I needed was an excuse to make contact.' I smiled at him as I took a pair of glasses down. 'So I went in and pretended that I had a flat to sell in the same building and before you could say Jimmy Somerville he'd gone and told me everything I needed to know.'

'That's not very professional,' I said, pouring us each a generous puddle.

'Nor's he, darling!' Paul sang. 'They don't call him old yo-yo knickers for nothing. My pièce de résistance was the chicken fillet I added to my boy bulge. What's this?' He was distracted by the shopping bag on the table, pulled it open and looked inside. 'My, my. What have we got here?'

'Felt,' I said. 'Lots of it. I'm making the Christmas concert costumes for Leoni's kids.'

'What are they going as? Snooker tables?' Paul unfolded length after length of green fabric. 'All I know is that it's a woman, she's the creative and exotic type and she doesn't have a husband.'

What? Another lone woman? Moving onto my patch? Well, we'll soon see about that. What if she stole Paul and Sally from me by turning out to be fascinating and scintillating company, showing me up as boring and dull? I would have no choice other than to eliminate her. Could be tricky. 'Oh.' I sounded dejected already. Why couldn't it be a single man? Someone exciting and kind and, let's face it, straight? Somebody who would turn out to be completely perfect for me.

That evening I felt as though I had had my nose well and truly put out of joint. I hadn't given it a single thought before Paul bowled up at my door with his ill-gotten gossip, but I suddenly felt violently territorial. I didn't want some trollop barging in and breaking up our little clique. I sulked in the bath for the best part of an hour, finished the bottle of Pinot Noir that he and I had started and watched the tips of my fingers pucker up. Getting ready for bed, I caught myself making more of an effort with my bedtime skincare routine (which normally consists of blinking into the mirror and thinking sod it), as though I might have to start competing at any moment with the jezebel shortly to take up residence beneath my floorboards.

The next morning, I was astonished to find my complexion looking (and feeling) pretty bloody marvellous. During the previous evening's huffathon I had slapped on just about every face cream sample I'd ever collected and all I could assume is that at least one of them had reaped some kind of noticeable result. Trouble was, I'd gone and thrown out all the little empties and their associated boxlets. I wouldn't stand a cat in hell's chance of identifying and isolating the wonder product now. Typical.

RICK WAS ALREADY in the kitchen triumphantly helping himself to a cup of coffee when I arrived for work. He was dressed in a dark blue suit, white shirt and grey silk tie, which, at this time of the morning, meant that he needed to impress somebody today.

'You're looking radiant,' he said.

'And you're not so bad yourself,' I replied while avoiding his gaze. I wouldn't want him to get any ideas.

The fact was Rick had undergone something of a

transformation recently. He had a little scare about six months ago with some unexplained chest pains. They were bad enough for him to cancel a long-standing arrangement with a golf course in Dubai and he'd booked himself in for an MOT with his Harley Street physician. Two days of exhaustive tests later, it turned out to be a meat pie that had disagreed with him. Yet his brush with a bout of acute indigestion had set off a few warning bells, so he turned over a new lettuce leaf the moment he got out of the clinic. Is it just my imagination or are men much better at sticking to diets than women? He's easily dropped at least a stone or two and I've not even heard him mention the biscotti word.

'Nice suit. Got a court appearance or something?'

'Very funny,' he said, but chose not to tell me why he was wearing the whistle.

'What's on my busy agenda today, then?' I asked.

Rick looked at his watch. 'I've left you a list on my desk,' he said. 'It's not everything but you'll get the general idea. If you could make a start on it, that'd be great. And if there's anything you're not sure about, ask me tomorrow. Gotta go.' He picked up his coat and headed off.

The house fell silent behind the closed door and I wandered into the study to collect my instructional list. There was only one scrawled piece of paper on the desk so there was no mistaking the single command. It said: organize Christmas.

I HAVE AN email address these days. It's Helen underscore Robbins at hotmail dot com. Has a certain ring to it, don't you think? Sara set it up for me and showed me how to access my mail in any internet café. It's a doddle, so she said, but I felt so self-conscious the first time I tried it out on the single screen in a little coffee shop down South Molton Street that I pretended to have remembered something terribly important and scurried out of the door. Sara marched me into another one later that same week and stood over me like a frustrated parent coercing their ten-year-old into a vile homework assignment. Satisfied that she had succeeded in dragging me into the information-rich society, she left me to it. I've never checked it since.

'I'm going to do all my shopping on the internet this year,' declared Marcus from one of the old wing-backed armchairs beside Julia's roaring fire. He rolled the ice around in his whisky soda. 'It'll only take me half an hour!' Leoni narrowed her eyes at him. 'You women, all running around like headless chickens on angel dust.' He laughed. 'I mean, what's Christmas? It's just a couple of days off work with a big roast in the middle of it, isn't it?' He looked around for support.

Leoni glanced at Julia. 'Is David like this?' she asked coolly.

Julia winked and smiled. 'Come and give me a hand in the kitchen,' and they left the room.

Marcus raised his glass at the only person likely to give him some back-up. 'It's true, though, isn't it, David?' he demanded. 'All the shops are packed with women in a complete tizz while us men sit back and do it all from the comfort of our laptops.' He smiled smugly to himself. 'We're more evolved,' he concluded. He didn't see the potato coming. It hit him smack in the side of the head then bounced to the floor. The look on his face was priceless.

Sunday lunch at Julia's house is always a thoroughly relaxed affair. She buys the whole enchilada in and won't even sully her hands with chopping a bit of parsley. 'It's supposed to be a day of rest,' she reasoned with me once. 'Yet Mum managed to turn it into the most stressful day of the week.' Goodness me, I remember it well. Being frogmarched to church in a hideous dress. The shouting and crashing in the kitchen while she burned the gravy and trashed every pan in the house. The lunchtime heated debate that would invariably get completely out of hand and end up with us all having a massive argument. The mountain of washing-up that Julia and I had to deal with and the way Mum would then come barging into the kitchen determined to make an enormous crumpeted tea that nobody wanted.

As far as aversion therapies go, it had certainly done the trick with Julia. To her, Sundays were sacrosanct, and on the rare occasions that she decided to throw her doors open to the hangers-on, you could be sure of a highly chilled afternoon experience. The five of us gathered round the gleaming dining table and watched David dismember the chicken and unload its apricot stuffing. There was a succulent piece of lamb too, and more fussed-about vegetables than you could shake a stick at.

'Chicken or lamb?' David asked me.

'Everything,' said Marcus, thrusting out his plate.

Want to know how to spot a public schoolboy from a mile off? Watch how they behave around food. Marcus's normally faultlessly polite manners fly straight out of the window as he adopts an every-man-for-himself stance. He doesn't seem to notice and we're all used to it. Even Leoni has stopped trying to head him off at the pass. Marcus watched, wide-eyed, as David heaped slice after slice on his plate before realizing that Marcus was never going to say 'when'.

'What are your plans for Christmas?' Marcus asked without being specific about whose.

The rest of us looked at each other before David volunteered, 'We're thinking of going away. We could both do with a bit of sunshine and we haven't pushed the boat out with a holiday for over two years now.'

'Is it that long?' asked Julia, surprised. 'I had no idea.'

David raised an eyebrow but didn't look at her. 'Julia's been so wrapped up in work. It's been impossible for her to take more than a few days off in a row.'

'I'm sorry,' she said. 'But I can't just go off and abandon my clients in the middle of a busy patch.'

'It's always a busy patch.' David continued to serve. 'If you were to get run over by a bus they'd soon learn to manage without you. Everyone deserves a holiday. Even you.' He wasn't smiling. The table was becoming tense.

'Bloody right!' said Marcus through a mouthful of lamb. 'Tell them all to go take a running jump!' Although he may come across as a bumbling buffoon, Marcus is actually a very skilled people person. Remember he's been trained to defuse doodlebug Leoni, which is no mean feat.

Julia smiled tightly. 'I don't hear anyone complaining about the income we enjoy. And were it not for that we wouldn't be able to bloody afford nice holidays. Or a million other things I could mention.'

This time David stared at her. 'Don't start,' he said. 'You know exactly what I mean. What's the bloody point in working your balls off for a stack of money you're always too busy to enjoy?' I felt my cheeks going hot and snuck a glimpse at Leoni. She was looking at me from lowered eyes and flashed them uncomfortably. We could feel the charge of Julia's angry silence. 'Or has it escaped your notice that you're hardly ever at home these days?'

'I'm here now, aren't I?' Julia snapped. 'If you had wanted some little hausfrau for a wife, why didn't you say so?' Her tone was scathing. 'You could have saved me the trouble of a demanding career and bought me a floral pinny years ago. I could have spent the rest of my life cutting out money-off coupons from second-hand magazines rescued from other people's waste-paper baskets. Silly me.'

David put the carving knife down and glared at his wife.

'Any more of that lamb?' asked Marcus loudly, holding up his empty plate.

'You've never finished that already?' Leoni scolded him. 'You big fat pig. What about everybody else? No one's even started yet!'

'I'm just showing my appreciation for the cook,' Marcus defended himself. 'Aren't I, Julia?' In one deft move, Marcus had forced Julia to remove her sights from David and train them onto him instead. She reluctantly met his eyes and her expression changed.

'Thank you,' Julia said. 'But I think you would have to class me as the re-heater rather than the cook.'

'She never cooks on a Sunday,' I said rather too cheerfully.

'I think that's a brilliant idea,' concurred a relieved Leoni. 'From now on, I'm not going to cook on a Sunday either.'

Marcus looked up. 'Promise?'

LEONI AND MARCUS had to get going shortly after lunch following a red-alert distress call from home. Josh had apparently tried to wire up two games consoles to the big television set in the sitting room and now the whole house had fused. Even the central heating had packed up and their Marxist babysitter was threatening a walk-out. They argued hotly all the way to the car about whose fault it was that the boys had turned into the kind of children that you see on Channel 4 documentaries for all the wrong reasons.

'Is everything all right with you and David?' I whispered quietly to Julia as we loaded the dishwasher. 'It's not like you two to argue in front of people.'

'I don't know,' she sighed. 'Maybe it's me but he's really getting on my nerves. He takes such a simplistic view of everything. Then he follows me around and keeps asking what the matter is. When I try to talk to him he either completely misunderstands what I'm saying and makes stupid suggestions, or tells me not to worry about it then changes the subject.' Julia stared into space. 'What is it with men? He mopes around as though I am responsible for his mood and I can't stand it. It just doesn't feel right at the moment. Nothing does.' She reached for a tea towel and wiped her hands. 'It's been like that for a while.' A shadow of sadness passed over her face. 'I feel like I'm missing out. Like life is passing me by,' she said. 'I never thought I'd say this, but I'm starting to feel old.' Julia sat down heavily on one of the kitchen chairs and began to cry.

David appeared silently at the door. We looked at each other. I gave him a pained expression and shook my head in a small way. He nodded and retreated quietly to the sitting room, softly pulling the door to as he went. I sat beside Julia and put my arm around her shoulders. 'Hey,' I said gently. 'What's all this about?'

'I don't know.' Julia used the tea towel to blot her wet cheeks. 'Some days I feel like I'm going mad. I get so cross with everybody around me. It's like I want to tell everyone to fuck off and run away, and live in the middle of nowhere all on my own. Then I wouldn't have to deal with anyone any more.'

'I think David's right,' I said quietly. 'You could really do with getting away. It'll do you the power of good.'

'Do you think so?' she asked hopefully. 'All I keep thinking is that I couldn't stand two weeks of his company twenty-four hours a day. It might just tip me over the edge.'

'What's he done to make you feel like this?' After all, one never knows what goes on behind closed doors. A little warning bell was going off somewhere at the back of my mind.

Julia attempted a vexed smile. 'Nothing,' she said. 'That's the whole point. He hasn't done anything at all. I don't even have an excuse for being like this.'

I rubbed her back and made sympathetic noises. 'You've been burning both ends of your candle for far too long,' I said. 'You don't have to prove anything to anyone, you know.' She didn't look particularly comforted, so I tried a little harder. 'We all love you and worry about you, Julia. You need to take care of yourself or you'll end up having another breakdown.'

I took a pair of freshly washed wine glasses from the draining board, poured the remainder of the claret and pushed one of them towards her. She lifted her head sharply. 'Never,' she said. 'I'm not going back there again. Not in a million years.' She picked up her glass and took a sip. 'Don't you think it's strange that neither of us ended up with any children?'

'I have thought about that sometimes,' I said. Truth was, I had thought about it quite a lot over recent years. The absence of children in Julia's life had been dealt to her as a cruel stroke of fate when she was still in her early twenties. Since being told she might never bear a child of her own, she had endured the indignity of numerous fertility treatments, none of which were successful, and had even entertained visions of adoption for a while before they became lost in the heartbreaking process only to find that it wasn't for them. Julia eventually resigned herself to her childless state and compensated for the emptiness by immersing herself in a high-flying career with a lifestyle to match.

'Do you feel that we've missed out?' she asked quietly. I could sense her fragility.

I threw my wine back in two swallows. 'Are you kidding?' I said. 'Have you seen what it's done to Leoni? If you ask me, you and I have had a narrow escape, my friend. Now where's that husband of yours? If he's pissing you off this badly the least he can do is open us another bottle of wine.' I got up and went to the door, glancing back at her over my shoulder. 'Mind if I stay over? I know it's becoming a bit of a habit. It's your silk pyjamas. They make me feel all louche.'

She shook her head and smiled at me. 'Thanks, Helen.'

David was sitting with the newspapers on the sofa pretending to read. He looked up as soon as I put my face around the door. I asked him if there was any chance of him sacrificing another bottle of Margaux, suggested that a cuddle might be in order for his missus, and went to use the telephone on the side table.

'Rick?' Sounded like he was in a bar, as usual.

'Hell!' he shouted. 'I'm having a beer in the Wellie with Spud. Wanna come and join us?'

'Sorry. No can do.' I plugged my other ear with a finger and tried to tune into his voice over the general background din. 'I won't be in till later tomorrow morning. Something's come up.'

'Nothing to do with that list I left you, is it?' He laughed.

'That wasn't a list,' I said. 'It was an insult.'

Festive Mince

Paul and Sally window-shopping
down Walton Street.

Chapter Six

PIGS IN BLANKETS

THE NEXT EVENING my sitting room resembled the seamstress's department backstage at the Royal Opera House. There was felt everywhere, tailor's chalk, pins, bobbins, bits of fabric and a tin of outsized buttons that I'd picked up in the local British Heart Foundation charity shop. There was no way that the measurements Leoni had given me could be right and the Dopey outfit was looking worryingly like a shrunken Robin Hood frock. I persevered long into the night and tried to clear my mind of the stack of foam rubber and coat hangers behind the other sofa waiting to be fashioned into a Millie-sized, wearable star.

Paul passed me in a hurry on the stairs the following

morning, trailing his usual mist of fresh, citrussy cologne. 'Morning, neighbour!' He kissed his hand and patted it on my arm as he rushed by me. 'The new girl's moving in on Thursday! I'm going to take the day off and watch the whole event from your balcony. Bye!' The front door swung shut behind him and I heard his light footsteps dash down the portico steps.

'Thursday?' I mumbled to myself and started engineering an excuse to join him. I'm not exactly stacked out with thrilling events in my life at the moment. This sounded like it might be the most entertaining slot on my social calendar for quite some time.

'GOOT MONGING,' CHIRPED HELGA the Russian cleaning lady as I pulled my coat off and hung it by the front door. 'Reek farting more coffee,' she said brightly. 'I get of shops to 'im.' And she trotted out into the street. Rick appeared from his study and rolled his eyes at me.

'Morning, Reek,' I said. 'I see the English lessons are coming on in leaps and bounds.'

'Christ knows what she's going to come back with,' he grumbled. 'It's taken me fifteen minutes to explain that we're out of coffee and get through to her what an espresso pod is. I might as well have gone down the shops and got the fucking things myself.'

I smiled and went to join him. 'Don't be too hard on

her,' I said. 'She's really trying and you know she thinks you're the best thing since Glasnost for getting her out of that immigration wrangle.' We both sat down in his study. 'So, what demands are you foisting off on me today, slave driver?'

Rick reached for his cigar box and pulled out a big Cohiba. He rolled it in his fingers, held it under his nose for a few moments then stuck it in his mouth. I struck one of the long matches from the rough earthenware pot by the humidor and held it for him while he puffed.

'I'm pissed off, Hell,' he said. 'I mean, really pissed off.'

'Oh, not you as well,' I moaned. He took no notice.

'I'm fed up with the way everyone takes me for fucking granted.'

'I don't take you for granted!' I protested.

'I know you don't,' he said. 'Or old Mrs Gorbachev out there. But you're about the only two.' He leaned back in his chair, pulled hard on his cigar and let out a long thin ribbon of smoke. 'I want to make some changes this year,' he said. 'I've spent every Christmas for God knows how long chasing a stream of exes and angry kids from country to country, and frankly I don't think any of them could give a flying fuck either way.'

Rick and I have developed a strange relationship. Although he hired me as a surrogate housewife to look after his home and personal arrangements soon after his fourth breeding partner had taken him to the cleaners and run off with her Pilates teacher (who happened to be a woman), I had become more like a common-sense mentor. I'm supposed to work three mornings and one full day a week, but it never seems to work out that way. At least fifty per cent of my time is devoted to playing agony aunt. It's all rather fun actually.

'What are you going to do about it?' I asked, mindful that this is the cop-out game that highly paid psychiatrists play with their patients. Get them to solve their own problems then take all the glory for yourself and charge them five hundred pounds an hour. Talk about money for old rope.

'Spud had a good idea,' he said and brightened up with a series of smaller puffs. 'Told me I should fake my own death and see what happens.' Rick put the cigar down in the ashtray. 'I think he's got a bloody good point there. Don't you? If you want to know how people really feel about you, there's only one surefire way to find out.' He picked up the cigar again and pointed it at me. 'Get yourself dead, sit back and watch.'

'You mean, like, do a Reggie Perrin?'

'Exactamundo.'

I regarded him solemnly. 'You are joking of course.'

Rick chewed on the end of his cigar and touched the side of his nose with his thumb. At that moment, we heard the front door slam, then scampering feet. Helga burst in through the door looking flushed and victori-ous. 'Is make round coffee yah!' she said, delighted with herself. She was wielding a big blue packet of Tetleys.

QUEUING UP AT the counter of our local Starbucks while the staff took as long as possible over every painful order, Rick huffed and tutted his impatience. 'Will you please stop that?' I said. 'It's very annoying.'

'I dunno how places like this stay in business,' he complained.

'You should have stayed at home.' Or, better still, gone out to get the coffees himself. I have no idea why he insisted on walking around the corner with me.

Rick started fiddling with the wafer biscuits on the display. 'I fancied a bit of fresh air.'

'In the middle of Victoria? You might as well stick your head up an exhaust pipe.' Rick smiled and reached over to pay for our takeaway lattes. 'Come on,' I said. 'Back to the jolly old grindstone.' Instead of taking off at his usual thundering pace, Rick dawdled, sipped at his cup and allowed himself to be distracted by the Monopoly-board house prices in the estate agents three doors up. I hung back patiently for a minute or two then wondered if I shouldn't just leave him to it. 'Shall I see you back at the ranch?'

'What?' Rick seemed to have forgotten that I was there. 'Oh, sorry, Hell. No.'

'You're not firing on all six today, are you?' I could tell when Rick wasn't quite himself. He takes on a certain vacant expression and chews his cigars more deliberately.

'Shall we walk for a bit?' he suggested. It was a fine enough day so I nodded my agreement and automatically headed for the short cut towards the back end of Buckingham Palace. Rick was in pensive mood and unusually quiet. I nudged his arm with my elbow.

'Try not to let them get to you,' I suggested earnestly.

'Easier said than done,' he replied. We walked half the length of the palace garden before exchanging another word. 'Christmas always makes me think of things I shouldn't think about. You know.' He shrugged at me. 'It's all turned into a bit of a mess.' Rick puffed hard on his cigar and frowned.

'Cheer up.' I gave him a bright smile. After all, I consider it one of those services that I'm paid so handsomely for. 'Things could be a whole lot worse.'

'Really?' he said flatly.

'At least you have a family, even if they are spread over every corner of the earth and like to give you a hard time.' He didn't seem any perkier, so I went for the direct comparison method. 'Look at me.' I took on a self-deprecating tone. 'I'd love to have a troublesome kid to worry about. Even just the one. You've got *five*. Instead I have to satisfy myself in the role of an ageing spinster who doesn't have so much as a single niece or nephew.' My pace slowed as my own words rang in my ears. 'I'm going to die old and alone, and nobody will remember me for anything.' In my attempt to find a small shred of encouragement to lift Rick's mood, I had managed only to depress myself unutterably. 'I'm doomed.' I sighed and sat heavily on the first vacant bench and sulked into my coffee.

'Thanks, Hell.' Rick patted my tweedy knee. 'I can always count on you to brighten my day.'

'Sorry.' I felt myself blush. 'I don't know where that came from.'

Rick drained his cup and wiped the froth from his face with the back of his hand. 'You know what,' he said, aiming his empty at a wire bin and scoring a direct hit. 'We ought to join forces against Christmas this year and swear a pact to protect each other from the ghost of Christmas past.'

'Good idea,' I joked back. 'You bring the cyanide and I'll leave the gas on.'

'HAVE WE GOT EVERYTHING?' Paul whispered loudly.

We had both sets of French doors pinned wide open with sofa cushions and had donned old clothes so that we could crawl along the floor and spy on the entrance undetected. He fiddled with his new walkie-talkie. 'Sally. Come in, Sally,' he hissed into the handset. It crackled for a couple of seconds before Sally's voice drawled out of it.

'What?'

Paul frowned at me. 'Not *what*,' he said into the mouthpiece. 'It's what, *over*.' He let go of the red button.

'Paul,' Sally replied patiently. 'I have to get this finished, so I don't have time for your silly games this morning. Tell me when there's something to see and I'll come down,' he said. We heard a sigh. 'Over.'

Paul beamed. 'By jove I think he's got it!' he said, then back into the mouthpiece, 'Roger Dodge,' crackle, crackle. 'Over and out.'

We waited and waited. Then I made us some lunch which we ate in the kitchen before resuming our uncomfortable positions for the next shift. Boredom soon set in, so we put the television on and watched a predictable episode of *Columbo* while keeping half an ear open for any signs of movement from below. The whole flat was freezing and I eventually insisted that we take the cushions up and shut the doors before we both died of hypothermia. Slipping the latch closed, I saw a white truck drawing up at the pavement.

'Paul! I think we're on!'

Paul jumped up from the sofa, grabbed his walkie-talkie and pressed the button in a rapid succession of squelching crackles. 'Come in, wild goose,' he screeched. 'We have eyeball. Repeat, eyeball.'

The handset hissed emptily for ages, then drawled lazily, 'I think you mean, we have eyeball, over.'

'Whatever,' Paul yelled back. 'They're here. Bring the binoculars.'

Sally arrived within moments and the three of us slid all the doors open and slithered out onto the balcony on our stomachs, pressing our faces up to our pre-selected gaps in between the battlements. To our mutual disappointment the three men in the lorry just sat there in the front. One produced a tartan Thermos flask and we watched them pour tea into tin cups and eat sandwiches from a brown paper bag.

Within fifteen arctic minutes, we had stealthily dragged out a couple of small rugs, a double duvet and the chenille throw from the sitting room. It looked like a chic little shanty town, with the three of us taking shelter beneath our makeshift al-fresco hide. A taxi rolled to the kerb and waited for ages before its lone occupant opened the black passenger door. A billowing coat of richly tapestried autumnal colours draped with two similarly ornamental scarves emerged. We couldn't see her face, just the crown of a deep purple turban with a long feather curling up from the front. She slammed the door of the taxi, shared a final word with the driver, then turned around and looked straight up and directly at us, our faces peeking out shamefully from between the balustrades.

THE BLAST OF fresh air through the flat had blown away the cobwebs and left everything with a fresh, neutral smell. After retrieving the upholstery from the balcony floor I locked up for the night and settled myself in front of the television with the leftovers from our covert picnic. Paul had left his green army-surplus water flask behind, which I soon discovered had been filled with what tasted suspiciously like sangria. Well, no point in letting it go to waste.

The evening news was uneventful, this being a slow day with relatively little shit hitting the fan. The local bulletin reminded us that it was National Chip Week, although quite what we were all supposed to do in its honour I'm not sure. I pulled the first dwarf costume off the tailor's dummy (yes, I do have such a thing) and tried to convince myself that it didn't look like a diminutive dress for an elf. 'It'll be better when it's on,' I mumbled to myself as I made a start on the other one. 'Otherwise I'm well and truly stuffed.'

'HAVE YOU INTRODUCED yourselves yet?' asked Sara, who had arrived at my door unannounced and was busily unloading a carrier bag of assorted ice-cream tubs into my freezer for no particular reason.

'I thought I'd let her settle in for a couple of days before I knocked on the door,' I lied.

'Chicken,' she said.

A flush rose in my cheeks. 'I don't know how I get myself into these situations.' I watched as Sara finally gave up trying to fit the last carton into the ice compartment. She pulled the lid off and stuck a soup spoon in it instead.

'Well, you can't hide up here forever, you know. It wasn't exactly a warm and friendly welcome to her new home, was it?'

I winced at the thought. 'As soon as I think of a reasonable explanation as to why the three of us were pinned to the balcony floor staring at her, I'll go and say hello.'

Sara reloaded her weapon and passed it to me. 'Are you sure she definitely saw you?'

'Positive.' I took the spoon from her hand and nibbled at the heap of ice cream. 'It was the weirdest thing. Like the cabbie had tipped her off or something. She turned around and looked straight up at us.' I felt a chill go down my spine just the way it had done two days ago. 'Paul noticed it too and said someone had walked right over his grave. She had all sorts of interesting stuff, mind you.' The fact is, we had only retreated so far and had hung close to the windows and watched the new neighbour's belongings being humped in by the removal men. Her furnishings looked like something off a film set, and she supervised the unloading and made much fuss about them being extra careful with three large, black trunks.

'Oh, well,' said Sara. 'At least you made a lasting impression.' She took the spoon back and scooped out another huge chunk of ice cream. 'And you only get one chance to make one of those.'

'Anyway,' I said. 'What are you doing hanging around here? Haven't you got some important wifely duties to attend to? Anyone would think you're trying to avoid spending time with your husband.'

'Shopping,' she said.

'What? For ice cream?'

'No,' she rolled her eyes at me. 'You know. Stuff for the house. Proper food for the fridge. I think Dudley's expecting me to start playing the corporate wife with polite cocktail parties and shit like that, but I can't be arsed. I got as far as Peter Jones with a list as long as your arm this morning then I suddenly lost interest.' That's one of the things about Sara. Although she turned out to be the best right-hand man my sister had ever known, when it came to Sara's free time she was concerned only with meeting her own needs. She didn't even feel bad about it. A guilt-free woman. Must be a new cross-breed.

'The way I see it, he's got a secretary, let her bloody

well sort it out,' she said. 'He must have managed perfectly well before I came along, so I don't see why he can't just continue doing the same.'

'I'm not sure that's how marriage is supposed to work,' I suggested.

'Yeah? Well, I don't see Julia skivvying in a frilly apron and I'm not about to do a major U-turn on my principles.'

I didn't realize she had any. I poured the coffee and wondered if I should say anything or keep my mouth shut. I was never quite sure just how blurred the line was between Sara and Julia these days. Sometimes it looked like an entirely professional relationship and at other times anything but. Yet if there was one person who might have the griff on Julia's sombre mood of late, it was Sara.

'Have you noticed anything about Julia lately?' I ventured as casually as my concern would allow.

'Like what?' she said, before answering the question herself without skipping a beat. 'You mean like her being a stressed-out harpie from hell? I'd have to be deaf, dumb and blind to have missed that one.' Her response took me aback momentarily, then seemed to be perfectly accurate.

'That's one way of putting it,' I said. 'I can't help but notice she's been a bit strung out. She's gone all quiet on me too. I was wondering if you might know what's up with her.'

'Life,' she said, with an uncharacteristically knowing nod. 'I reckon she's running out of steam, which means that sooner or later she's going to have to face up to the demons she's been running away from for the last twenty years.'

Sara was still concentrating on her spoon and missed the look of fleeting shock that must have creased my face. The conversation had just become very uncomfortable from where I was sitting. This was my sister we were talking about. Whatever demons Julia had to deal with were her business. I suppose I was a little unsteadied by Sara's nonchalance.

'You know what your sister's like,' she said. 'So long as she's up to her eyeballs in a million things, she's happy.' She daydreamed for a second before adding, 'I don't know how David puts up with it.'

'What on earth do you mean?' I tried to sound surprised even though she wasn't saying anything I hadn't already considered.

'I dunno,' she said. 'But if I had a bloke like him you wouldn't catch me spending my whole life chasing the next big buck. God knows, it's not as though she even needs the money any more. The company's minted and I reckon she could retire if only she'd listen to her accountant, but she won't have it. David's tried to surprise her with a long weekend away four times in the last year and each time she's found an excuse to let him down at the last minute. If you ask me, she's pushing her luck.'

'I had no idea,' I said quietly, forgetting my initial defensive stance.

'Yeah? Well, last time I'm pretty sure he got on a plane and went by himself. Julia wants to watch herself there.' Sara tipped me a sage expression and pressed her spoon back into the tub. 'Men will only try so hard and for so long, then she really will have something to get her knickers in a twist about.'

Since when did Sara get a Ph.D in relationships? Maybe these few months of marriage have given her something of a crash course. If what she was saying was right, then things were far worse than I had thought. 'Thank God she's got you,' I said.

Sara looked up at me. 'I'm your sister's number-one fan,' she said with a serious note in her voice. 'If it weren't for her, I'd have ended up chained to my dad's morgue of a law firm pushing conveyancing forms around for the rest of my days. Now,' she said, 'now, I've got ambitions.'

And so it comes around. The natural generational cycle where the young get older and the schoolchildren we once saw making their way to the bus stop in the morning become the new wave of hungry wolverines taking over the jobs and spaces we assumed would always be ours. Sara scraped the bottom of the ice-cream tub, flipped the spoon into the sink and saw herself to the door, blowing a kiss through the air behind her. I reluctantly dragged myself off the kitchen stool and resumed my hopeless position behind the ridiculous star-shaped foam armature that I was failing miserably to clad in felt with a bottle of stinky Copydex glue and a staple gun.

THERE'S NOTHING QUITE like starting the day with a nice firm stiffie from the postman. As the festive season advances, the slim possibility of an invitation mixed in with the bills adds a certain frisson of excitement to one's daily doormat lottery. It was from Julia – one of those deep-embossed gilt-edged cards that people like her get, to a private viewing of a new exhibition by a young artist at an overpriced gallery in Cork Street. She had stuck a Post-It note on the front asking if I fancied a jolly. Julia doesn't normally bother with these things but seemed unusually keen to go, which was excellent news, seeing as my diary appeared to be completely empty between now and the next century. That said, my heart did sink at the prospect of rubbing shoulders with a gallery full of highbrow culture vultures. I don't know anything about art, which means I would be bound to spend the entire evening panicking about what to (or more importantly what not to) say.

'Oh, go on, Helen,' Julia persuaded me on the

telephone later. 'Or are you still hoping that if you stay in for long enough Mister Right is going to waltz up and ring your doorbell? You need to get out and meet new people. It'll be a good crowd.'

'You know I don't like art galleries,' I snivelled. 'I always feel so intimidated. What if someone tries to talk to me about the pictures?'

'They won't.' She laughed. 'They're just there for the free champagne and to see who's wearing what. Nobody's interested in the art. All the good stuff's already sold or reserved anyway. Always is.'

'Why don't you go with David?' I suggested. 'At least he knows what he's looking at.'

'I don't want to.' Julia went quiet for a moment.

'You're not still arguing with each other, are you?' My heart felt heavy and I could tell that she would avoid the question. There was a long pause.

'I've heard someone's going to be there,' she said quietly.

Sounds ominous. 'Oh yes? Like who?'

She seemed reluctant to answer, then said, 'Stan.'

Now there was a name I hadn't heard from Julia's lips for a very long time.

The pair of us remained quiet while she allowed me some time to absorb it. Stan, as she calls him, was the man we were once all convinced she was going to marry. The love of her life, no less. She had met him while she was at the height of her show-stopping youthful beauty at a polo match in the Great Windsor Park. Julia was there in a promotional capacity for one of the big Champagne houses where she worked in the public-relations department, drumming up interest from high-profile quaffers in the right enclosures. On the second day of play, she had gone into one of the hospitality tents to buttonhole some important guests and had emerged several hours later totally besotted. The man she would later refer to as Stan West was the highly eligible son of one of the oldest families in Europe. The pair of them fell hopelessly in love.

He showered her with fine jewels and exotic holidays and she settled into the first-class lifestyle of a titled aristocrat as easily as anyone of such dazzling beauty would. She was born to it. Mum had to be prevented from calling every newspaper and magazine in the country and Julia was on cloud nine for seven glorious months. The proposal came the following February. Julia had been a bag of nerves the moment she learned he was whisking her away to Paris for the weekend. She had wanted to go before, but he had told her that Paris was a vicious, gargoyled city filled with ghastly people and that its only role in the realm of great world destinations was as the perfect place to pop the question. He took her to dinner at the restaurant Jules Verne, perched at the summit of the Eiffel Tower, where they dined on oysters and she waited patiently for the most important moment in her life. It had been perfect, and at the precise second when she said yes and he slipped the enormous diamond on her finger, she told me that even if the great tower had collapsed there and then killing them both, she would have died the happiest woman on earth. Mum had her hair permed and wore trenches in the carpet, anticipating Julia's knock on the door at any moment to introduce us to our future in-law.

By the time they returned to London it was over.

None of us saw her for weeks then months while she shut herself away and cried a river. Dad and I talked about it a lot and consoled Julia as much as we could, given the constant obstacle of her answerphone. Mum was devastated, too, having made elaborate plans in her head for her own early retirement playing some kind of European Queen Mother. 'She should have told him straight away or never said anything at all,' Mum wailed, adopting her usual I-told-you-so stance. 'Any idiot knows that the most important thing to a man like that is an heir.'

I ARRIVED EARLIER than I had intended. Had it not been for the persistent drizzle I would have loitered outside and waited for Julia in the brisk evening air, but there was no way my hair would survive so I walked in and tried to look arty. I accepted a glass of Champagne from one of the loaded waitresses and stood in a corner pretending to appreciate a rather ugly painting of I'm not quite sure what.

'Magnificent, isn't it?' said the man I suddenly found standing next to me. I looked at him in a nervously noncommittal way that I hoped answered his question without my actually having to speak. 'Are you a fan?' he asked. My smile froze. This is precisely what I had wanted to avoid. Finding myself being harangued by the art critic from the bloody *Observer* while I try to thaw out in a corner with a free glass of bubbly. He was still waiting for a reply and I was starting to feel idiotically conspicuous.

'I'm afraid not,' I conceded. 'This is the first time I've seen – ' I realized I had no idea if it was a man or a woman. I gestured towards the canvas – 'any of this.' Phew.

'He's a genius, don't you think?'

I sipped at my glass and nodded.

'Painted this one with his mouth, you know.'

'Really?' I asked, becoming a little more interested.

'But the ones over there – ' he indicated the far wall of the gallery – 'those are the ones he got all the press attention for. Extraordinary work,' his voice was full of admiration. 'Simply extraordinary.'

I turned to look at them through the gaps in the crowd. They looked like a bigger version of some of the daubs Millie used to bring home from nursery school when she was about three. 'Amazing,' I said.

'Isn't it?' he agreed, making no effort to move away. My heart sank.

'There you are!' shouted Leoni. Well, hallelujah. I was just weighing up whether or not I could pull off a convincing faint. Where she had appeared from, I have no idea. I hadn't even known she was coming. She had a glass of Champagne in each hand. 'Julia's two minutes away apparently.' Leoni took a big sip from each of the flutes. 'Isn't this the bloke who paints with a brush stuck up his arsehole? What a complete load of old cobblers,' she said loudly. 'You just wouldn't want something like that in your house, would you? It's unhygienic for a start.'

The man looked horrified and began to protest. 'Ricardo Ackland is the most exciting new artist to emerge from the London scene in the last five years,' he insisted.

Leoni laughed. 'Really?' she said, gently knocking his arm with her elbow. 'I think he's having you on. Ever heard of the emperor's new clothes? My kids could knock you up half a dozen of these in about ten minutes. In fact,' she raised both her glasses towards him, 'I reckon you and I could make a fortune.'

Just as he looked as though he was about to have Leoni ejected, Julia swept in front of the three of us to announce her arrival. Our jaws dropped in unison. She looked utterly spectacular in a long line black dress swathed with a luxurious wrap of bronze-satin-lined velvet. Her glossy hair had been expertly dressed into a pile of not quite perfect curls loaded high on her crown and secured with an exquisite antique tortoise-shell comb set with precious stones. Julia had showed it to me once many years ago, shortly after Stan had given it to her, saying that it was an heirloom piece from his grandmother's museum-quality collection. She hadn't worn it, or anything else he had given her, since they parted company. I had often wondered what she did with it all, whether she had sent the whole lot off to auction, returned it or hidden it away. As she told me some time later, she could not bear to be parted from a single piece.

The gallery man recognized her instantly. 'Julia!' he enthused, leaning in to kiss her cheeks. 'So good of you to come! I took the liberty of putting a red dot on the bleeding heart.' He led her away to see the canvas he had reserved for her.

I stared at Leoni. She stared back at me. 'Have I missed something?' she said. 'Or does Julia look like she's about to pick up an Oscar? Did you *see* that dress? Hello?'

'I don't know,' I replied nervously, looking round the room. 'But I've got a bad feeling about all this.'

'Oh for God's sake, Helen, what?' She clutched my arm. 'I'm not a complete idiot you know. Julia's quite obviously spent at least four hours in a salon and Christ knows how much down Sloane Street by the looks of that outfit. To buy a painting? I don't think so. '

I lost sight of Julia and Leoni pierced me with questioning eyes. The noise in the gallery was rising as the Champagne flowed and Leoni strained the side of her head to hear me over the clattering racket. 'I think Julia's expecting to run into an old friend of hers this evening,' I told her. 'They were very close once.'

Leoni's eyes widened. 'You mean an old boyfriend?' I nodded discreetly. 'Where?' She started craning her head. 'Is he here yet?'

'Stop it!' I hissed at her. 'This is not a laughing matter. She wanted to marry him, but it all went horribly wrong and she ended up with a broken heart.' Leoni squinted at me. 'He's a count,' I whispered.

'Oh yes?' Leoni was still trying to scan the room. 'Well, thanks for filling me in. This'll be interesting.' She finished both her drinks and dumped the empty glasses on a sculpture plinth. At that moment Julia appeared through the crowd with a huge smile on her ' face, leading a handsomely dressed man by the hand. He was tall and distinguished-looking with soft brown eyes set into olive skin, and sensitive manicured hands that appeared never to have done a day's work. Upon reaching us he dipped a small bow. Julia beamed proudly. Leoni scowled at him.

'May I introduce my old friend, Count Stanislas von

Westenhöltz.' Julia flushed as she said his name. 'He's from Transylvania.' I put my hand out to greet his. 'Stan, this is my little sister, Helen.'

'Enchanted.' He smiled and squeezed my hand gently. 'I have heard a lot about you. I am sorry we never met before.'

'And this is Leoni.' Julia's smile faded when she saw the expression on Leoni's face.

'Count?' screeched Leoni. 'Did you say *Count*? Oh my God. I thought you meant—' She cut herself off abruptly, then fiddled with the collar of her emerald-green blouse.

Stan smiled down at her imperiously. 'You do not have a drink?' He noticed her empty hands. 'Let me bring one for you.' And with that he turned and disappeared into the gathered crowd. Julia watched his every move and seemed lost in an unbreakable spell. Leoni looked at me, held her hair out sideways, and did a big jaw-dropped cartoon face at the pair of us.

'Holy moley!' she said. 'I wouldn't bloody kick him out of bed for eating crisps!'

Julia sighed and said nothing.

'Are you OK?' I asked her. She nodded. 'I had no idea the two of you had kept in touch.'

'We didn't,' she replied softly.

Leoni raised one eyebrow. The one that says Big Fat

Lie. 'So it's a complete coincidence that we're all stand-ing here when he walks in, and you just happen to look like Miss World today?' She caressed the fabric of Julia's exquisite shawl. 'And I suppose this is some old thing you found at the back of your wardrobe?' But Julia wouldn't be drawn.

Stan returned empty-handed, much to Leoni's dis-appointment. 'They're out of Champagne,' he explained. 'And I really don't think you will want to drink the wine. It's not very good.' He addressed Julia. 'You know how these things are.' She nodded. 'I was thinking, if you are free, perhaps we could have dinner together.' Julia didn't look at either of us and there was a moment's awkward silence. Stan tore his eyes from Julia and gallantly added, 'I mean all of us of course.'

'That would be brilliant!' Leoni enthused. Stan smiled politely and Julia seemed unsettled.

'That would be lovely,' I thanked him. 'But Leoni and I won't be able to join you, I'm afraid.'

'What?' said Leoni. I slipped my arm around her waist, pinched hold of the little roll of love handle and gave it a firm squeeze.

'We had an early supper before we came,' I told him. 'Didn't we, Leoni?'

Leoni nodded her head furiously. 'Yes! Completely forgot! Must have worms!'

Stan made a convincing show of disappointment. Julia glanced at me through lowered eyes but continued to hold her silence.

'If you're absolutely sure,' he said, then turned to Julia. 'What do you think? A cosy little table at Rules? We could catch up on old times.'

Julia cocked her head at him. 'Stan West,' she said weakly. 'I can't think of anything else I would rather do.'

Note to Self

Stop eating and drinking your way
around the festive freebies in Waitrose.

You're beginning to draw attention
to yourself.

Chapter Seven

SANTA'S LITTLE HELPER

I WAITED NERVOUSLY at the door, inspecting the posy of purple anemones resting on top of the wicker welcome basket I had fussed over for two hours. In it I had put a couple of the jams and chutneys I'd bought at the farmer's market last Saturday, some posh biscuits, nice tea, a jar of vanilla sugar and a bottle of wine. There was no getting out of it any longer and I had decided I might as well face the music and get it over with. The door opened and a dark shadow fell across the landing. A ripple of fear ran down my spine as I looked into my new neighbour's unsmiling face.

'Hello,' I started innocently. 'I live upstairs.' I shakily offered the basket towards her. 'I just wanted to pop down and introduce myself and say welcome.'

She looked at me, looked at the basket, then back at me. Judging by her hefty frame I wouldn't stand a chance if this were to get a bit ugly. Her bulk was upholstered in a long, drifting kaftan, weighted down with an eclectic collection of pendants and necklaces fashioned from big, colourful pebbles, pieces of wood and, if my eyes did not deceive me, some kind of animal teeth. Her hair was covered with a turquoise scarf, secured in a large knot at the side of her head and fastened with a rather racy jewelled brooch. She reached out to touch the basket but didn't take it, then stepped back and pulled her door wider. 'Please,' she said in a startlingly low voice, 'do bring it in.' I stepped tentatively into her flat. Her ceilings were lower than mine, windows smaller, and the light felt different, I suppose because there was generally less of it.

Closing the door behind us, she turned to me and smiled questioningly. She was one of those women whose age is nigh on impossible to guess. On first inspection, I would say anywhere between sixty and eighty, give or take half a dozen years. Her face was pale and powdered with pads of rouge in that old-fashioned rose red shade, a streak of crimson lipstick, dark blue eyeshadow and lashings of block mascara. Clearly, she was a woman who was used to taking the trouble.

'You had to bring it in,' she explained, taking the basket from my hands. 'When a gift comes to your door in the hands of a stranger, you must never accept it before they have stepped across your threshold.'

'I'm Helen,' I said, offering my hand. She looked at it, took a breath and sandwiched it in between her soft palms.

'Helen,' she repeated quietly, then closed her eyes for a moment. Opening them again she patted my hand and let go. 'You are a good person, Helen. I think you and I will become great friends.' Her spontaneous smile was warm and mischievous. Then she pointed at herself. 'Rosa,' she said. 'Call me Rosa.'

Rosa had put the basket on top of one of her trunks. She now lifted out the bunch of flowers and picked up the jar of sugar. 'Oh! Vanilla,' she observed approvingly. 'We'll have some in our tea. Make yourself at home.' She took me into her sitting room and gestured towards two huge settees, both of which were shrouded in piles of tapestried throws and heaps of cushions. I did as she said and waited while she went to the kitchen. The whole room was draped in luscious fabrics. Not just in the curtains, but over the dark furniture, hanging in cascades from the walls and gathering loosely on the carpet. It felt otherworldly, with strange

ornaments cluttering all the surfaces and a few mysterious, abstract paintings leaning against the skirting
waiting to be hung.

When Rosa came back a few minutes later I found I
was feeling quite at home. The tea in the glass pot was
magnolia pale with tiny yellow flowers floating in it.
The posy of anemones now sat in a painted china vase
on the tray. Rosa served the tea in high Moroccan
glasses, put half a spoon of sugar in each and a sliver
of cinnamon, and placed each one on an ornate silver
saucer. I watched the steam curl upwards from the
glass and wondered how I was going to pick it up.

'Let it cool,' she said, as if having read my thoughts.
'It's better that way. The flavours become much more
intense.'

'Thank you,' I said. 'I hope you'll be very happy
here.'

Rosa leaned towards me. 'Are you?'

The glimmer in her eye was infectious and I
returned her smile. As impertinent as the question
sounded – and believe me, the way she put it, it did –
I think that older people are allowed to make such
direct enquiries. They have a lot less time than us to
fritter away on small talk.

'That's a good question,' I answered. 'Yes. I'm very
happy here.' I gave it a little more thought, wanting to
demonstrate my prowess as a good conversationalist.
'In fact, and I know this isn't very sensible – ' I let out

a nervous laugh – 'this was the only flat I saw. I came in and I knew immediately.' My hand wandered towards the glass but Rosa wagged a finger at me. 'I suppose it just felt right,' I finished.

'Excellent,' Rosa observed. 'You have the gift of intuition.'

'Really?' Suddenly her approval seemed inexplicably important to me.

'Of course,' she said. 'We all have it, but most people lose their inner eye by the time they reach their teens.' Rosa leaned forwards to the low, carved coffee table where the tray was settled and lifted the chequered cloth she had used to cover a mounded plate. Beneath it was a pile of cucumber sandwiches, crusts removed and cut into small squares rather than triangles. There was no way she could have rustled them up in the time it took her to make the tea. Anyone would have thought she had been expecting company. She offered me the plate then handed me a napkin.

'Where have you moved from?' I asked her.

'The Dorchester,' she replied through a delicate mouthful of sandwich.

I wasn't sure I had heard her properly. 'Dorchester, Dorset?'

'No,' she said. 'Dorchester, Park Lane.'

It took a few moments for the penny to drop. How can anyone possibly live in the Dorchester? This was the kind of response that demanded a stream of questions, but I felt it would be impolite. Rosa's shoulders betrayed a small chuckle as she watched me twitching with curiosity.

'Golly,' I said. 'I've never met anyone who lived in the Dorchester before.'

'We're a small club,' she said. 'But we do exist.'

'Why did you move?' I accepted two more sandwiches onto my open napkin. 'Sorry. It's none of my business. I didn't mean to ask such a personal question.'

'Not at all, Helen,' she said. I liked the way she said my name. It felt regal and important. 'I told you, you and I are going to be great friends, so you can ask me anything you want.' She wiped the ends of her fingers on the napkin and replaced it on the tray. 'Not that I promise to answer you,' she laughed. Her smile then faded and she pressed her crimson lips into a rueful pucker. 'They developed a problem with Babushka, which was quite ridiculous seeing as the two of us have been together for so long. Personally, I think it was nothing to do with her. They've changed so many of the old faces that we had become accustomed to and manners are not what they used to be. So I said to them, if you don't want Babushka, you don't want me.' She affected a little sniff. 'Then I left. I expect it was something to do with that odious little man who was responsible for destroying the Grill Room. Have you seen it?' I shook my head. 'Shocking. Utterly shocking.'

'Who's Babushka?' I asked.

'She's my . . .' Rosa trailed off and thought about it for a moment. 'Companion. Although I have to say she has been rather crotchety lately, what with all this upset. We are getting on in years, both of us.' She gave me a little nod. 'One gets stuck in one's ways. She won't be here until next week. I must get the place exactly right for her or she won't be happy with it at all.'

'Where is she now? Back at the Dorchester?'

'Gracious, no.' She tut-tutted. 'She's gone for a little holiday in the country.' Picking up her glass she nodded at me to do the same. 'Try your tea,' she said. 'It will be perfect now.'

I tasted it and it was.

'LOOK, RICK,' I SAID sternly. 'Don't you think you're taking this a bit far?'

'No,' he stared back at me petulantly. 'From now on, if any of the bloodsuckers want anything, you can bloody well tell them to call my lawyer.'

'That's hardly going to nurture a more loving relationship with your families.'

'Good.' He started flicking crossly through his car magazine then stopped and cocked his head at the page. 'Yeah,' he said, shoving the fat cigar back between his teeth and holding the magazine up. 'That's the one. What do you think, Hell?' He turned it round and displayed the gleaming photograph with clean, silver lines. I reached out and took it from him for closer inspection.

Picking out a new toy (Rick allows himself at least one a year) has been his favourite distraction activity for the past eight weeks. The Maserati was never the same after he impaled it on a bollard, so he called the dealer and told him to come and take it away. It's been chauffeur-driven cars for Rick since then. And car magazines. Loads of them. Why he decided to rope me in on the act I don't know. Our tastes are oceans apart. Every time he flapped a copy of *Supercar* in front of me I ended up saying something along the lines of 'wouldn't be seen dead in it', or 'have you any idea how ridiculous a man looks driving around in a tart's handbag like that?' He questioned me at length about the whys and why nots, and even made a few notes and stuck them in his wallet.

The magazine lay spread open in my lap, the centre-fold a portrait of a sleeping beast oozing power in the best possible taste. 'Now that – ' I tapped my finger lightly on the page – 'is a nice car.'

Leoni pulled up in the disabled space outside the glass-fronted brasserie and limped in to greet me at one of the tables facing the road.

'You'll never get away with it,' I told her. 'They're really strict around here and if you haven't got a blue badge you're a sitting duck.'

'Let them try it.' She kissed me hello. 'It'll be them that ends up with a disabled sticker.' She sat down and dumped her handbag on the floor beside her, shrugged her shoulders out of her camel coat and draped it over the back of her chair. Taking the menu from my hands, she gave its familiar contents a cursory scan then raised her eyebrows at me. 'Eggs Benedict?'

'That's exactly what I had in mind,' I replied.

'With a kir royale,' she said.

I glanced at my watch disapprovingly.

'After a cappuccino,' she conceded. 'Have you heard from Julia?'

I rummaged in my bag then motioned to the waiter to distract her. 'Have you?'

'I asked first,' she said. 'And no, I haven't.' The waiter came and we ordered. 'I'd bloody love to know what's going on there.' Leoni handed the menu back.

'I couldn't believe it when she told me,' I said. 'It was twenty years ago.'

'Do you think they've been in touch all this time?' Leoni leaned back to make way for the coffees and continental bread basket.

I shook my head. 'No,' I said. 'Definitely not. She got an email from him out of the blue. Julia had been mentioned in a meeting between some bigwigs in Milan. One of her clients was over there buying real estate or something.' I picked up a piece of bread and tore off a crust. 'Stan happened to be at that conference for some unknown reason. Said he couldn't believe it when he heard her name, so he made a note of Julia's company and tracked her down.'

Leoni spooned the cocoa-dusted froth off her cappuccino and ate it like a sundae. 'I wonder what he wants,' she said.

I chewed on my bread and mulled it over. 'I bet he's wondered over the years what happened to her,' I speculated. 'They really were in love. It can't have been easy for either of them.' My mind returned to that distant time. 'It was over just like that.' I snapped my fingers softly. 'Goodnight Vienna. They never saw each other again.' I shook my head sadly at the memories. 'For all I know, they never even spoke to each other on the phone after they broke up.'

'It's all very mysterious,' Leoni said mysteriously. 'But if you ask me' – I didn't – 'he's after something.' She put down the spoon. 'They always are. I'll bet he's married.'

'Divorced,' I said. 'Two kids.'

'So he got what he wanted then.' I had given Leoni the whole nine yards when we left the gallery.

'Looks like it.' I turned my attentions to the coffee. 'Julia said they went for dinner and talked the whole thing over. Poor thing,' I said. 'It must have been terribly emotional for her. She told him she's completely accepted that marriage had been out of the question.'

'Bastard,' mumbled Leoni.

'No he wasn't.' I pinched her hand playfully. 'He told Julia that he has regretted it every day since and asked for her forgiveness.'

'I knew it.' Leoni tapped the table. 'He's after something and doing a big psychological number on her. Now that he's got an heir and a spare, probably wants to play bloody Transylvanian step-families with Julia.' Leoni picked up her cup, downed the cappuccino in one and looked at me with doe eyes. 'Please, miss, can we have those drinkiepoos now?'

With the pair of us busily trying to get the waiter's attention to order Leoni's liveners, neither of us noticed the clampers locking a yellow boot on her car until it was too late. She marched outside, clean forgetting to limp, shouted at the two men and asked them if their children knew what they did for a living before stomping back to the table. She picked up her glass and addressed the waiter. 'Might as well make it a bottle,' she shouted. Then looking at me without apology, 'Well, it's not as though I've got to drive anywhere now, is it?'

*

SALLY ANSWERED THE DOOR with the telephone in his hand and a toothbrush sticking out of his mouth. He continued talking with the phone tucked in the crook of his neck and beckoned me in. I wandered through to their sitting room and helped myself to a good long look at his latest piece of work spread out on the drawing board by the window. He's an artist, and a very good one too. The unfinished illustration pinned beneath the parallel motion was full of life. I heard his lazy padding footsteps returning.

'Sorry,' he drawled, shaking his hands round his head and pulling a little salsa move. 'I'm feeling a little crazy today.'

'I don't want to disturb you.'

He kept dancing and grabbed my arms, forcing me to crash onto the sofa with him. 'You never disturb me.' He winked. 'But let's leave the front door a little bit open in case Paul comes back and thinks we're being naughty.'

Good idea. I won't go into it right now, but trust me. 'I'm having a dinner party,' I said. 'A big one.'

'What's the special occasion?' Sally smiled his big Colombian half-moon.

'We're going to welcome our new neighbour,' I said. 'She's really bloody interesting.' I thought of Rosa. 'A bit weird, mind you.'

Sally covered his smile with his hands and widened

his eyes. 'Did she say anything about us spying on her when she arrived?'

'Not a word. She didn't even mention it.'

Sally nodded approvingly. 'That's pretty cool. Yeah.'

'So you'll tell Paul?'

'Sure. What day?'

'I thought Friday would be good.'

Sally got up and consulted their diary, wrote it in and came back to me. 'I'm bored,' he whispered cheekily with a note of mischief in his voice. 'Shall we mix a jug of margaritas and watch daytime TV?'

DIFFERENT THINGS ARE important to different people. I, for example, believe there is no substitute for a nice big dining table with comfortable chairs, crisp white linen, heavy cutlery and sparkling crystal. Although I don't like to broadcast it, you might as well know that I have the benefit of a rather tidy little nest egg courtesy of my husband's early demise, which, provided I am careful, should be sufficient to see me through my dotage quite nicely. Of the few luxuries on my wish list, the grand dining paraphernalia had been at the top. I asked everyone to arrive at seven thirty sharp so we could all be there to welcome the guest of honour when she appeared at eight.

'What's she like?' Paul was on drinks duty in the

kitchen. I had quite enough to deal with, having decided to birch myself by rustling up a Nobel Prize-worthy dinner for ten. Despite swearing to myself that I would keep it simple (when will I ever learn?), the sight of all the seasonal fayre in the local purveyors of fine produce had sent my pulse racing. I couldn't help but succumb to temptation, broke the budget and went just a little bit mad. Besides, I had a sneaking suspicion that Rosa's culinary bar, honed as it was by the Dorchester, was probably set far higher than your average new girl, and I didn't want to let the side down.

'She seems really nice,' I said. 'Eccentric, but nice.' Wrestling the goose back into the oven for its final blast, I topped off my appraisal with a sweeping assumption. 'I think you'll like her.' Right. Vegetables: check. Sauce: check. And don't forget to get the torte out of the fridge. 'That's it.' I clapped my hands. 'I think we're just about ready to sound mess call.' Paul handed me an icy gin and tonic.

'Is this bloody Beluga?' boomed Marcus as I brought the last two starters to the table. As usual, he had begun eating before everyone was served, even though that had meant him digging into Leoni's, much to her chagrin.

'I cannot deny that it is,' I said, feeling a little embarrassed at such an ostentatious dish. I had hoped-that no one would notice my shameless extravagance. The thing is, you see, that my friends are not entirely aware of my financial circumstances. I had a bit of a financial hiccup some time ago and learned a few crucial lessons about how money can affect people and relationships. I now stick firmly to the traditional principle of never mentioning such vulgarities. It's one of the reasons why I still have a job. Like a perfect smokescreen. It's no bother either. I like working for Rick. I think I'd be at a loose end if I didn't and I don't doubt that he would be too. I put a plate in front of Marcus and took the last to my seat at the bottom of the table. Rosa held court at the head. It seemed a fitting moment for me to say a few words before unleashing my spectacular menu.

'Before we start – ' Leoni grabbed Marcus's arm, already halfway to his gaping jaws with another loaded mother-of-pearl spoon, and wrestled his hand back down. 'Thank you, Marcus,' I said. He looked inconvenienced. 'I think we should propose an early toast to Rosa to wish her health and happiness in her new home before we all get stuck into the vino collapso.'

'Hear, hear!' shouted Marcus then shoved the spoonful in his mouth while Leoni wasn't looking. We all raised our glasses then tucked in. 'So where have you hailed from?' Marcus was talking to Rosa but looking at his food.

'The Dorchester,' she replied.

'Dorchester?' Marcus repeated.

'No, Marcus,' I said, spooning a little more caviar onto his plate. '*The* Dorchester.'

My clarification was met with stunned silence. Even Marcus stopped eating. The initially shy curiosity that everyone had displayed around the new acquaintance was soon abandoned and became an all-out barrage of questions. Rosa turned out to be an extraordinary supper guest who knew the kind of gossip about famous people that never makes it into the press. She knew these sensational events to be true, because most of the time she had been there.

'I've heard that Rock Hudson used to keep a suite at the Dorchester when he was in London,' said Paul.

'He was very sweet.' Rosa replied. 'Most charming.'

Paul ventured a little further. 'Is it true about . . .'

Rosa dropped her spoon and began nodding immediately. 'Absolutely,' she said. 'I have never seen anything like it in my life. Where he got the pygmies from I don't know. I think they may have been shipped in from the Amazon.' Paul was enchanted. Rosa beckoned him to come closer and leaned into his ear.

Paul listened, his smiling mouth opening as wide and as shocked as his eyes. He turned sharply to face her. 'No!' he said.

'It's true.' Rosa was deadpan. 'With Liza Minnelli and her chihuahua. But you must promise me that you will never tell a living soul.' She apologized to the rest of us. 'I know it's rude to whisper. Forgive me.' Her eyes shone with a distant memory. 'And Helen, this is the most fabulous dinner. Where on earth did you learn how to cook like this? You could teach the chefs at the Dorchester a thing or two.'

'She does it to make the rest of us feel inadequate,' Sara said through a mouthful. 'It's a special gene. You've either got it, or you haven't. I can't even boil an egg.'

Dudley looked up. 'Have you ever tried, darling?'

'Why should I? You're rich. You can afford to pay someone to boil eggs for us.' Sara was unrepentant. 'Besides, I thought you married me for sex, not snacks.'

'Sounds all right to me!' Marcus guffawed, as he tends to do when anyone mentions reproduction or bodily functions. 'Leoni's a terrible cook anyway.' He looked at his wife. 'How about it, darling? You can give all the kitchen duties a miss from now on and I'll settle for a bit of the other instead.'

Leoni scowled at him. 'I'd rather spend the rest of my days shackled to a stove.'

Rosa's pale-green eyes sparkled. When everyone had finished their first course she got up and helped me in the kitchen, despite my protestations. 'This is quite the most wonderful evening I've had in a very long time,' she said, tying a full bin liner and flapping open another. 'I'd forgotten what it was like to entertain

friends and make a wonderful mess without room service.' We recruited Marcus to struggle the goose to the
dining table then settled in for some serious eating.

Julia and David were unusually quiet, although at
least David made an effort to keep up. Julia seemed as
though her mind was elsewhere. I saw Rosa looking at
her intently on several occasions, but Julia appeared
unreceptive to her efforts at conversation.

'Are you feeling all right?' Sara asked her. 'We've
hardly heard a dickie bird out of you all evening.'

Julia attempted an unconvincing smile. 'I've had
a ferocious headache all day,' she said. 'I've taken a
couple of Nurofen but it just won't budge.'

'Nurofen?' spat Paul. 'They give that stuff to babies.'
He got up from the table and threw down his napkin.
'Wait here,' he said, scurrying towards the door. 'I'll
be back in two shakes of a lamb's tail.'

Julia turned to David. 'I think I may have to go
home,' she told him.

'Whatever you want to do, darling,' David replied
heavily. 'I'll get our coats.'

Julia protested immediately. 'No. Why don't you
stay here? No point in us both being party poopers.'

'Don't be ridiculous, darling. I'll take you home.'

'Please.' Julia pressed him. 'I'm no company anyway.
I'd rather be on my own.'

David raised his hands in submission and retook his
seat. Leoni and I made a point not to look at each

other and we all ignored the awkward silence. Mercifully, Paul broke the ice when he bounded back in a couple of seconds later and everything returned to normal. 'Here. Swallow a couple of these.' He put a blister pack in front of Julia and refreshed her water glass. 'In half an hour, you won't even remember you had a headache. In fact, I defy you to even know what your name is.' Julia reluctantly took her medicine and rang for a taxi. Everything felt a little strained for a while until Julia's cab arrived. David watched her leave then raised his eyebrows to the rest of us.

'I must apologize for my wife,' he said with resignation. 'She's been under a lot of pressure lately and isn't feeling herself, I'm afraid.' I knew that Leoni would be pulling faces at me so kept my eyes firmly locked on David.

'Best thing for her,' bellowed Marcus. 'Woman with a headache? Bloody worst thing known to mankind, David. At least she won't be here chewing your balls off for drinking too much.' He filled David's glass right up to the brim. 'Get that down your neck and I bet you fifty quid I can eat more goose than you.' Marcus slapped a fifty-pound note on the table with all the panache of an East End market trader and emptied his glass in one gulp. David laughed and seemed to relax visibly.

'If I may make a suggestion,' said Rosa. 'Why don't we indulge in an amusing parlour game after dinner?

I think I may have just the thing to provide a little light distraction.'

Some time later, after David had thrown in the towel and conceded defeat in the face of Marcus's competitive eating disorder, Rosa slipped downstairs to her flat and came back carrying a black box draped with an ornately embroidered silk scarf. With the dining table cleared, she asked for the lights to be turned down then lit the four candles she had brought with her and began to rearrange the chairs.

'What's she doing?' whispered Leoni, who was supposed to be helping us clear away the dishes but was managing not to lift a finger.

'I haven't the faintest idea,' I said. 'Why don't you take the brandy through? I'll bring the coffee.'

'She's got something under that scarf,' she hissed.

Sara stopped what she was doing and tried to get a look over Leoni's shoulder. 'Maybe it's a strip poker set for the aged. That's why she wanted all the lights dimmed. Bet she wants to get a closer look at David's credentials. Did you see the way she was eyeing him up over dinner?'

Soon Rosa seemed satisfied that her table was ready and clapped her hands softly. 'Is everybody ready? Do come and take a seat.' We all chattered back to our chairs. 'Helen, would you mind putting the kitchen lights off, dear? It's much better if we can use just these.'

Sitting between Rosa and Paul, I felt an eerie hush descend over the room. We looked at each other, our faces glowing in the golden candlelight, and waited. Rosa removed the scarf from the table to reveal an ancient ouija board, complete with an old-fashioned planchette and faded lettering. 'Tonight,' she said, 'we are going to hold a seance.' I felt my blood run cold. Contacting the dead? Given my circumstances? No, thank you very much. Why couldn't she have come back with a special edition Monopoly set or Twister?

'Oh my God, that's *too* scary!' squealed Paul, bouncing in his chair and pulling at Sally's sleeve in mock terror.

'Cool!' said Sara, rubbing her hands together.

Leoni's eyes widened. 'Bloody hell. Are you sure this is a good idea? I mean, don't people end up throwing themselves out of windows and all the walls start bleeding?'

'You've been watching too many of those old Hammer horror films,' Rosa said. 'But if anyone doesn't want to join in, that's quite all right. We can put it all away and play a nice hand of cards instead.'

'Well, I'm game,' said Dudley. 'It's the live ones you have to watch out for.'

'Me too,' said Marcus. 'In fact I wouldn't mind contacting the old man and finding out what he did with all those bonds he used to have. Great wodges of the things. The old dear hasn't the foggiest idea where he used to keep his money tied up. Bloody died of a heart attack without leaving so much as a note.' Marcus tutted. 'Silly old bastard.'

Rosa waited patiently for us to settle down then asked, 'Is everyone ready?'

We all nodded.

'We need complete silence for this. Now, I want you all to concentrate very hard and banish all thoughts from your heads.' We all pretended to clear our minds and watched sneakily as Rosa mumbled to herself and lit several incense sticks. She smudged the smoke around the table and took a few exaggerated breaths. 'All right. Let's all hold hands and form a circle.' I found Paul's hand to my left and Rosa's to my right. The silence grew. Rosa began in a low, monotonous voice, repeating, 'Is there anybody there?'

There was no sound for a few moments, then a small squeaking voice said, 'I see dead people.' Dudley glared at Sara. She stopped grinning. 'Sorry,' she said. 'I was only messing about.'

'If we are to enter the spirit world,' said Rosa quietly, 'we must do so with gravitas and respect.' I noticed Paul nudge Leoni. Rosa continued. 'Is there anybody there?' We all waited, the nail-biting tension mounting. Zilcho.

Suddenly the flame of one of the candles flickered. Leoni's sharp intake of breath gave us all a jolt. 'Did you see that? Oh my God. I'm going to have a heart attack.'

'It was you breathing heavily,' Marcus said.

'No it wasn't!' she snapped at him. 'It moved. I saw it.'

'Oh, do shut up, darling.'

Leoni pouted and returned her attentions to the mystic circle. Rosa closed her eyes and continued her deep breathing exercises. Our hands remained clasped together and several long minutes passed in silence. I peeped across at Leoni. She did her snarling I'm Bored expression. I shrugged my shoulders. At that moment Rosa sat up bolt upright. 'There's something in the room with us,' she announced before lowering her voice and speaking to the presence. 'If there is somebody here from the spirit world, give us a sign.' A car horn blared from the street outside.

'Shit!' screeched Leoni. 'I'm freaking! What if it wants to kill us?'

'It's OK,' soothed Sally. 'I don't think that counts.'

'Shhh!' urged Rosa. 'There's something coming through. A message from the other side.' She opened her eyes. 'Everyone, quickly, put a finger on the planchette.'

'The what?' said Sara.

'The pushy thing,' said Paul knowledgeably.

'This is creeping me out.' Leoni shuddered and

knocked back Marcus's brandy before adding her index finger to the pile.

'Who are you?' said Rosa. Nothing happened.

'Do you have a message for somebody in this room?' The marker twitched. We looked up at each other, some of us showing more obvious signs of alarm than others. Leoni's upper lip glistened with nervous perspiration. Quite deliberately, our fingers unanimously slid along the board and came to rest on the word *Yes*.

'I don't believe what I'm seeing,' said Dudley, his eyes widening.

'Be quiet,' hissed Sara. 'This is just starting to get interesting.'

Rosa asked in a more commanding tone, 'Who is your message for?'

The planchette began to move again. This time towards the letter H, then the E, then the L. Then it stopped.

'It's for Helen!' choked Paul. 'It has to be! Oh my God. I'm so scared!'

Leoni was quivering in her seat. There came a sharp tap from beneath the table. We all jumped out of our skins and held our breath.

'Quiet!' urged Rosa. 'Don't break the circle of concentration.' She looked up towards the ceiling. 'Bring us your message!' she commanded. 'Send us a sign!' The tension was unbearable. Marcus's brow was jewelled with perspiration, Rosa swayed from side to side, grasping our hands and moaning rhythmically, Paul's eyes were bulging, even Sara was chewing her lip. The silence was abruptly shattered by the loud serrated noise of the door buzzer. Leoni let out a bloodcurdling scream and Paul fainted to the floor.

'That's it!' shouted Marcus. 'I've had enough of this! Who's been knocking on the table and making the candle flames go funny? Eh? Come on! Which one of you was it?' He jumped up from the table and turned on the lights, spinning round to examine our faces. We all squinted at each other under the sudden glare but everyone looked innocent.

Rosa adjusted her dishevelled turban and smiled. 'It's quite all right, Marcus. Everybody gets a little nervous at their first seance. Next time will be a lot more relaxed.'

'Next time?' His voice was near to hysterical. 'Are you mad? What am I saying? Of course you are! Why else would someone want to scare my wife half to death as after-dinner entertainment?' Marcus mopped his fevered brow with a handkerchief and steadied himself against the back of Leoni's chair while she clattered the brandy bottle against the lip of her shaking glass.

Sally was attempting to rouse the gently moaning, carpetized Paul, slapping his hand and calling his name. Sara barged up with a glass of water and threw it into Paul's face. He immediately began to splutter and came to his senses. 'Where am I?' he whimpered theatrically. 'What happened?'

'Oh, get with the programme and stop being such a drama queen,' said Sara. 'We could have had a full-blown *Ghostbusters* moment there. You're such a cream puff.'

Somewhere amid the melee, I remembered that the doorbell had gone. Before I could stop to consider whether or not it was a headless torso in clanking chains, I hit the buzzer. A few moments later Julia appeared at the top of the stairs.

'Hello?' I said. 'Shouldn't you be at home by now?' She gave me a sad smile. I stepped out onto the landing and pulled the door to, lowering my voice to a whisper. 'That is, assuming you were going home and not somewhere else?'

'I got the funniest feeling in the taxi,' she said. 'Almost like there was a voice in my head telling me to turn around and go back.' I felt a pull on the door handle. David appeared behind me.

'Julia?' He looked confused.

Julia looked up at him. 'We need to talk.'

To-do List

Cook fifty-eight tons of food for Leoni.

Organize Rick's life.

Hire a private detective to follow Julia.

Remake kids' costumes.

Never have a dinner party for Rosa again.

Ring the Samaritans.

Chapter Eight

IT'S GONNA BE LONELY, THIS CHRISTMAS

Being a little blurry-eyed the next morning, I almost overlooked the cerise envelope that had slithered under the door. Taking it to the kitchen with me, I slit it open with the paring knife and perched on a stool while the kettle did its thing. My eyes darted to the bottom of the long letter. It was from Rosa. Either she's an early riser or she must have written it last night. I admire that in a person, swift thank-you notes, although this looked more like an epistle. Eyes returning to the top of the page, I began to read. By the time I got to the bottom my mouth was agape.

After the compliments about the dinner party the night before and some lengthy apologies for scaring the bejesus out of Leoni, she had gone on to say she thought my sister was deeply troubled and needed keeping an eye on and that I had a problem she could help me with. It was all rather strange really. I wondered if I hadn't gushingly made friends too quickly with a woman who appeared amazing on first impression but who had rapidly turned out to be a nutter. I decided to pop down to ask her for an explanation. Upon reaching her door I found a prescient note stuck to the knocker. It said, *Gone to fetch Babushka*, and was signed off with a flourishing 'R'.

Great. We are about to receive the nutter's live-in Latvian girlfriend and if she's already been kicked out of the Dorchester, heaven only knows what havoc she's going to wreak here. I retreated to my kitchen, made a cup of tea and sighed at my growing list of other people's responsibilities.

WHENEVER DECEMBER BECKONS, I find that my thoughts turn to reflecting on the year drawing towards its close. One thing's for sure, I've learned a lot. The world today is a very different place from the one I grew up in. Not many cars on the road. Hardly any yellow lines. People's doors left open for the neighbours. And the summers seemed longer. It's not like that now. Everyone living at a hundred miles an hour. Consumerism gone mad. Kids terrorizing adults. Yes, it's a brave new world all right, but I've found my little space in it, although, now and again, I cannot pretend it wouldn't be nice to have someone to share it with. Consulting my own list of things-to-do-before-D-day, the absence of a special person for whom to choose a perfect present was painfully conspicuous.

I put the tray down on the low table in the sitting room. The loo flushed from a far corner of the flat. Julia appeared, smoothing the line of her cherry-red skirt, sat on the sofa on the opposite side of the table and pushed off her shoes. 'That's better,' she sighed, running her fingers through her hair as she watched me pour the coffee. I remained silent until I finished arranging the cups, sensing her tension.

'Headache gone?' I asked absently.

'Yes,' she said. 'It was a real stinker. Nice of you to suggest coffee this afternoon.' What she actually meant was she knew very well that I had an ulterior motive, like wanting to have a word with her in private. So come on. Out with it.

'Well,' I said without looking up, 'I didn't really get to see much of you last night.'

'It was a lovely dinner party.' She headed for neutral ground. 'Sorry I dashed off like that.'

'So?' I said to her.

'So what?' she replied. We looked at each other squarely, locked in a temporary stalemate until one or the other gave way.

I let out an exasperated puff and put my cup down on the table. 'You know exactly what,' I said. 'You want to watch yourself, Julia.' We don't stress each other's names very often, and when we do, it's usually to make a point.

'There's nothing going on.' She picked up her own cup and saucer. 'If that's what you're getting at.'

'I'll take your word for it,' I said rather too aggressively. We both backed off quickly. Then, softening my voice: 'I'm just worried about you,' I said. 'I think you're a bit vulnerable at the moment and if you're having a bad patch with David the last thing you need is to go and get sidetracked by somebody else.' Julia stared into her cup. 'I know that you two were madly in love but it was a long time ago. You can't go back, Julia. Not unless you're one hundred per cent sure that it's absolutely what you want.' She nodded silently. 'Think of David, if nothing else.' I stopped talking and drank some of my coffee.

'It's like the years just drop away,' she said in a small voice. 'Like going back in time. I even feel different. The way I used to feel then.' Julia smiled at me with sadness in her eyes. 'I know it's ridiculous,' she said. 'I know that none of this makes any sense, but I can't go on for the next ten years doing exactly the same thing as I've done before. I'm forty-three going on fifty and what have I done with my life?'

I got up, came round to her sofa and rested my hand on her knee.

'Be careful with your heart,' I said to her. 'He's already broken it once. The important thing is what you have now.' We sat together quietly for a while, the atmosphere heavy with regret for things that cannot be regained. Then, I slapped my thighs hard with both hands. 'Hark at me, giving you advice about relationships,' I said self-mockingly. 'I couldn't spot a decent bloke if he landed right in front of me. How about a bit of cake to go with that?' I rose to my feet and went briskly to the kitchen to fetch the walnut gateau I had knocked up during yesterday morning's *Woman's Hour*, before I started cooking the main event. Reaching the cake tin out of the cupboard and pulling off the lid, the shock of what lay within gave me such a jolt that I felt every hair on my body move. 'Mouse!' I screamed as the whole thing crashed to the floor.

WITH A MERE four weeks to go it began to dawn on me that I may well have bitten off more than any sane human being could comfortably chew. Coming straight in at number one in the pre-Christmas disaster charts were the costumes for Leoni's children. I laid them out on the bed, sat on the dressing-table stool with a mug of hot chocolate and tried to convince myself that it wasn't as bad as it looked. But it was. The boys' dwarf outfits were a complete catastrophe, and as for my foam Star of Bethlehem, well, let's not even go there. I chewed my lower lip until it was sore, then picked up the phone to Leoni.

'Helen!' she announced merrily into the phone.

'How did you know it was me?'

'We've got a new Nimrod phone where the numbers come up,' she said. 'I got it from Argos so I can spot if it's Marcus's mother. Forewarned is forearmed.'

'Shrewd move,' I said.

'What's new, pussycat?' She sang a bit of the tune.

'Nothing much,' I lied. 'But I need you to check a few measurements for me so that I can make sure the children's costumes are the right size.'

'Sure,' she said cheerfully. 'What do you need?'

'Height, shoulder width, hips, waist, inside leg for the boys, and nape to knees.'

'Uh-huh.'

'Are you writing this down?' The momentary silence spoke volumes, so I offered to hang on while she got a pen then made her repeat each part of the brief back to me.

'I can't tell you how much I appreciate this, Helen,' she said. 'You're a bloody superstar.'

'I know,' I said. 'But the superstar's running out of

time, so quick as you can please. And for God's sake double-check them, OK?'

'Rightie-ho,' she said, then lowered her voice. 'Marcus is being all huffy with me because I've told him he's got to do the Christmas cards this year. I've given him a list as long as the electoral register, three moth-eaten address books, and told him to get on with it.' She sniggered softly. 'I've even added some bogus ones.'

'Is he doing them now?'

'You're joking,' she said. 'He has no idea how long it will take, seeing as he's never written so much as a note for the milkman before. I'll bet you he's going to try and make it look like a really easy five-minute job, then he'll get into a complete panic about it at the last minute.'

'Like you do, you mean.'

Leoni's tone became menacing. 'I bloody hate Christmas cards.'

GETTING A DECENT RESTAURANT reservation at this time of year can be a bit touch and go.

'Who chose this place?' said Julia.

'Me,' I replied proudly.

She sat back while the waiter flapped a napkin into her lap. 'Very impressive,' she approved. 'Not a Christmas hat in sight.' With this probably being our last girlie lunch of the year before the schools break up and Leoni goes off radar, I had buttered Rick up and asked if he could get me a table for four at his favourite haunt. He's taken me there a couple of times and it wasn't the kind of place where you'd be likely to run into a rowdy table of tinsel-topped photocopier salesmen.

'I thought you had to wait months to get in here,' said Sara, glancing at the sumptuous interior with low, golden lighting. 'Even Dudley's secretary couldn't manage it when I wanted to come for dinner. Miserable cow. She's got a real attitude problem. We call her Mrs Danvers.'

'Let's just say I got lucky,' I smiled. We raised our glasses and said cheers.

'Talking of office parties,' said Leoni, 'we've got Marcus's do coming up in a couple of weeks. It's a dinner dance at that place on the embankment. Something on the river. Can't remember now.'

'Really?' said Julia. 'God. I haven't been there for years. Used to be a favourite haunt with Princess Madge when she was a gadabout, didn't it?'

'Dunno,' said Leoni, pulling her bread in half. 'All I do know is that Marcus tried on his dress suit last night and looked like a fat girl's socks.'

Sara was scrutinizing the menu. 'Bloody hell,' she said. 'They've got everything here. What are you going to wear?'

'I'm not sure yet. It depends on how much money I can extract from Marcus. Why did I have to marry a miser who's as tight as a gnat's chuff?'

'Oh, goody,' Sara said. 'Sounds like a shopping excursion on the horizon.'

Leoni shook her head violently and swallowed. 'No way,' she said. 'I'm pocketing the dosh then I'm going to borrow something from one of you lot and stick it in a new carrier bag.' She put down her menu. 'What are we all having?'

We ordered different dishes so that we could taste each other's and maximize our gastronomic experience. To sit in front of fine cuisine that someone else has slaved over and relax for a couple of hours with your favourite company is roughly as good as it gets. Leoni found the truffles in her sauce a little peculiar so we swapped plates and she tore into my osso bucco with reckless abandon.

'How's David?' I asked Julia as Leoni flashed her eyes at me.

'He's fine,' she said evenly. 'We've booked the holiday so I suppose at least that's one thing we won't be arguing about now.'

'I thought you said you didn't have the time,' Sara said.

Julia kept her face masked and emotionless. 'David arranged it, so I didn't have a great deal of say in the matter.'

'Why haven't you given me the dates? I've told you before, so long as it's in the diary, I can field it.'

'Yes, yes.' Julia looked irritable. 'I'll get them from David tonight.'

'Going anywhere nice?' I said airily.

The way she spat Hawaii, Julia might as well have said Belmarsh. Leoni sensed it was a good time to change the subject. 'I could have murdered the woman on the train with me this morning. She sat there right there in front of me making phone call after phone call, talking and laughing really loudly about her stupid, inane life. Everyone in the carriage was glaring at her but she didn't take a blind bit of notice.'

Sara was nodding. 'I hate people who do that.'

'Don't tell me,' I said. 'You decided to enlighten her.'

'I stood it for a lot longer than I should have done if you ask me.' Leoni made her vampire face. 'She started dialling another number and I shouted at her, "That had better be a fucking emergency call, love, because if I have to listen to one more of your asinine conversations you'll be needing a bloody ambulance."' Even Julia let out a mighty roar.

I pointed my glass at Sara. 'And what about you?' I asked her. 'Looking forward to your first Christmas as a married woman?'

Sara raised her eyebrows. 'We're going to my parents,' she said. 'So God knows how that will pan out. At least I won't have to think about cooking, although I've had some worrying reports about what's been coming out of my mother's oven these days. She's still tinkering with her prescriptions and now that Dudley's sent her off to his own private GP and offered to pick up all her bills, their bathroom cabinet looks like the bloody Rowntree Macintosh factory.' We all made little clucking noises. 'Dad's thinking about retiring, which has thrown her into a flat spin. She keeps telling him that most men die within two years of drawing their pension, so if he wants to live a long and happy life, he'd better stay at work.'

'She's a bloody card, your mum,' said Leoni. 'At least she's not lying in bed in a candlewick dressing gown waiting for the onslaught of old age.'

By the time I got home it was already getting dark. I noticed the lights on in Rosa's flat. Stopping briefly at her door, I reminded myself that I'd had a couple of glasses of wine and a Limoncello. Or was it two? Either way, now was probably not the smartest of times to tackle a sixteen-stone liberty-taker. I headed up the stairs, let myself in and got comfortable on the sofa with a cup of mint tea. Does wonders for indigestion, and wine seems to afflict me with terrible heartburn these days. Cheese after six is completely out of the question. Noel Edmonds was scurrying around on the television set whipping his audience up into a blue-rinsed frenzy and I watched a callow young man go red as he pretended not to be gutted at having turned down a fortune in favour of opening a box containing 50p.

There was a gentle rap on the door. Peering through the spy hole, I saw Rosa waiting on the landing. After what felt like a remarkably long day I'd kind of run out of steam about the contents of her strange letter. I wasn't really in the mood for a ding-dong and was tempted to ignore the knock and go back to the television, but she stared into the other side of the lens as though she could see me standing there and smiled. I reluctantly pulled the door open. Before I could say anything, I saw that she had brought something with her.

'Helen,' she said, as though about to bestow a dame-hood upon me. 'I'm not disturbing you, am I?' She rearranged the enormous burnt-orange bundle in her arms, lifted it up and presented it to me. 'This,' she said proudly, 'is Babushka.' Babushka granted me a supercilious glare with flaming yellow eyes then closed them slowly while Rosa fussed her luxuriously furry neck. 'May we come in?'

My first reaction was to ask if her companion was house-trained, but they made such an arresting couple that it seemed only natural to treat them both with the utmost deference. Rosa made her way to the sitting room and checked that the French doors were closed. 'I have buttered her paws,' she explained. 'I wouldn't want her wandering off and getting lost.' She bent to Babushka's ear. 'Would we, darling?'

'Would you like some mint tea?' I asked her.

'That would be lovely,' she said. 'But I'd much rather have a large brandy if you have one.'

I poured Rosa a drink, replaced the cap, then threw caution to the wind and joined her with a small one for myself even though I was still feeling a little acidic. Should be OK. I bought a big pack of Rennies yesterday which ought to see me through the night. I'll tuck one in each cheek like a hamster before retiring.

'Thank you for your note,' I said, handing her one of the snifters. She took it from me touching my hand as she did so.

'I wondered if you might think it a little forward,' she said, settling herself and the purring monster on the sofa.

'It was rather unusual, I'll grant you.' I sat beside her and looked down at the cat in her lap. 'I thought it somewhat surprising that you should think I have a problem.' I smiled brightly to indicate that all was well in my little life, although God knows she could take her pick of any number of fault lines if you want to get all analytical about it. 'I wasn't sure how to take it.'

Rosa smiled back but didn't answer. 'And how is your sister?'

I raised my eyes to hers in submission. 'You were

right about that one,' I conceded. 'But I think she'll be OK. I don't know.' Rosa nodded silently and looked sympathetic. I took a small sip of the brandy and felt its heat burn my throat. 'So,' I said, 'what did you mean about me?'

Rosa looked down at Babushka and stroked her with long movements of her ring-laden hands. 'Did you hear that, Babushka?' she whispered. Babushka purred like an engine and returned her gaze with glowing eyes. Rosa looked up with a big smile and winked at me. 'My intuition tells me that you need a cat – ' she took a sip from her glass – 'to catch a mouse.'

'MY FEET ARE fucking killing me. Can't we stop for a pint?'

'Nope.'

'Oh, go on, Hell. Look. Why don't you take over and I'll pay you ten per cent on everything you buy?'

'Will you please stop complaining. You're beginning to get on my nerves.'

'Right. That's it.' Rick stopped in the middle of the aisle and dumped the bags he was holding. 'I'm not taking another step until I've had a drink and a drag on a cigar.'

I suppose it was inevitable that it would come to this. For a man of such vulgar wealth Rick had a remarkably acute aversion to shopping. He's quite happy to order stuff off the internet, usually late at night when he's been at the Armagnac, but the thought of walking into a store and choosing something is anathema to him. I lead him to the only café in the shop where you're allowed to smoke.

'Here,' I said, pointing at a free table. 'You park yourself there and I'll find the waitress. This is a thirty-minute pit stop and no more, understand?'

'Oh, for fuck's sake, Hell. You're worse than Mr Indicator.'

I should probably explain that Mr Indicator is Rick's personal trainer. Rick calls him that because of the way he flaps his arms about when demonstrating star jumps. Rick sat down. I placed the order. When I got back to the table, Rick was trying to take his shoes off.

'Don't do that!' I barked at him. 'If your feet are hurting that's the worst thing you can possibly do. Put them back on afterwards and they'll feel like they're full of broken glass. You have to rise above the pain.' I showed him how to take a few deep breaths. 'Don't think about how much your feet hurt. Think about how much you're achieving in just one day of Christmas shopping.'

'You're all bloody mad,' he said. 'I don't know why I let you talk me into this.' The waitress arrived with our drinks and Rick fell on his beer like a desert rat.

'Because it's about time you started putting a little more effort into your family for a change,' I told him.

'It's all very well throwing money left, right and centre and getting your secretary or old muggins here to do your dirty work. This time you're going to choose all the presents yourself. You never know, you might even experience a bit of the joy of giving.' I rolled my eyes. 'How would you feel if I didn't even know what I'd got you for Christmas?'

Rick pulled from his mouth the cigar he had been frantically trying to light. 'Have you got me a present?' He looked all chuffed.

'Well, no.' I couldn't bear to see the disappointment on his face. 'At least, not yet.' I sighed. 'Oh, for heaven's sake, Rick, that's not the point. It's you we're talking about here.' Our sandwiches arrived. 'Look, eat your lunch and we'll crack on. Gift shopping doesn't do itself, you know.'

Rick munched on his sandwich while I consulted our list. Instead of doing all his shopping for him, as he had tried to insist, I had written out the names of the people he needed to buy presents for and demanded that he take at least one day to attend to it. Stubborn as a mule, he refused point-blank and dug his heels in. So I went on strike. Within forty-eight hours he had relented and hauled up the white flag. Now here we were in Selfridges and I might as well have chosen to drag a dead horse around the place. Rick turned out to be completely hopeless in anything except the home entertainment department. I'd had to sit him down at one point and explain to him the basic principles of shopping for other people. If you've got lots of money and it's for a female aged fifteen or over, head for the expensive handbags. If it's for a male, buy some kind of electronic gadget. If they're too old to have teeth of their own, play it safe with a Val Doonican record. See? Piece of cake. He'd nodded, clicked his head this way and that, loosened his shoulders with a couple of rolls and said, 'Right.'

The practical part of the exercise didn't go as smoothly as the theory. Every time a pretty sales assistant accosted him with her wares, Rick's brain dropped into his trousers. I had to keep steering him away and reminding him that no, it wasn't his magnetic personality, they were all on commission.

Sandwich demolished, Rick slumped back in his chair and had another go at lighting his cigar. 'OK,' he said. 'Who's next?'

'Helga.'

'Well, that's easy,' he said. 'We'll get Spud to forge her a British passport. That'll keep the KGB out of her hair.'

'Very funny,' I said. 'I think you should get her a nice coat. The one she's wearing has seen better days.' I moved down the list. 'And something for your secretary.'

We looked at each other and racked our brains for a couple of minutes. Neither of us could think of anything. 'Handbag?' Rick finally suggested. We both nodded and I made a note.

By six o'clock Rick was almost weeping with fatigue. He got himself and his mountain of shopping bags into a cab and went home to unweld his shoes from his blistered feet. I was feeling pretty smug when I let myself into the flat. Big man with his big business and big ideas, reduced to a gibbering imbecile after less than seven hours of retail therapy. Lightweight. I left my handbag by the door and turned on a few lights. It had been raining and the street lights left streaks of white in the droplets on the windowpanes. Pushing my shoes off and trying not to wince, I shuffled into the kitchen in search of a tasty little fridge morsel and a well-earned glass of wine. Babushka was lying in wait in the corner, half in, half out of the cupboard where the mouse had last been seen.

It wasn't until much later that I had the first notion that something might not be quite right. I treated myself to an indecently long bath with a dash of Radio 4, ate half a box of chocolates while allowing my hair to dry 'naturally' (couldn't be bothered to blow-dry it), and watched a pointless documentary on Channel Five about fat people who eat their own bodyweight in junk food and drink fifteen gallons of Coke a day, then wonder why they look the way they do. Is it just me or has telly gone right downhill these days? The chocolates had left me feeling sweet-toothed and munchy so I was on my way to make some proper cocoa when I noticed that Babushka hadn't moved a whisker. Literally.

'Babushka?' I said, as though talking to a plumber lying under the kitchen sink. 'Are you all right?'

My cheeks went hot. I tentatively put my toe towards the cat and gave it a little nudge. The mug dropped from my grip and smashed on the floor. My hands rushed to my face. Oh my God. Absolutely no response.

'What am I going to do?' I howled at Paul about thirty seconds later after hammering on his door.

'Nice pyjamas,' he commented as I fell in. 'What's up?'

'I've killed her cat!' Sally looked across from the sofa and switched off the TV. 'She left it with me to deal with the mouse in my kitchen and now it's dead!'

'What on earth are you going on about? What cat?'

'Rosa's cat! The one that got barred from the Dorchester!'

Paul looked at Sally quizzically. 'Do you think we should have her sectioned?' Sally steered me towards the sofa by the shoulders. Paul flapped around for a moment then pressed a brandy into my hands. I threw it back and thrust it at him for a refill.

'Start again,' Sally said. 'Slowly.'

I tried to get my breathing under control. 'There's a dead cat in my kitchen. It's Rosa's. She's going to kill me. I can't tell her. She'll be devastated. Oh, God, I'm going to have to move out immediately. Shit, shit, shit.' I pounded my forehead.

'Double shit,' said Paul.

'Triple shit,' agreed Sally.

The three of us crept downstairs to my open door as though about to deal with a burglar. 'In the kitchen?' whispered Paul.

'Why are we whispering?' said Sally.

'Sshhhh!' we hissed back.

I couldn't bear to look, so Sally went and did the manly thing. 'It's dead all right,' we heard him say. He came out of the kitchen with something in his hand. 'And here's why.'

Solvent Abuse

Run out of alcohol?

Crushed-up firelighters make an
excellent rock 'n' roll alternative.

.

Chapter Nine

ROASTED CHESTNUTS

WITH HINDSIGHT, I CAN see that I panicked. I just couldn't think of any solution other than to get myself out of there as fast as my little legs would carry me. It took me less than two minutes to blindly sling half a dozen essentials into a bag and tear out of the door. I heard Paul calling to me, 'Where do you think you're going?' but I was already halfway down the stairs. I didn't even look over my shoulder. When the taxi driver asked me where to, I hadn't the foggiest, so he drove around in wide Kensington circles for a while, passing the same landmarks half a dozen times, before I told him to stop outside one of the better hotels near the museums.

The doorman stepped down the kerb and helped me out of the cab. 'Checking in, madam?' Well, it seemed as good an idea as any. The glossy weather girl on reception found it a bit of a struggle to deal with a walk-in customer with no reservation and had to go and get the duty manager, who then insisted on making painful conversation with me about where had I come from, was I on a special shopping trip and how nice the lights are down Regent Street this year. Yes, yes. Just shut up and get on with it, will you? I felt like a criminal. What if I'd been spotted or, worse still, followed? My heart pounded at the thought of Rosa bursting in through the hotel entrance and running at me with a javelin. When I finished filling in the registration form and handed it back, the manager did a double-take at my home address.

'Oh,' he said. 'I see you're local?' I was in no mood to return his inquisitive smile. He quickly rearranged his expression to professional mode and handed me a key card. 'Room three-oh-six. The lift's just along there and if you—' but I was already long gone.

If you need to hide, a hotel room's not a bad place to start. I sat down and tried to gather myself. OK. Take a few deep breaths. What's the worst that can happen here? Then I felt really sick. There wasn't much room for pacing so I opened the window and stuck my head out above the street below. It was a much busier thoroughfare than the one I lived on, and despite the lateness of the hour there was enough toing and froing to distract my attention for a few minutes. Closing the window and sitting on the edge of the bed, I reminded myself that there was only one way to deal with those occasional days that turn into a complete nightmare, so I changed into my saggy bottoms and Lindisfarne T-shirt, brushed my teeth and swallowed a sleeping pill. As my sister often preaches, things always seem better in the morning.

I woke up at seven to find myself clutching the sheets in the grip of a full-blown anxiety attack. I'd been having a dream about my debit card not working in Waitrose and being naked in the middle of the organic section. Then I had a bucket and mop and was trying to clear up a ketchup spillage in aisle fourteen where an assistant had run amok with a load of Loyd Grossman curry sauces. So this is how my subconscious works through stressful situations, is it? I must try to broaden my horizons.

Breakfast was nice, but then again breakfast in hotels is always nice, provided you're not staying in a Travelodge. Deciding that today was bound to hold one or two hideous moments I went for the full Monty and fuelled myself in preparation for losing my appetite later in the day when Rosa tried to rip out my entrails. By the time I arrived on Leoni's doorstep I was wondering if that extra sausage might not have been such a good move.

'Helen! Brilliant!' Leoni dragged me in by my coat-sleeve. 'You've got to come and see this. They've got that woman on *This Morning*. You know, the one who got done for stapling her husband's knackers together while he was asleep after she caught him having it off with her best friend.' Leoni flung herself back onto her favourite sofa and buried her arm in the biscuit tin. 'Phillip Schofield's face was a picture when Fern was describing what she did. He kept trying not to hold onto his crotch.' There was no tearing Leoni away from her favourite programme, so I made us a pot of tea and waited at her kitchen table until the advertisements came on.

'Leoni?' I called her. 'Can I borrow you for a moment?'

My face must have given her half the story before I had opened my mouth. She sat opposite me, twitching nervously. 'You all right?'

'I know this might sound like a strange question, but did you happen to put a pile of rat poison down in my kitchen?'

Leoni lit up. 'Did you get it?'

'I suppose you could say that,' I mused.

'Bloody fantastic! What did I tell you? That'll teach the little bastard.'

'Leoni,' I sighed. 'Rosa's cat found the poison. Now it's dead and I'm on the run.' Leoni blinked at me. 'So your well-meaning gesture has killed my new neighbour's beloved pet and I'm in the doodah right up to my neck.'

'Shit,' said Leoni. 'What did she say?'

'I haven't got that far yet.'

'You mean she doesn't know? Bloody hell, Helen, you might want to borrow one of my riot shields before you knock on her door.'

'I thought you might like to break the news to her yourself seeing as it was your fault it went and committed suicide.'

'Piss off!' she said. 'It's not my problem if her cat's too sodding stupid to know the difference between a kitty kibble and a cyanide pellet. Besides, she'd probably turn me into a frog or something.' Leoni was twisting her hands, a sure sign that she's under pressure. 'Can't you get her a new one? One that looks the same?'

'Oh, yes, that's highly likely, isn't it? We're not talking about a bloody goldfish, here.' All of a sudden the stress of yesterday's furry corpse started creeping up on me. 'I don't know what I'm going to do.'

'Where's the body?' Leoni asked.

'Good question,' I said. 'Last time I saw it, it was hanging out of one my kitchen cupboards.' It began to dawn on me that doing a runner might not have been such a great idea. 'Can I use your phone?'

Sally took for ever to pick up, and when he heard my strained voice at the other end of the line, he started laughing.

'It's not funny!' I said. 'Any sign of Rosa?'

'Nope.'

'What have you done with it?'

'You mean, what has Paul done with it.' I could hear the beaming smile in his voice. 'He wrapped it up in a Missoni scarf and rang for an undertaker.'

'For a *cat*?'

'Oh yes. But you'd better get back here before Rosa comes looking for you. Paul says you can do the rest of your dirty work without him.'

Leoni's doorbell sounded and I nearly jumped clean out of my skin. Spot the woman with the guilty conscience. Leoni went to answer it. The ensuing noise brought my paranoia to an abrupt halt and I went to see what all the fuss was about. Outside, a truck carrying topsoil and turf was backing up the side of Leoni's house while she walked behind it, beckoning madly and yelling to the driver, 'Yep! OK! Come on! Loads of room!' Then the lorry hit a tree. Leoni turned her hand into a stop sign. 'That'll do!' she shouted.

'What on earth are you doing?' I asked.

'You think you've got problems? Our lawn looks like Boris Johnson's hair.' Leoni started marching up the garden. 'Come and have a look at this!' I followed her across the chargrilled grass and saw the huge crater left courtesy of Marcus's Bonfire Night Chinese cluster bomb.

Dawdling all the way home, I stopped off at the hotel to pick up my bag, thinking that I must have looked like a complete lunatic last night the way I had behaved, then created another diversion by popping into the hairdresser's around the corner for an impromptu blow-dry. I had deliberately left my mobile phone on the side table before haring out of the door the day before, so if anyone was trying to get hold of me, they would just have to wait a bit longer.

'So, just a wash and blow today, is it?' The hairdresser assigned to me couldn't have been more than half my age. She was speaking to me in that invisible manner. To someone like her I'm just cluttering up the planet with my nondescript features and sensible coat. She pointed me towards a sink manned by an even younger girl with lots of painful-looking facial piercings. Her heart certainly wasn't in her job and I felt uncomfortable lines of water trickling down the back of my shirt. She dried my head roughly with a scratchy towel then left me sitting in the chair looking like an angora hedgehog. I wouldn't have minded quite so much were it not for the fact that I was being so cruelly displayed in the window.

The hairdresser reappeared and began attacking my hair with a brush. 'Ooh!' she exclaimed. 'It's quite fine, your hair, isn't it?' Fine? Do you mean *thin*, young lady? I resisted the urge to spill my free cappuccino over her shoes. 'I think I'll get some volumizing mousse in that,' she said. 'Give it a bit of body.' I ignored her. 'Are you going somewhere special?'

'No,' I said. Oh please, just get on with it.

'That's nice.' She started piling mousse in my hair and rubbing it in much too hard. 'Go out and give yourself a little treat, that's what my mum always says. I go round and do her hair for her every week. She went blonde on Saturday. It's called Flaming Passion. Dad loves it. I'm doing him highlights tomorrow. Like old wossname. Rod Stewart.'

'Mmm,' I said. The whole point of my stopping off for a bit of pampering, apart from putting off the inevitable, was so that I could get my brain in gear and think about how I was going to tackle Rosa. The last thing I needed right now was to be subjected to a blow-by-blow account of Little Miss Sunshine's bleached, frolicking parents. 'Actually, I'm not really in the mood for talking today. So if you don't mind.'

'Oh!' She sounded surprised. 'Sorry. I'm always in the mood for talking, I am! Even my mum says to me, you know what? You talk too much! I told her, you know where I get it from, doncha!' She cackled like a Gatling gun. 'Shall I bring you some magazines to look at?' I forced a smile and she started pointing at my head while mouthing 'magazines' to the pierced apprentice. My eyes wandered to the street outside. It was a dull grey day, but looked like staying dry. There were a few people milling about, some stopping to look in the shop windows, others taking a mid-morning break at the café opposite. It was then that I spotted Rosa, coming out of the newsagent's with a *Telegraph* tucked under her arm and heading for the coffee shop. My stomach did a somersault.

'Magazines!' I bellowed at the girl who was still rifling through a pile of old *Tatlers* and *Marie Claires* beside the till. The whole salon jumped to attention. I leapt out of my chair and snatched the one from her hands, sat back down and hid my face behind the centrefold. The chatterbox stopped talking at that point, exchanged a look of alarm with the junior and finally got to work on drying my hair. When I next looked up from the page, Rosa had gone.

I crept into the flat as quietly as I could, returning the heavy front door to the latch without a sound and taking the stairs close to the wall where they would be less likely to groan my presence. The first thing I noticed was that the kitchen was spotless. There was no sign of any of the counter-top debris I had left behind or the cup I had smashed on the floor. I noted a faint whiff of Dettox. There was no mistaking Paul's domestic handiwork. That man's nothing short of a marvel around the house. I wondered if he had been like that as a child and whether or not it provided an early indicator to his sexual disposition. The second thing I noticed was Julia's coat. It was hanging neatly on the stand by the door. Strange. I hadn't noticed it there before and I was certain she hadn't left it behind on the night of the dinner party. Perhaps I was having a senior moment.

My hastily assembled overnight bag only took a couple of minutes to unpack, so I sat on the stool in front of the dressing-table mirror and fretted. I suppose I could wait until Rosa knocked on my door, which was bound to be any time soon, or I could bite the bullet and take it on the chin. I think it was boredom that forced me to make the right decision. For so long as I was hiding up here, I couldn't make any noise. Deprived of radio, television and hoovering duties, I skulked downstairs to Rosa's flat and knocked on the door, hoping that she wasn't in.

Rosa answered in a raspberry poncho printed with birds of paradise. Her turban was missing, leaving her unruly mop of red hair free to be itself. The smell of freshly brewed coffee hung temptingly on the air. Her face was virtually expressionless. 'Rosa,' I started. But before I could roll out my speech, I suddenly felt so terrible that all I could manage was a pathetic sob. 'I'm so sorry!' I said.

Rosa stepped out onto the landing for a moment, put her arm around me and said, 'Shhh. Your sister's here.' So that explains the coat. 'We're having some coffee. Come in and join us.'

Julia was sitting at the small table in the corner of

the room, apparently deep in thought. In front of her was a set of cards arranged into a complicated spread. She looked up and seemed startled to see me.

'Hi,' I said. 'This is a surprise.'

'You're not kidding,' she said. 'Where have you been? I tried ringing you earlier to say I was on my way over but you didn't pick up.'

'My phone's out of charge,' I fibbed.

'That's OK. I let myself in.' She nodded at Rosa. 'I think Rosa must have thought it was you.'

'Oh,' I said. Rosa had disappeared off to the kitchen to fetch another cup, leaving us alone for a moment. There was nothing I could say to explain my predicament to Julia in five seconds, so I kept quiet instead. When Rosa came back she took a seat on one of the sofas and avoided making eye contact with me. I wondered if she already knew, in that supernatural way of hers. If she did, she wasn't letting on. Julia rose from the table to join us and we all sat together with our coffee. I tried to relax but it's hard to swallow when your throat is tight with fear and your heart is jammed in your mouth.

'Julia and I have been spending a little time getting to know each other,' Rosa said cagily.

Julia toyed with a biscuit. 'I'm not sure if that's what I'd call it,' she said. 'Rosa wanted to do me a tarot reading and now I feel like a burglar's just gone through my underwear drawers.'

'Rosa,' I said gently. 'I thought we agreed the other day that the occult's not necessarily a normal or friendly way to get to know new people.'

'Nonsense, dear,' she said. 'There's nothing occultish about any of it. You can dismiss it as a load of old hocus pocus if you want to, but I think people like nothing better than to try and catch a glimpse of what fate is about to throw at them.' She poured herself some more coffee and popped a small piece of biscuit into her mouth. 'Besides, I didn't hear Julia put up much of a protest, did I?' Rosa tipped a wink at Julia, who was still sporting a deadpan expression. 'And it's nothing to do with me. Your sister chose the cards herself, one way or another. I'm merely the interpreter.'

'What did they say?'

Rosa wagged a finger at me. 'It's not me you need to ask. That's entirely up to Julia. It's her future, not mine.' I saw a small smile pass across Julia's face.

'Rosa,' she said playfully. 'You're incorrigible. I swear you almost had me going there for a moment. Still, it's all good fun, isn't it? I must ask you to do it again for me some time.'

Rosa gave her a knowing look. 'Of course. It would be my pleasure. But I must warn you, they will tell you exactly the same thing next time. The cards never lie.' She finished her coffee, got up and went back to the table, clearing the cards into a neat pile and folding them up in a silk scarf. She saw me watching her every move then held the pack towards me. 'Would you like to choose some?' she said.

'No thanks,' I replied too quickly.

'Oh, go on, Helen!' Julia goaded me. 'It's a laugh! You might find out you're about to meet a tall, dark stranger.'

Rosa was smiling at me and waiting for my response. 'Why don't you pick out just one?' Being outgunned I agreed, reluctantly, and Rosa spread the pack on the coffee table, all face down. 'Take your time,' she said. 'See if there's one card that you feel drawn to.'

How do I get myself into these things? No, I didn't want to choose a bloody card. I wanted to stand up and say look, Rosa, I know this is going to be unbearably painful and that you'll never speak to me again, but your sodding cat's dead. It's currently rotting in some ghastly pet crematorium near Crawley, just in case you want to go and identify it yourself, and I swear I'll never borrow anything from you again for so long as we both shall live. I stared down at the cards. There were loads of them. One or two seemed to be more prominent to my eye, so I thought better not pick either of those up, because I didn't want to play the game. Finally, I just pointed at any old one. 'That one,' I said.

'Are you sure?' asked Rosa. I nodded. She picked it up and looked at it, then turned it round to show me.

Well, it just had to be, didn't it? The grim reaper peered out from under his hoodie. I felt myself go pale.

'Death,' Rosa said, rubbing her chin. 'Very interesting. Very interesting indeed.'

'Bloody hell,' Julia pitched in. 'Must be her dead husband.'

'Look,' I blurted to Rosa. 'There's something I have to talk to you about.' Like the coward that I am, the next sentence got stuck somewhere in my throat.

'Do you want me to leave?' Julia had misinterpreted my stilted manner as a hint for her to scram.

'No. Don't go. This is going to be hard enough as it is.' Too right. In about five seconds, I might just need someone to keep Rosa from ripping my gizzards out. 'Rosa, I'm afraid something terrible has happened to Babushka.' Rosa took a seat and fixed me with her green eyes. 'I don't know how it could have happened, but she ate some rat poison that had been left in my cupboard.' I felt my cheeks begin to burn. 'I am so desperately sorry.' Rosa didn't say a word. Just sat there with a hollow expression, stared at the rug and let out a big sigh. 'It must have happened when I was out at work, because by the time I got back, it was too late. I know I should have come straight down and told you, but I panicked. I didn't know how I was going to face you. It was wrong of me, I know, and I feel like a complete heel.'

Julia's hand was across her mouth, as though she didn't dare trust herself to speak. She widened her eyes at me instead. I stared down into my lap waiting to take my medicine. Rosa sat in silence, which is probably the worst thing she could have done. I had come prepared for histrionics. Please say something. Anything. Stand up and shout at me. Smash a couple of plates over my head or something. Eventually Rosa got up from the sofa, went to the cupboard in the corner of the room and took out a bottle of whisky. She poured a generous measure into a glass, brought it over and stood right in front of me. 'Here,' she said. For one horrible moment I thought she was going to douse me with it then flick a lit match at my head. To my relief, she placed the glass in my trembling hand then retook her seat. She appeared remarkably calm for someone who had just lost her dearest friend.

'Do you have any idea what you have done?' she said.

'Yes. I know.' I took a big slurp from the glass. 'I'll never forgive myself. And I know I'll never be able to make amends.'

Rosa raised her hand at me. 'On the contrary. Babushka has been hell-bent on ruining my life ever since I had her done.' Julia and I looked at each other. 'Oh, yes,' Rosa nodded, casting her eyes about the room to conjure memories. 'She destroyed four Indian silk rugs the Maharaja of Jaipur gave me, pissed in every pair of shoes I own, and as for our hotel suite, well – ' she rumpled her face and made a distasteful expression – 'I'm surprised they didn't throw us out months ago.'

'Excuse me,' Julia interrupted us. 'I'm completely confused here. Who exactly are we talking about?'

'My cat,' Rosa said matter-of-factly. 'Vicious little sonofabitch.'

'Thank God for that,' Julia said. 'For a moment there I thought we might have to dispose of a corpse.'

'Talking of which,' said Rosa.

'Erm, yes.' I said. 'Well, I fled to Sally and Paul in a panic when it happened and they sent her off to a pet crematorium in Sussex. We thought we had better do things properly. I assumed you'd be crushed.'

'Really?' said Rosa with a twinkle in her eyes. 'Let's see now. Perhaps we could have a little fun here.'

We spent the rest of the afternoon sitting around plotting, drinking tea and listening to more of Rosa's stories about the rich and famous she had variously partied with, married, divorced and married again. Her third marriage dissolution had left her eye-poppingly wealthy, so she dispensed with any further notions of future ex-husbands and from that day forward lived her life exactly as she pleased. She was never short of interesting invitations and, as it turned out, was a trusted psychic advisor to some of her more illustrious acquaintances. 'I like the Californians best,' she confided. 'All that sunshine sends them quite mad, you know. Some of them couldn't even make a decision about what they're going to wear in the morning without consulting their guru of the moment first. The thing that really foxed them about me was that I would never accept any kind of payment.' She chuckled to herself. 'If you take money out of the equation, it leaves some of these hotshots quite confounded. They seem to take great comfort in paying people obscene fees. It really is most odd.'

Just when she was about to break a promised confidence about a mindbending impropriety at a party hosted by Freddie Mercury in the late seventies, we heard footsteps coming up to the portico. Rosa glanced out of her window. 'It's Paul!' she said excitedly. 'Shall we?'

I let Paul settle in for the agreed ten minutes before pounding at his door.

'What is it now?' he greeted me sarcastically. 'Horse's head in your bed?'

'It's Rosa.' I flapped my arms and tried to sound menacing. 'She's reported you to the RSPCA for murdering her cat and then trying to hide the evidence by sending the body away for disposal.'

'*What?*'

'I have no idea how she found out. You know what she's like. She's called the police and everything. I think they're on their way here right now.'

Paul's face became ashen. He made gulping noises and was barely able to catch his breath. 'Sally!' he shouted. 'The police are coming for me!' Sally appeared from the bedroom door and feigned ignorance. 'Hide me! Get me out of here! Oh my God. I'm going to jail!'

I winked at Sally, who remained completely cool and unruffled, as usual. 'So,' he said sagely to the stricken Paul. 'You do a little time, make a few friends . . .'

'Are you insane?' Paul was shaking Sally by the shoulders. 'Have you any idea what happens to people like me on the inside?'

'Uh-huh,' tutted Sally. 'But they say you get used to it pretty quickly. I hear they come down real hard on people who abuse animals. You English. You've got a real thing about your pets.'

'Jesus Christ!' Paul was beginning to hyperventilate. 'Somebody do something! Phone Julia! Get me a lawyer!' Just then we heard a loud banging on the front door downstairs, followed by an opening, then slamming shut, and voices crackling through a walkie-talkie. 'They're here!' Paul howled. 'Don't let them take me away!' Heavy footsteps started up the stairs. Paul stared at Sally for a moment then fled into their bedroom.

It didn't take us long to find him cowering in the wardrobe quivering like a jelly behind a Gucci overcoat. Sally flung it to one side and Julia took the photograph while Paul screamed like a girl. 'And that,' said Rosa, reaching her hand in to help him out with a smile, 'is what you get for trying to pull the wool over my eyes.'

Gingerbread Men

Such is the madness of modern politics
that these are now called 'Gingerbread
People' in my local supermarket.

Make them yourself and let men be men.

I like to remove all doubt about their
gender by icing little willies.

Hang some on Granny's Christmas tree.

Chapter Ten

THE REAL MEANING OF CHRISTMAS

THERE USED TO BE a time when certain things were kept special. Take Sundays, for instance: being hauled off to church, returning home to sit in front of a lump of roast charcoal, its species identifiable only by the accompanying pot of apple, mint or horseradish sauce, having to tackle the mountain of carbonized pans piled up in the sink, then sitting around for the rest of the day bored senseless, waiting for the onset of bedtime while the parents assailed each other with the usual list of domestic gripes and inconsequential neighbourly scandals.

The Keep Sunday Special brigade was finally out-voted by the atheist majority who preferred to worship at the tills, and millions of teenagers everywhere were liberated. Our western society has been successfully homogenized into one big round-the-clock retail experience. Bloody good job too, judging by the list that had since split and multiplied into several even longer ones. Buying presents for one's girlfriends is easy. The main obstacle in my case is not getting carried away. The super-dooper bumper gift boxes in Jo Malone might well cost about a hundred million pounds each, but oh, the heavenly smells inside them. I couldn't help myself, bought two, and hoped that my meagre self-control would be sufficient to prevent me ripping them both open myself and going through the whole lot before they made it anywhere near the bottom of someone else's Christmas tree.

I wandered around some of the lovely boutiques down the back streets and kept my eyes open for something for Rick. His overexcited response at the notion that I might get him a present had settled under my skin and I was determined to surprise him with something special. But what do you get for the man with everything? I don't really understand man stuff. If you buy them clothing it's bound to be wrong or not fit. He's already got every gadget this side of Tokyo. I don't know anything about art, as you've probably already gathered, so a picture is out of the question. He's sold his boat, so no point in getting him anything nautical. I was quite relaxed about finding him something until after my first few shopping sorties, when I realized that this was possibly the most difficult task I had set myself since young Millie stamped a slice of cherry pie into my cream velvet-pile carpet.

Be warned, this is what happens when you find yourself completely out of practice on the man front. True, I did have a boyfriend a while ago for about five minutes, but he wasn't up to much. Nor was I for that matter. I found to my disgrace that I accidentally slipped back into the role of stupid, simpering woman without her own brain. Not my finest hour. I resolved to avoid further relationships until I could learn how to get a more reliable grip on my faculties.

It was Wednesday before I caught up with Rick again. He'd been in Vienna for a long weekend. I have no idea who he went with, although why that should bother me I don't know. In fact, it doesn't. I have no idea why I should even mention it.

'All right, Hell?' He was freshly showered, hair still wet, when I let myself in and found him rummaging through the drawers in his study. 'Good weekend?'

'Spiffing,' I said, with a soupçon of sarcasm. 'You?'

'Yeah.' He found the box of cigars he was looking for, sparked one up and sat back in his big leather chair with a smile. 'Not bad. Not bad at all.'

'Business, was it?'

'Maybe.' He blew out a thin line of smoke and stifled a smile. 'Maybe not.'

'I see,' I said. I'd spent enough time with the man to know that he was in one of his mysterious moods. These are usually peppered with snippets of bizarre conversation and Rick going off into short trances every now and again. He rolled the cigar around in his mouth and concentrated on the ceiling.

'Hell?' Oh, here we go. 'I've been thinking.'

'Oh yes? I thought I could smell something burning.'

'No. Listen.' He looked all serious. 'I've been mulling over some of the things you said to me and I reckon you might just have a point.'

'Really?' I had no recollection of the particular conversation.

'Yep.' An awkward moment passed where he waited for me to say something and I couldn't remember what we'd been talking about. 'I reckon I've probably got a bit selfish in my old age. I suppose living on your own for a long time can make you like that.'

'Tell me about it,' I said.

'Life's been good to me, Hell.' Well, this was a turn up for the books. 'I can't grumble, really – ' he gestured around the room. 'So I've been thinking, maybe I should make more of an effort. You know, put something back in.'

'What? Like giving to charity?'

'Nah.' He waved his cigar at me. 'That's too easy, that is. I've been writing out cheques willy-nilly for years. Doesn't make me feel any better though, does it? It needs to be something more. Something special.'

I wondered if Rick had received a severe blow to the head while he was away.

'So . . .' I wasn't sure where to go with this. 'Did you have something specific in mind?'

Rick shrugged his shoulders. 'Dunno,' he said. 'I'll think of something.'

I walked home from work that day. It was a cold, crisp evening, but I was wrapped up warmly and felt in need of the exercise. I'm lazier than ever about fitness these days, though heaven knows this is precisely the time when I should be making more of an effort. Julia had been much luckier than me in the gene-pool stakes. Hers gave her Father's height and raven locks while I was left to make do with my mother's altogether more modest artillery. The only reason I'm not a size twenty-two is that I have a morbid fear of obesity. My grandmother was a whale of a woman who seemed unable to comprehend any recipe that didn't call for four pounds of lard. I make the best of myself, you could say, and painfully resist the excessive levels of indulgence I am predisposed towards.

The trouble with any form of workout, even a brisk stroll, is that it makes you really hungry. Or is that just me? By the time I reached my front door I was fantasizing about roasted hazelnuts dipped in dark Belgian chocolate and dusted with cocoa powder. Specific, yes, and understandable, seeing as a box of them had inexplicably appeared in my handbag when I accidentally made a purchase in the swanky confectioner's I passed on the way home. God, I'm so weak.

I sat munching my illicit bonbons and lifted the telephone in search of some company. Julia's answerphone was on so I left a message. Then Leoni's phone rang for ages. The babysitter eventually picked it up, grunted at me that they were out and hung up before I could give her my name. Charming. A little chat with her would have tided me over quite nicely. Next, in a moment of complete madness, I found myself dialling Rick's number. Realizing immediately that this was scraping the bottom of the barrel, I put the phone down before it connected. I was tempted to take myself off to the cinema to drool over Russell Crowe with a bucket of popcorn, but then the sugar hit landed so I stuck the television on instead and fell asleep in front of the *CSI* double bill.

I KNOW IT MAY not look like it, but I've actually been extremely busy over these last few weeks, cooking for England. With the culinary assistance of her secret agent, I was determined that Leoni would win a reprieve after last year's humiliation when she tried to defrost the still-frozen turkey in the dishwasher. Solid with permafrost after a second cycle, she made Marcus take it into the garage and chop it in half with an axe.

Leoni was late. By the time she arrived with Millie in tow I'd had sufficient time to bake an extra batch of gingerbread men. Wiping my hands on the tea towel as I let them in, I wondered if I should question the two plastic traffic cones Leoni had hauled along with her. Probably not. It'll only be really complicated.

'I don't mind bringing the car,' she said. 'Even though it means I won't be able to drink this – ' she waved a litre bottle of Sainsbury's soave in front of me. 'But what I do mind is not being able to bloody well park.' She manhandled the cones in through the door and left them by the coat stand. 'Do me a favour next time, will you? Go and stick these in one of the spaces outside?'

'Are you kidding? You've bought your own parking cones? And what do you expect me to do with them? Stand around in the street until there's a free space then rush at it like a lunatic?'

'Bought? Don't be stupid. I nicked them from our next-door neighbours. They've hired a skip and these were lying in the road next to it.'

I gasped at her chutzpah. 'You'll get yourself into serious trouble one of these days, Leoni. What if your neighbour saw you?'

Millie was holding onto the bottom of her mother's coat. 'Mummy says she's a stupid ugly cow,' she said earnestly.

'That's nice.' I gave her a little hug. 'Do you want to come in the kitchen with me and put the icing on some gingerbread men?' Millie nodded enthusiastically. I had bought some little squeezy tubes of ready-made coloured icing specially for her. I perched her on one of the high stools in front of the batch. Leoni nipped off to the bathroom.

'What's a skelington?' Millie asked, squeezing most of the red tube directly onto the work surface.

'It's not skelington.' I tried to guide her hand towards the nearest gingerbread man. 'It's ske-le-ton.'

'What's a skelington?'

'Why are you so interested in skeletons all of a sudden?' Perhaps they were doing them in school.

'Mummy says she has lots of them in her closet, but Auntie Julia has more.'

Out of the mouths of babes. I feigned normality. 'Does she?'

'What's a closet?'

Leoni got back from the bathroom, picked up a gingerbread man and bit his head off. Millie frowned at her.

'You and Marcus,' I said. 'Did you go out some-where nice on Wednesday?'

'Eh?' She looked surprised. 'How did you know?'

'Babysitter answered the phone.'

'Blimey,' Leoni said. 'So it can communicate after all.'

'I wouldn't go that far.'

'No,' she said. 'We were at Relate.'

Me and my big mouth. I was genuinely shocked, but not surprised. I know that all relationships have their ups and downs, but Leoni's seems to have more downs than most. 'Don't worry,' she said, reading my mind. 'It's nothing serious. I told him he's let himself go and I don't fancy him any more. He then accused me of being a binge-drinking old slapper so I snipped the buttons off all his shirts.'

'Bad Mummy,' said Millie gravely.

'No, it's not bad Mummy.' Leoni corrected her. 'It's very clever Mummy.' She met my eyes. 'It's the best thing I've done in years. Took him ages to work out that there wasn't a single shirt left he could put on.'

'Leoni! What on earth did he do?'

'What could he do?' She broke the legs off the gingerbread man and started munching on them noisily. 'He had to sew them back on, didn't he?' She started laughing. 'Have you ever seen someone trying to sew when they're really angry?' ·

'Poor Marcus.' I tut-tutted.

'Rubbish,' she said. 'He had no right to speak to me like that. Binge drinking indeed. You know, I'd always been very moderate until they brought out those ridiculous guidelines. Two units a day? Is that it? Try telling that to a Frenchman.'

'Actually,' I started, 'the French are quite abstemious when it comes to—'

'Some pinstriped imbecile sitting in an office in Whitehall telling us all how to live our lives and printing billions of leaflets at vast cost to the taxpayer. And as for the men, they're allowed twice as much of course. Where's the equality in that?' Pointless to argue, so I nodded. 'Besides, I quite like going to Relate. The woman we've got this time is really nervy. I wonder what her story is? She said that Marcus and I should find a common interest we can enjoy together.'

'Like what?'

'Well, Marcus suggested sex, at which point I was able to shout, "See what I mean?" She went bright red and said she meant she wanted us to find something outside of the house. Marcus then said sex in a field, which seemed to make her very uncomfortable. It was quite funny actually. We had a real laugh about it on the way home.'

From her cheery tone it sounded like she was right. Nothing serious to worry about this time. Just Leoni's little way of imposing her point of view for a while and getting some extra attention. Goodness knows they've been to counselling that many times I expect they have a filing cabinet all of their own. 'I don't know how he puts up with you.' I smiled at her while pulling all the neatly labelled foil containers out of the freezer.

'Because﹒I'm bloody adorable,' she said, watching the mounting pile. 'Holy— ships in the night.' (Millie was there.) 'Is all this stuff for me?'

'Yep. It's all labelled and completely foolproof. You won't have to do anything except thaw and reheat, and some of it can go straight from the freezer into the oven or microwave.' Leoni was transfixed and I felt immensely proud of myself. 'There's everything. Home-made mince pies, all the veggies, stuffing balls, little eats for entertaining. I've written you a checklist of what to pull out and when.' Yes, I'm a regular Delia Smith. 'So just shove it all in your freezer and it'll come together like clockwork when the festivities hit. Just you wait and see.'

Leoni's eyes were like saucers. 'You're a—' She bit her lip and struggled valiantly to stop herself using the fuck-word. 'You're a brilliant person genius.' And she gave me an enormous hug. It felt particularly good.

'Now, don't you hang around here any longer. That lot will start defrosting any minute so you need to get it home before it spoils, or I'll have to kill you, I'm afraid.'

'Thanks, Helen.' Leoni was beaming from ear to ear. 'Thanks a million.'

Helping Leoni pack the feeding of the five thousand

into the boot of her clapped-out car, I saw Sally and Paul walking towards us laden with shopping bags and looking very pleased with themselves. On noticing me, Paul said something to Sally, who then loped easily to my side and put his hands over my eyes.

I heard Leoni's voice. 'Hello, sexpot.' Then the sound of them kissing.

'Paul doesn't want her to see the bags. She might get a clue.'

'Ooh, presents!' Leoni squealed. 'Have you got mine in there?' The quickening footsteps announced Paul had caught us up. He rustled past me to the steps. Sally let go of my face and draped his arm around Leoni's waist.

'Have you been a good girl this year?'

'I've been sensational,' she said, fluttering her eye-lashes at him.

'Then you have nothing to worry about.'

'Helen?' The voice on the other end of the phone was at once both critical and guilt-ridden.

'Hi, Mum,' I said, then launched into my standard apology. 'Sorry I haven't rung for a while. I keep meaning to, but then the time just slips by and . . .' I trailed off.

'That's all right, dear. We understand that you girls have your own lives now.' I heard her sigh. 'Your father and I don't want to be a burden, you know. If you don't have time to call and say hello, well, we understand. It was the same for us once.' I sat down and let her get on with my regulation grilling. 'Although we had children of course. And when you have children you never have time for anything.' She paused and tutted, allowing her barb to penetrate. 'But it's a different world now, I suppose. Everybody dashing around at a hundred miles an hour. Nobody has time for anyone else, least of all for us old folk.'

'Yes, Mum.'

'So I suppose you're getting yourself all ready for Christmas? Must be bedlam where you are. Why on earth you would want to go and live in the middle of London is beyond me, I must say. All those foreigners everywhere. And the prices! Hmmph. I can't imagine anyone paying four pounds for a cup of coffee. Ridiculous!'

'Yes, Mum.'

'Still, I suppose you know what you're doing.' Another sigh. 'And I expect you've already heard that Julia and David aren't going to be here?' I didn't answer immediately. 'I thought so. I'm always the last to know. Well – ' this time she went for more of a huff and a puff – 'if she didn't want us to come for Christmas, all she had to do was say. She didn't have to go and leave the country. I don't know what the world is coming to.' I was about to answer when she cranked herself up a gear. 'When I told your father, and you know how he likes to spend Christmas down there, he said he wasn't in the least bit surprised. Men, hmm? I don't suppose it occurred to him for a moment that I might have wanted to go on holiday myself, did it? Oh no.' I started flicking through a magazine. 'And it's quite obvious that you're not going to invite us so we've made our own arrangements.'

'Now hang on there just one minute,' I interrupted. 'That is exactly what I was going to do as a matter of fact. I thought it best to wait until Julia had decided on her own plans before calling you about it.' My heart was beating faster and my hackles rose. 'But no, you have to come steaming in with your size elevens and have a go at me before we've even said hello properly.' And here we were again, arguing about nothing, locking horns and sighing in exasperation.

'Well, you're too late,' she said tetchily. 'We're going on a cruise.' She paused for dramatic effect. It did the trick. Mum and Dad on a cruise? Together? Dear God, I hope they've taken out extra life insurance.

'Oh, Mum. You didn't have to go and do that! You know how much you detest travelling. Every holiday you've taken for the past ten years has turned into a complete disaster, what with your delicate constitution and all those allergies. You know very well that I would have loved to have you both come and stay with me for Christmas.' I quietened my voice. 'How could you think anything else?'

'Nonsense, dear. We're going because we want to. It's a British firm, so there'll be none of that trouble with the food this time. Your father hasn't been on a sea voyage' – *Voyage*? Going up in the world now, are we? – 'since his national service.' Poor old Dad. I can only imagine how that conversation must have gone.

'I think he might find life on the ocean wave much changed since then,' I said, but she wasn't listening.

'So I'll pop a note in with your Christmas card and let you know when we'll be sailing. Mrs Critchley has kindly offered to keep an eye on the house for us when we're away, water the plants, that sort of thing. I'll lock all the valuables away. I know very well she's always had her eye on my Lladró shepherdess. So you won't have to worry about us and there'll be no inconvenience.'

'Give my love to Dad,' I said, suddenly missing them both awfully.

'He's up the garden with his parsnips. I do wish he wouldn't insist on using that awful horse manure. It smells abominable. Why he can't have it treated first I don't know. Wash it or something.'

'Yes, Mum.'

We said goodbye and I replaced the handset. It rang back at me immediately.

'Hello?'

'Look out,' said Julia. 'Mum's on the warpath. I've told her that David and I are going away for Christmas.'

'You don't say.'

Size Zero Christmas Lunch

Stuffed shrew.

Chapter Eleven

CHEZ MARCUS

I'VE GOT A SERIOUS case of Winter Skin at the moment. It doesn't matter what I slap on or how much of it, I seem to have a permanently flushed expression and my cheeks feel like sandpaper. My complexion used to be great, not a single blemish anywhere. My pores were enviously branded 'invisible' by the lady at a Clinique counter when I was about twenty. Eyebrows held a good shape. Hair (on my head) shiny if not traffic-stopping. Now it's all about how long I can go without a colour at the local hairdresser's. My upper arms and thighs are no longer suitable for public display, and as for the bit in the middle, well, the less said about its general lumpiness the better. Perhaps I should set a little fund aside and have it all hauled back into place and lipo-sucked in another ten years or so. A long way off, I know, but time does have a habit of accelerating as the years flit by.

Whether or not to suffer the self-inflicted torture of a pre-Christmas diet is one of my annual dilemmas. If you're going to pack on the best part of a stone during the two-week armistice anyway, what's the point? Diet now or diet later? It's hardly an alluring conundrum. I buckled and opened one of the Jo Malone double deluxe packs instead and rifled inside for something that might ease the beauty situation. Fully aware that I'd probably be a whole lot more successful if I tried cutting out a few biscuits and cakes instead, I made up my mind to postpone the great weight debate with a well-reasoned 'Hey, it's Christmas. Wear something wafty and black, and divert attention from your expanding waistline by smelling fabulous instead.'

The flat needed a really good going over, so I turned up the radio, put on an old tracksuit that had lost its personality half a dozen washes ago and resolved to put a little more gumption into my cleaning routine. Stretching out with the feather duster, I could feel my triceps transforming themselves into svelte Madonna arms. The infectious first few bars of 'Young Hearts Run Free' burst out of the radio and I positively bounced around with the Pledge. An hour into my domestic disco, I turned off the vacuum cleaner and noticed the door buzzer was yelling. There was significantly less spring in my step when I went to answer it.

'Rick?' On a Sunday? I hope this isn't going to turn into one of his complicated whims, like shopping for a yacht. He trudged up the stairs miserably. 'What are you doing here?'

'Thanks,' he said. 'Good to see you, too.'

Oh dear. He had that certain hunch to his shoulders. The one that says he's in gloomy mood and feeling sorry for himself. 'Everything all right?' I held the door open and ushered him in.

'I guess,' he said. 'Just woke up feeling a bit, you know, this morning.' He shrugged his shoulders. 'Fed up. For no particular reason. Wanna go out for lunch?'

'Sorry, I can't. I'm going over to Leoni's this afternoon. In fact – ' I looked at my bare wrist – 'I'm probably already late.'

'Oh,' he said. 'That's nice.' Rick stood where he was and made no move to leave.

'How is she?' Yes, they've been introduced. I drafted Leoni in to help me out with a decorating project for Rick some time ago. He's met the whole crew once or twice due to circumstances beyond my control, but I try not to make a habit of it.

'She's fine,' I said. 'Marcus is cooking a big Sunday roast today, which is a first.'

I think it's all part of his New Man regime since their latest round of counselling. Leoni almost died laughing when he offered his services, and in order to make things as difficult for him as she possibly could, she insisted on asking me to join them. And Julia, and David. He finally put his foot down when she started dialling Sara's number, so she called it a day at five heads plus the children. For someone who's never cooked anything more complicated than beans on toast with a dash of Lea and Perrins before, you had to admire his confidence.

'It must be great to have such a close bunch of friends,' Rick said forlornly. 'My social life usually means trying to impress a date who probably doesn't like me anyway, or being stuck with a bunch of tossers I'm trying to set up a deal with. I can't remember the last time I had a proper home-made roast. I get sick of eating in restaurants.' He sat down on one of the kitchen stools and glanced inside my empty coffee cup.

'Look, did you want something or can we catch up tomorrow? I really do need to get myself ready.' I gestured down at my scruffs.

Rick shuffled around on his seat. 'I don't suppose I could tag along?' I stared back at him while the penny dropped. 'No.' He stood up. 'Of course not. I dunno what I was thinking there.'

Sometimes I can be terribly slow on the uptake. It hadn't crossed my mind that Rick might be in need of a little family time. I did wonder if I should call and check with Leoni first, but Marcus might have blown a gasket so I decided to harness the element of surprise to our mutual advantage. There was also the fringe benefit that came everywhere with Rick. While he remains carless, he has himself chauffeured around in roomy luxury vehicles. His run-around bill is a real shocker every month.

My 'don't be silly' was immediate. At least I wouldn't have to hang about in the freezing cold waiting for an oxidizing lump of public transport to arrive. Rick brightened instantly with a huge smile. He stood up as if to hug me then quickly sat down again, made a call, and soon a smooth Lexus slid up outside. In the meantime I made a rapid dash to the bedroom and changed into something a little less Jerry Springer. When I got back to the kitchen, Rick had even done the bit of washing-up I'd left in the sink.

The chauffeur started pulling into Leoni's drive. 'I wouldn't park there if I were you,' I warned him. 'Better back up and drop us off out front.' Rick heaved himself out of the car, together with the staggeringly expensive wines and chocolates he had insisted we pick up on the way. I'm not surprised his generosity is legendary. I could live for a fortnight on what he just spent in the food hall. Leoni was utterly delighted when she saw what I had brought along and threw herself at Rick with a gushing hug. He blushed and looked humbled.

'Bloody fantastic!' Leoni shouted at us. 'Marcus will

have a blue fit!' She ran off into the house to break the good news.

'I should probably warn you now,' I said discreetly to Rick, but before I could go any further, the twins came scrambling out of the house, bawling abuse at each other and dragging a rope. Attached to the end of it was Millie's dolls' house. They ran off up the path that runs beside the house, scraping it behind them. Three seconds on, Millie came wandering out of the door, screaming and crying, arms held out in front of her like a zombie. I looked at Rick. 'You get the picture.'

Rick was smiling. He stuck a fresh cigar in his mouth. 'I'm gonna feel right at home here,' he said, clanking up the drive ahead of me with his boxed vineyard. 'Sign for the car, Hell.'

David and Julia were standing awkwardly in the doorway of the dining room holding complicated-looking drinks. I kissed them hello and Rick shook hands with David. Julia leaned into my ear with a smile. 'Spending the weekend with your boss? What's going on here?' I shoved her off.

'Rick fancied a good old family Sunday lunch so I thought I'd drag him along.' Julia and David pulled a face at each other and pointed towards the kitchen door.

'I'm not sure if you picked the best day to get one of those around here. He won't let anyone in there except

Leoni,' Julia said. 'Looks like he's about to have a heart attack.' Marcus's profusely sweating head appeared from behind the kitchen door, his eyes widening in panic when he saw the spontaneous extra diner. He must have thought Leoni was winding him up.

'Rick!' he shrilled. 'Good of you to join us!' It sounded absolutely genuine. 'Can I get you both a drink?' He disappeared before either of us could answer or specify, then came back with two more of the same concoction that Julia and David were nursing. Thrusting the glasses at us, we were barely able to say cheers before he'd fled back to the cooker.

'See?' said Julia.

'Blimey,' I said.

David nudged Rick on the arm. 'It gets a whole lot better.' The four of us shuffled into the dining room. Julia put her finger up to her lips and we all strained our ears towards the kitchen. We could hear Marcus getting grumpy with Leoni, asking her in whining tones how to do this, how to do that.

'Are you cooking lunch or not?' she steamed. 'Because I might as well do it myself for all the time I've spent running around bloody demonstrating everything and resetting the smoke alarm.'

'How am I supposed to get it right if you won't tell me anything?' Scuffling sounds. Then Leoni, shouting.

'No! You blithering idiot! Not like that! It'll stick to the pan!'

When Leoni banged out of the kitchen, the rest of us tried to look as though we'd been having an interesting conversation. Leoni flushed us through to the sitting room, where we made a start on Marcus's rather odd pre-lunch cocktails. 'Don't ask me what he's put in them,' she said after taking a huge slug of hers. 'He's probably trying to kill off our tastebuds.'

Marcus appeared at the door and started nodding Leoni towards the kitchen. She remained seated and gave him a supercilious glare. 'What do you want?'

'Could you come in here and give me a hand for a minute please, darling?'

'No I bloody well can't. Why? What can't you do this time?'

Marcus looked like he wanted to strangle her. 'It's about the gravy.'

Leoni smiled at us triumphantly. 'What about it?'

Marcus answered her through gritted teeth. 'How do you make it?'

Lubricated by half a glass of Green Goddess, Leoni took a great deal of pleasure in explaining the exact science of perfect gravy constructed with complicated stocks made well in advance. Like she's ever used anything but granules. Marcus stomped back to the kitchen.

'Not married again, yet?' Leoni asked Rick. (She's never hidden the fact that she rather likes him.) 'We're all dying to know about your love life.' Here it comes.

She's only had half a drink and she's already hell-bent on going through everyone's dirty laundry.

Rick looked perfectly relaxed. 'How could I be when you're already taken?' He's such a charmer.

Leoni preened. 'A mere detail,' she said matter-of-factly. 'Watch this space. I'll be getting divorced myself one of these days. It's only a question of time. Marcus and I don't really like each other at all, just in case you haven't noticed. But there's the children to think of and I'm not bloody well doing single-parent family while Marcus gets to enjoy his freedom, so we'll have to put up with each other until they've gone.' Leoni drained her glass, oblivious to her open-mouthed audience. 'Anybody for another one of these?' She held up her empty so we all followed suit and handed ours over. The sound of Millie's crying amplified as she neared the sitting room. Leoni took no notice. Julia rose from her seat immediately to see to her, scooping her up in her arms and mopping her tears with a hanky.

'Whatever's the matter?' Julia said gently. Millie sobbed pitifully and buried her face in Julia's shoulder. 'Are those horrible boys being nasty to you again?' Millie nodded without lifting her head. 'Shall we go and duff them up?' Millie stopped sobbing. 'Shall we, pooch?' Julia gave her a playful wobble. This time Millie lifted her tear-stained face and smiled at Julia. 'Good,' Julia said. 'That's better. Now, where do they keep their favourite things?' Millie pointed upstairs and Julia took her off. David was smiling after them, lost in his own thoughts.

'Got kids of your own?' Rick asked.

'Afraid not,' said David. 'You?'

'Loads,' said Rick. 'For my sins. Ungrateful bloodsuckers.'

They were interrupted by Marcus's raised voice as Leoni returned with a tray of recharged drinks. 'How do you thicken it?'

Leoni yelled back at him while politely passing the tray around. 'How many times have I got to tell you? Gravy powder!' Then whispering to us: 'Sure I bought some back in the mid-nineties.'

Some time later Marcus leaned out of the kitchen door holding an ancient Bisto box. 'What do you do with it?'

Leoni reached one of her rapid-boil flashpoints. 'You read the side of the fucking packet, for Chrissakes.'

Marcus closed his eyes and took a deep breath, counted to ten, and rose above his wife's unseemly outburst. 'All right,' he said. 'There's no need to be like that.'

Leoni waited for him to go back inside. 'Even if it's edible, which I seriously doubt, it won't make any difference.' She rearranged the fruit in her glass. 'He knows very well that I'm in love with Gordon Ramsay.

It's that bit at the beginning of his TV programme when he walks along and starts peeling his clothes off.' Leoni stared into space for a moment. 'I quite like a bit of rough.'

'They're not all they're cracked up to be.' Rick continued his conversation with David. It was painful to watch. David smiled politely and joined in as best he could given the circumstances. Rick wasn't to know. He just assumed that their childless state had been a matter of choice rather than a brutal fait accompli. Julia came back to the room smiling. Whatever she and Millie had just done, they both seemed satisfied that it was just deserts. Julia settled herself on the sofa again and Millie climbed into her lap. 'Shame, though,' concluded Rick. 'You and Julia look like you'd suit a couple of kids.'

Having missed the entire conversation, this last comment came as something of a shock to Julia. Her face dropped. 'Excuse me?' she said. 'What have you been talking about behind my back?' David was lost for words.

For once, Leoni managed to say something approaching sensible. 'Rick's on a crusade to try and make everyone breed so that they have to suffer just like the rest of us.'

Julia was momentarily flummoxed. 'What is it with everyone going on at me about children these days?' she said, sounding more wounded than she probably intended. 'That's three times in the last fortnight and I'm getting a bit fed up with it.'

'Darling?' David put his hand over Julia's. 'Has something happened? Someone said something to upset you?'

Rick sensed that he'd trodden on an emotional landmine. He held his hands up. 'I'm sorry,' he said. 'I'm always like this. Don't engage my brain before I put my mouth in gear. I'm probably just jealous of people who've decided not to have any. They only grow up to hate your guts, anyway. What a knobhead, eh?'

Leoni looked at Rick. 'Do you mind not saying knobhead in front of the C-H-I-L-D?'

'It's OK,' Julia managed a small smile. 'Don't take any notice of me.'

LEONI WAS WRONG about one thing. The lunch Marcus finally produced was way beyond edible. It was a triumph. Only Marcus was so hot and flustered by the time he managed to get it all to the table that he was scarely able to manage a bite. Rick hit the spot by pulling the best bottle of Burgundy from the box, heaving the cork out and leaving it beside Marcus as the cook's treat. Once the wine appreciation began, the men started to get competitive with each other and began telling tall tales filled with their own puffery.

When lunch was over, we womenfolk left them to powwow and went to clear up.

If we thought Marcus had made a mess of the garden, it was nothing compared to the kitchen. Vegetable peelings littered the floor. Gravy dripped from the side of the cooker. Pots and pans piled everywhere, all of them trashed. The three of us stood there open-mouthed and Julia had to restrain Leoni to prevent her running back into the dining room and beheading Marcus with the carving knife. It took us almost an hour to clear up the devastation, but it was no hardship really, thanks to another half bottle of the sweetly delicious vintage Sauternes Rick had so thoughtfully brought in to us with the rest of the chocolates. We sat at the kitchen table when we were done and finished them off.

'You're quiet,' Leoni said to Julia. 'It's getting to be a bit of a habit. Something on your mind that you're not sharing with us?' Julia didn't answer, acting as if her mouth was fully occupied with the chocolate she was eating. Leoni soldiered on. 'Nothing to do with that Count Dracula friend of yours, is it?'

'Pipe down,' hissed Julia. 'For God's sake, Leoni.' Julia nodded towards the dining room where the men were enjoying Rick's cigars and swapping filthy jokes. 'Are you trying to make things any worse than they already are?'

'Sensitive, aren't we?' Leoni narrowed her eyes. 'If I

didn't know you better . . .' She got up from the table and put her glass on the draining board without finishing the accusation. You could have cut the atmosphere with a knife. Julia got up silently and left the room.

'Well done.' I shook my head at Leoni. 'Ever considered joining the diplomatic corps?'

'It's her that's the problem,' she said. 'Not me. The only person she's thinking about is herself. Wallowing in it, that's what she's doing. Have you seen David? Poor bastard looks knackered.' I couldn't help but nod my agreement. 'He only wants to help, but oh no, she just keeps shoving him off and shutting everyone out. Makes you wonder what's got into her. Or should I say *who*?'

Saints forgive me for what I said next, hushing my voice to a whisper. 'Do you really think she's having an affair?'

Leoni pursed her lips and poured the last of the wine into her glass. 'Does the Pope shit in the woods?'

With the conversation now too hot to handle, we left it there and went to join the men. Julia was nowhere to be found until we heard muffled noises from upstairs. Leoni and I went to seek her out to check if she was OK and to offer the apology that she was no doubt expecting. She was sitting with Millie on her pretty white bed sewing Teddy's eyes back on. 'I was going to do that,' said Leoni softly. 'Thanks.' Julia wordlessly handed Teddy back to Millie, who was delighted his eyesight had been restored and showed him her *Hungry Caterpillar* book. 'Sorry,' said Leoni awkwardly. She's never been one to go in for big, flowery apologies and still believes for the most part that she is never wrong.

Hearing the pea shingle crunching from the path below her window, Leoni pulled the curtain back and peered down. 'Oh, that's just great,' she mumbled. The doorbell went. Leoni froze, told us to keep quiet and left Marcus to answer it. The low doorstep conversation soon became heated, with angry voices drifting up to Millie's room. Marcus shouted for Leoni to come downstairs. She looked at us and slit her throat with a silent finger. On her husband's third command she left the room in a huff and trudged down the stairs.

'I know it was you,' said the man, pointing angrily at Leoni. 'Or those bloody kids of yours. Why don't you keep them under control? I should call the police and have you all done for antisocial behaviour. You're a menace. All of you.'

Marcus was trying to keep things calm and civilized. 'Now, let's not jump to conclusions here. I'm sure there's a perfectly reasonable explanation.' Judging by the colour of his face, the bloke at the door might be well advised to go and have his blood pressure checked. And his cholesterol levels. Panting and puce, he scowled at his neighbours. Marcus looked at Leoni hopefully, but not entirely convinced. 'Darling,' he said, 'I don't suppose you know anything about a couple of cones that have gone missing from Gerald's skip, do you?'

I WAS NOW ON my third attempt at the children's costumes. Whether it was Leoni's measurements or my general inadequacies as a seamstress, I couldn't rightly say. A bit of both, probably. I used to be brilliant at sewing. My soft furnishings were once the envy of all my suburban neighbours, but there's a big difference between lining a couple of swags and creating a full-on London Palladium special. How many tons of felt and foam I had got through is anyone's guess. Certainly enough for me to have caught the attention of the staff in the haberdashery department. With the benefit of hindsight I thought it best to try a different tack, so I went freestyle and attempted to judge all the measurements by eye. All I can say is that it's not looking overly promising. I shoved the whole lot behind one of the sofas and went to answer the door. It was Paul, wrapped in a cashmere overcoat and bearing a Christmas card.

'Am I your first?' He had a mischievous glint in his eye. I took the card from his hand and welcomed him in.

'You're just trying to make me feel guilty because I haven't done mine yet.' Paul followed me into the kitchen. 'Tea? Coffee? Something a little more bracing?'

'No thanks,' he said, rubbing his trim tummy. 'I've already started on the nuts and if I take on board any liquid I might explode.' He pulled a few more cards from his pocket. 'So I'm going to take a little stroll around the block and post the rest of these.' I couldn't help but feel a pang of disappointment that he wasn't staying. Reading my thoughts, he pushed me on the arm. 'I'll only be a few minutes. Want to come up and watch TV with us? You can keep me away from the Brazils, although I'm not making any promises about the Colombian.'

When he had gone I opened the envelope. As far as Christmas cards go (and let's face it, there are some monsters out there), this was a work of art. When opened, a tiny mobile lifted on a fine wire, suspending a flurry of hand-cut paper snowflakes in the window of the card. It was absolutely charming. Looking on the back to see where it had been bought, there was no mark. The message inside read: *Join us for Christmas lunch?*

I cannot begin to tell you how I felt on reading those words. I had honestly, truly thought I would be having my parents here and that I'd be busy dealing with the usual run of family politics and picky eating. Dad's OK. He'll eat anything provided it's slathered in gravy or custard accordingly. But Mum is from the old school

of domestic science and can't handle any kind of devi-
ation from the traditional. Although I can't say that I
wasn't a tiny bit relieved at being excused yuletide
duty, I'd subsequently had terrible visions of sitting on
my own in a paper hat faced with a stuffed poussin
and a litre of hock. I put the card on display in the
middle of the mantelpiece, sat down and counted my
blessings.

Important Reminder

Pick up half-a-dozen copies of the naked calendar from the local fire service before they sell out (again).

Chapter Twelve

IT'S THE THOUGHT
THAT COUNTS

I'M STILL NO FURTHER down the line with Rick's present. Everyone else is pretty much sewn up but the Rick Gift, as it has now become known, is starting to drive me potty. It's all become rather stressful. On the upside, I had a stroke of genius when I found myself walking past one of those hippy new-age shops. Although I was certain they would laugh their heads off when I told them what I wanted, they merely asked, 'What size?' and away I went five minutes later with an enormous gift-wrapped crystal ball for Rosa. It weighed an absolute ton and put paid to my shopping plans for the rest of the afternoon.

Marcus likes gadgets so I got him one of those sticks you poke in your computer when you want to feel like James Bond. I'm not sure what they do exactly, only that you can add it to your keyring so everyone can see you have one. He'll appreciate that. I went browsing around the second-hand bookshops one Sunday afternoon, had a word with the nice chap who specializes in foreign-language titles, and he found me a few trashy romance novels. In Russian. Helga looks like the kind of woman who's not averse to a bit of bodice-ripping between the pages. Every woman needs a little romance in her life. Something she can daydream about while the kettle boils.

I had to completely rethink my plans for Julia. I can't bear the thought of not exchanging gifts on the day, so I ditched my original idea to surprise her with the enormous vase she's had her eye on and went in search of something small I could sneak into her luggage. Julia has really eclectic tastes so I went to see her man down the Portobello Road. He used to have a stall there many moons ago but has since upgraded to one of the cupboard-sized shops. Sometimes it's closed for weeks while he goes off on his travels scouring the world for antiques and oddities. As his reputation has grown, so have his prices, but Julia has been loyal to him for so long that he always cuts her a persuasive deal. She has that effect on people. I took a photograph of the pair of us in case he had forgotten me. He had. The picture did the trick just nicely. Sara kindly volunteered to come along in case I should need a second opinion, which, for once, I didn't. The miniature Limoges enamel box he suggested was practically perfect in every way.

'I don't see many men about spending hours agonizing over their shopping like this,' she said. It seemed she wasn't too wide of the mark. The men were generally outnumbered ten to one by hysterical women tearing from one outlet to the next. 'Why do they leave it all until the last minute? I've seen men doing a commando roll under the security shutters at closing time on Christmas Eve.'

'That's if you're lucky,' I said sagely.

The taxi driver eyed our bags as we piled in. 'Christmas shopping?' We mumbled yes and continued our conversation. Or at least tried to. This was one of those cabbies who treats his passengers like a captive audience. 'My wife's been at it since July,' he yelled back at us. Sara pretended she couldn't hear him but instead of taking the hint, he put his speaker on and came back at us amplified. 'Can you hear me now?' he said grinning.

'Take a wild guess,' Sara said. At that moment we were both thrown forwards by him slamming on the brakes. An elderly woman had dared to not quite finish crossing the road, and instead of slowing down to allow her sufficient time, he'd hit the accelerator and thrown her into a panic.

'Did you see that?' he shouted. 'Bloody unbelievable. You know, I spend most of my day saving lives.' Sara and I looked at each other. 'It's true. I've saved hundreds of pedestrians. Not that anyone's ever thanked me.' He tutted and shook his head. 'What you bought then?'

'A meat cleaver to hack my husband's head off with,' Sara replied.

The cabbie laughed. 'That's a good one!' he said. 'I'll have to tell my wife that!'

'Have you bought her present yet?' I asked him.

'Nah,' he said. 'I'll do all that on Christmas Eve.'

You know when the novelty is wearing off because the music in the stores starts to drive you insane. There's only so much any person can take and if I walk into one more shop to hear Slade screaming that it's Christmas, I may well do something I'll live to regret, like tearing the speakers off the walls and kicking their woofers in. After a couple of days of relentless and not always fruitful shopping, I was glad to get back to work.

'You know what, Hell?' Oh, do tell me, Rick. 'You were right about all this.' I had just finished boxing up the parcels and Rick was helping me move them nearer to the door to make it easier for the courier man when he arrived. 'I'm feeling pretty good about getting that lot sorted. Thanks for that. You can consider me a changed man.'

'See?' I said.

'Yeah.' He nodded enthusiastically. 'I could really get into this.' The doorbell rang and the man from DHL jumped a mile high when Rick wrenched it open not a split second later.

Loading the boxes into the back of his van and noticing the festive address stickers I'd used, he nodded after Rick. 'Blimey, mate,' he said. 'What's your name? Father Christmas?'

Rick stuck the cigar back in his mouth and wandered back to his study, deep in thought.

'WHAT DO YOU THINK?' Leoni said, turning round to check her rear view in Julia's cheval mirror. We were trying to cobble together a sensational evening outfit without Leoni having to spend any of the money she'd wrestled out of her husband. I had bagged up everything I owned that I thought might have potential, Sara had done the same, and we'd brought the whole lot over to Julia's house where she had thrown open her walk-in closet doors and added her own contributions to the pile.

'Perfect,' we said.

'Does it make my bum look big?'

'Nope. Looks great.'

'Do you think it's a bit mutton dressed as lamb?'

Like that's ever bothered her before. Julia weighed up whether or not to tell the truth. After all, Leoni was standing there in one of Sara's rather risqué dresses and showing a great deal more décolletage than most women would dare.

'Of course not!'

For some reason that escapes me, I thought fit to give her the benefit of my opinion. 'You might want to try a little jacket with it.' Leoni's eyes darted back to the mirror with a renewed sense of criticism. She turned this way and that, then noticed where Julia's eyes were focused.

'You mean my upper arms, don't you?'

'No!' I protested too much. 'They're *grr-reat*. I was just thinking that you might get a bit chilly.' There wasn't that much fabric to keep her warm.

'Look,' Julia sighed. 'You've tried on everything that all of us have, so if you can't find anything among this lot – ' she waved her arms at the mounds of clothes all over the bed and floor – 'you're going to have to go out and buy something.'

Leoni stamped her foot. 'No bloody way,' she said. 'I've put the money Marcus gave me into my collagen jar.' (Leoni's been saving on the quiet towards surgical salvation for some time now.) 'This'll do just fine.' We cleared up the devastation, sorted the clothes back into whose was whose and went downstairs to the kitchen to make a sandwich. Leoni offered to help, which meant standing in the way and eating most of the ham before it reached the bread.

'This Friday, isn't it?' I asked, shoving her away from the fillings.

'Yep.' Leoni opened another packet of crisps. 'If you don't count the Relate sessions, I haven't been out with Marcus for ages.'

'Looking forward to it?'

'I suppose.' She thought about it. 'So long as he doesn't talk about work all night or do his bloody party piece.'

If there is one thing that should be etched onto my memory for ever more, it's Marcus's party turn, although I'm not sure that he'll be rolling it out again in a hurry after ending up in hospital the last time. He had to have three stitches in his head. Julia came into the kitchen with a few perfectly preserved Bond Street carrier bags and an envelope.

'Right,' she said to Leoni. 'Take your pick from this lot, then we'll pack up your outfit and see if we can find you some bogus till receipts to match.'

WHENEVER THE TELEPHONE starts ringing in the middle of the night, my first thought is that something's happened to my parents. They're getting to that age when bits start to fall off and the unexpected becomes ever more likely. A man's voice rose from the receiver.

'Is that Helen Rubens?'

'Close enough,' I croaked.

'It's Sergeant Clarke from Paddington Green,' he said. 'Sorry to disturb you so late. We've got a friend of yours here who's in a bit of a state.' I heard some commotion in the background which may or may not have been related. 'I wonder if we could ask you to come down to the station?'

'Who is it?' Like I needed to ask. It's been a while since I've been dragged from my bed at stupid o'clock in the morning to deal with one of Rick's nocturnal crises. 'And what's he gone and done this time?'

It was freezing outside and bucketing down. By the time I had made my way across town in a bad-tempered taxi that took me half a sodden mile to find, I was chilled to the bone and looking like a drowned rat. The check-in desk at the police station was predictably busy for the time of year and rank with the smell of drink. Two young women wearing stained party clothes were slumped in plastic chairs by the door. A scruffy man argued with one of the officers behind the desk about why couldn't they give him a lift home in a panda car because he paid his taxes. I crept up to the counter and tried to go unnoticed by the motley crew.

'I'm looking for Sergeant Clarke,' I said quietly to the sturdy officer with the beard.

He smiled back at me. 'That would be me. What can I do for you?'

'I'm Helen Robbins. I mean Rubens. Although it's Robbins.'

He looked at me cautiously while I vainly tried to explain which option was, or was not, my name, then a wave of recognition passed across his face.

'I see,' he said, motioning to one of his colleagues to take over. 'Good of you to come out on such a horrible night. We'd have kept him locked up 'til morning but it's pretty busy in here and we could do with the extra room. Do you want to come round?' I was buzzed through a security door and taken down a few corridors. 'It's that time of year,' the officer explained. 'We get all sorts to deal with, although your fella's won tonight's prize for most entertaining customer.'

'He's not my—'

'He's in here.' He stopped at a big cream metal door and opened the viewing hatch. I peered inside and there, sprawled across the prison bunk snoring like a rhinoceros, was an enormous, fat Santa, resplendent with outsized belt buckle and fur-trimmed booties. Sergeant Clarke banged his fist gently on the door. 'Wakey, wakey, Mr Wilton. You've got company.' Rick remained comatose so the sergeant opened the door, went in and gave him a shake. 'Come on, Sleeping

Beauty.' Rick woke with a snort. For a moment he seemed not to have the faintest idea where he was. Then he saw the officer and smiled.

'Sharge!' He clung to the policeman's uniform and tried to pull himself upright. Sergeant Clarke helped him with good humour. Then he saw me. 'Hell!' bellowed Rick. The gust of fumes nearly knocked me over. 'Ishn't she great?' He grinned drunkenly at the officer, then wobbled his head towards me and lifted a finger to his lips. 'Sshhhh,' he slurred, then started giggling.

'We found him staggering around Soho Square making a bit of a nuisance of himself,' the sergeant explained. 'The arresting officers couldn't just leave him there in case he came to any harm. There's some dodgy characters around at that time of night. When they tried to get him into the back of the police car, a couple of tramps attacked the officers saying that he was the real Santa Claus.' The sergeant laughed, took Rick by the arm and helped him towards the door. 'He'd only been going around with a big red sack giving food and money to all the down-and-outs.'

'Wheresh my bell?' Rick pulled on the sergeant's arm and looked around the cell with one eye closed.

'It's all right, big fella,' smiled the officer. 'You'll get your bell back.' Then to me: 'He made a lot of new friends tonight. Probably shouldn't have accepted the drinks they gave him, mind you. It might look like

Special Brew but you don't want to know what those people put in their cans.' From the reaction Rick got when we helped him past the front desk, he'd made a few new friends at the station too. He kept trying to wink and do a thumbs-up at everyone. 'Here,' Sergeant Clarke said to Rick, and handed him a big shiny bell with a black handle.

'Cheersh, shaarge.' Rick gave the sergeant a big salute and took the bell. 'Yo, ho, ho!' he said, then waved the bell in the air above his head. It didn't make any sound. Rick turned it over and stared into it, thoroughly confused. Even from where I was standing I could see the clapper had been sellotaped against the side. This escaped Rick's notice and he tried ringing it again. He frowned and looked at me. 'Dushn't work,' he hiccuped.

'Come on,' I said. 'Let's get you home.'

Rick's affectionate attempt in the taxi to lean his head on my shoulder was hampered by the girth of his padded Santa suit. He kept trying to hold my hand while telling me how fantastic I am.

'Now, Rick,' I warned him. 'You've got your beer goggles on, so I'm going to do you a big favour.' My stern voice forced him to look at me, his face adopting a silly oh-I'm-really-scared expression. 'Stop talking, otherwise you're going to feel very embarrassed in the morning.' I put my finger up to my lips. 'Not another word.'

Getting him in the house was easy. I just opened the front door and in he fell. I pulled on the rug on the polished-wood floor to slide his body clear of the door, hauled his boots off, covered him up with a duvet from upstairs and shoved a pillow under his head. He was out cold, but I said nightie-night anyway and crept quietly away.

The next morning, after a lengthy lie-in to make up for my *sleepus interruptus*, I made my way back to Rick's house in Victoria. His road is surprisingly peaceful considering it's slap-bang in the middle of one of the busiest parts of London. Tourists everywhere, clicking cameras at everything that moves and peskily asking directions. I side-stepped a young Japanese couple who seemed to be heading my way with a crumpled street map and got safely behind Rick's front door.

Rick was in the sitting room in his dressing gown, lying semi-conscious on the wide leather sofa with an ice pack attached to his head. I went to the kitchen and found Helga sitting at the table flicking through *Hello*. Her lips were moving. The second she saw me she got up and started apologizing. 'I nyet see,' she cried. 'I open door and, bang!' She banged her fists together. 'Rick head. On door. Bang!' She shrugged that it wasn't her fault. 'He lie there. In floor. I say – ' she pounded her fists on her chest – 'who make sleep like that?' She shook her head at me. 'I try open door, but nyet. So I bang with door. Bang! Bang! Bang!' She did the actions of smashing the front door onto Rick's cranium while she tried to move the obstruction she couldn't see. I heard a low groan from the sitting room and went back in there.

'Rick?' I whispered, bending over him. He lifted the ice pack from his forehead to reveal the most enormous shiner and a fine collection of bruises. 'Oh my God!' I said before I could stop myself. 'You look like you've fallen in front of a bus.'

'Thanks,' he barely managed. 'And for using me as a fucking draught excluder.' He winced with pain as I lay the ice pack back across his head. 'I tried to move but the belt buckle had got caught on the rug. I was pinned down by the duvet. Christ almighty,' he moaned. 'I thought she was trying to kill me.'

I perched on the edge of the sofa. 'Can I get you anything? Have you taken any painkillers?'

'About half a bottle.' He pulled up the corner of his ice pack and peered at me with one eye. 'I suppose I should say thanks for coming to get me last night,' he said. 'Not that I remember very much about it. A sackful of sarnies and fags from Sainsburys. A can of Special Brew . . .' He struggled to recall the events of the night before. 'And some bastard broke my bell.'

'It's not broken,' I said. 'They taped the clapper up and gave it back to you. You were too pie-eyed to notice.'

Rick covered his eye again. 'That's the last time I

play the Good Samaritan. Trying to spread a bit of the old Christmas spirit and look what happens. God, I feel rough.'

'Don't be daft! Your mission was more successful than you might think. There are now at least two vagrants in Soho who are convinced you're the real Santa Claus. They tried to attack the police when they carted you off.'

'Really?' Rick said. 'That's nice.'

'You honestly did look great.' I omitted the finer details of Rick's appearance by the end of the night. 'Every inch the real thing. It was a brilliant outfit.'

Rick gave a long sigh and another groan. 'Urgh,' he said, referring to his acute hangover. 'It's a creeper. I'm gonna have to go upstairs and crash out in bed.'

'Need help?' I asked as he hauled himself up from the sofa.

He held his hand up to say no thanks, and leaned on the wall until he found his feet. 'I'll be fine,' he said, and shuffled off towards the stairs. 'Oh, Hell?' He paused for a second and pointed to the costume piled up on the floor in the hallway. 'Do you think you could take that lot back for me? Phone my secretary and ask her where she got it from, will you?'

Angela doesn't like me. Rick says it's just my imagination, but I know women well enough to spot the ones who hate my guts, and she's way up there on the list. The first time I met her, the day I went to his West

End office for my interview, she looked me up and down as though I'd just crawled out of an organic salad. She's the kind of woman my mother used to refer to as 'brusque'. Angela's been Rick's secretary for about a thousand years, never married and thinks it's her job to protect Rick from anyone armed with a pair of functioning ovaries. You know the sort. Savagely maternal. Inappropriately overprotective. Severely sexually frustrated. Very possibly still *hymen intactus*. When I called her to ask where I should take the Santa suit back to, she sighed and tutted, then put me on hold for a couple of eons just to demonstrate her superior position. I was about to hang up when she flicked her switch and barked an address at me. She hung up halfway through my thank you.

Although cooking for Rick isn't part of my remit, it is definitely an integral piece of my need-to-please personality, so I nipped to the shops, rustled up a juicy steak sandwich and took it up to him before leaving. 'Eat something,' I said. 'It might help make you feel human again.'

'I doubt it.' He rolled over and saw the plate, his reddened eyes widening instantly. 'Then again – ' he caught a waft of the delicious aroma – 'I suppose I might be able to manage a couple of bites.' I turned the heating up a notch and left him to it. On my way to the address I'd been given somewhere round the back of Covent Garden, I couldn't stop fretting over how Helga had tried to smash his head in that morning. That eye did look mighty bad. I made an executive decision all by myself and rang Rick's doctor's to ask if they wouldn't mind paying Rick a house call just to check him over. The lady who answered the phone was very accommodating and promised the doctor would look in on him later that afternoon. Then my taxi pulled up outside the costume shop. I looked up at the window display and realized that all my problems were over. Or at least, three of them were.

IT WAS THE PERSISTENT, loud banging from downstairs that drove me to Rosa's door that evening. I still felt absolutely awful about Babushka having gone to the great litter tray in the sky. You don't have a pet for that long without getting attached to it, even if your relationship is totally dysfunctional. But Rosa was in an upbeat mood when she opened the door to greet me.

'Helen!' She flapped her black batwing arms around me like a seventeenth-century vampire and kissed me on the cheeks. 'Come in and tell me what you think.' I followed her inside and found Sally in her sitting room putting up one of the pictures that had been propped up against the skirting board since Rosa moved in. He was holding it against the wall, long arms stretched high above his head.

'Here?' He looked over his shoulder towards us and

gave me one of his big moonbeam smiles. Rosa and I cocked our heads at the painting, a modern composition mainly of, well, shapes. In different browns. It was strangely mesmerizing, although I couldn't tell you why.

'Perfect,' said Rosa. I nodded my agreement.

Sally nailed a picture hook to the wall. 'We've been talking about Julia,' he said, carefully lifting the frame into place and settling it until it was exactly level. 'And about the mysterious things that can happen in life.' I don't particularly like it when I hear other people speaking about my sister when she's not around to answer for herself. It's OK for me to do it. But not for anyone else.

'I'm sure she'll be pleased that you were concerned about her.' I caught Sally wink at Rosa and let it pass.

'So.' Rosa stepped up beside me and hung a batwing round my shoulder. 'What do you think of it?' She bucked her head in the direction of the newly hung artwork. The three of us stood there for a while, quietly appreciating the extraordinarily weird picture that was growing on me with every second that passed.

'I like it,' I said with conviction. 'Don't ask me why, but I do.'

'Good,' she said.

Sally took a bow in front of Rosa. 'May I go now, your majesty?'

'Dear boy,' she said, kissing him on the head. 'I can

see why my destiny led me here. Thank you, Sally, you sweet, sweet man. And don't forget about my little invitation. There's nothing like being the centre of other people's idle gossip.'

'You can count on me,' Sally replied, then leaned down to kiss me goodbye and whispered in my ear. 'It's a Picasso. You should see what's hanging in her bedroom.'

Mince Pies à la Freddie Mercury

Make the pies to your usual recipe.

Once cooled, sprinkle liberally
with icing sugar and cocaine.

Serve immediately.

Chapter Thirteen

TINSEL TOWN

WE MUST BE GETTING close now. People's behaviour patterns are shifting. Bus drivers with tinsel stuck to their bulletproof Perspex screens don't pretend not to have seen you at the stop. Newspaper vendors happily give you change instead of mumbling swearwords under their breath. Shop cashiers pin little scraps of shimmery nonsense to their uniforms and may even spoil you with a smile. It does make a difference. Why we can't all muster a little more effort for the other eleven months of the year, I really don't know. It's amazing what a can of spray snow and a string of fairy lights can do for humanity. The United Nations Security Council should think about that.

The office party season has definitely started, signalled by the women on the buses and tubes wearing some variation of the 'day-to-evening' fashions featured in this month's women's glossies. Who do they think they're kidding? You can't transform an office outfit into instant evening wear, no matter what the magazines say. But it's fun to watch. Especially the ones who are wearing crippling new shoes entirely unsuitable for the escalators at Tottenham Court Road.

Rick was taking his merry band out to lunch at the Star of India. 'Everyone loves a curry,' he assured me. I assumed he had left for the office first thing that morning, before I arrived, to show his face around, as he puts it. There was nothing waiting for me on his desk, no mess, no unpaid bills, no instructions or requests, so I guess that meant I had not a lot to do. I took a cheeky seat and rocked backwards in Rick's big chair, reached forwards for a cigar and stuck it between my teeth. I picked up the phone. 'Yeah?' I said. 'Nah, mate, have him killed and dump his body in the Thames.' I replaced the receiver, laid back in the comfort of the deep leather and put my feet up on the desk. Being Rick felt good. I lifted the phone again and made a real call.

'There you are!' I said when Leoni finally answered. 'I've left two messages for you and you haven't called me back.'

'Sorry,' she said. 'The kids have got so many bloody

arrangements at the moment that I don't know whether I'm coming or going. I'm either dropping off or picking up or turning up at the wrong house at the wrong bloody time.' She sounded genuinely stressed, which is much quieter than her normal state, like her batteries were running down.

'I was going to offer to take the children off your hands on Friday evening if you like, before you go to Marcus's do. They can stay over at my place so you and Marcus can nurse your hangovers in peace.'

'Stay over?' Leoni was clearly confused. 'At your place? Have you completely lost your mind?'

'It'll be fine!' I said with well-rehearsed conviction. 'The boys can bunk up in the spare bedroom together and Millie can cuddle up with me. We'll go out for ice cream and see the new Pixar movie at the cinema.' I was ad-libbing now. I didn't actually have a clue what I was going to do to entertain them between Friday evening and the appointment I had arranged for them on Saturday morning. Still, it can't be that difficult to keep three small humans occupied for a few hours until bedtime, can it? I had already rung my insurance company to check I'd be covered in the face of hurricane Joshua and William, and everything breakable would be safely locked away.

'Really?!' Leoni was overjoyed. 'Well, if you're absolutely sure! That would be bloody marvellous!' And with that, she neatly fell into my trap.

Rick's house is very quiet when there's no one here. Helga doesn't come in on a Wednesday. It's her day off. I asked her once what she likes to do when she's not at work. She looked at me as if I were mad. 'Russian sings,' she said. I think she meant 'things', but I could be wrong. Sometimes when the house is empty I have a sneaky chill-out in the sitting room with the big plasma screen. It's like being at the cinema. Brilliant picture. Surround sound. But I couldn't possibly live with one at home. They're a bit *Footballers' Wives*, don't you think? There are loads of good films on this week. They're rolling out all the seasonal favourites again. When I opened Rick's TV guide and saw *White Christmas* in the late-morning slot, I do believe I actually said 'Yessssss' out loud.

An hour and a half of tinseltown's finest sleighbell production propelled me straight into silly mode. I flicked the television off and lay there on the couch, soaking up the festive atmosphere courtesy of Bing Crosby. When I came to my senses, I realized something was wrong at Rick's place, and galvanized myself into taking some drastic action. Armed with the Harrods account card he had issued me with ages ago to take care of his household requisites, I headed straight to Knightsbridge and insisted they arrange for immediate delivery of the goods I hurriedly tore from the shelves.

I'm normally long gone by the time Rick gets back

at the end of his day, but today I had decided to put in a whole bunch of overtime. Anyway, I thought he'd probably be a couple of sheets to the wind after the office lunch party and I didn't want any repeats of him doubling as a draught excluder.

'Hello?' Rick shouted, having returned to find all the lights blazing and the chain firmly across the door. I raced out to greet him, bracing myself against it to prevent him entering any further.

'Don't come in!' I squawked, rudely covering his bruised eyes with my hands. To my surprise, he didn't smell of anything stronger than his usual cologne and a double espresso.

'What the bloody hell are you doing?' He was smiling.

'Sorry!' I was flustered. 'Just give me a minute!' I pushed him through to the downstairs cloakroom and told him not to come out.

'What's going on?' he shouted through the closed door.

'Nothing!' I yelled back. 'I thought you might come home drunk and I was worried about you doing yourself a mischief again.'

'I never drink with the staff. Is that why you've locked me in the bog?'

I finished what I was doing and turned all the lights off. Speaking through the door, I said, 'OK, you can come out now.'

The door to the loo opened and out stepped Rick into the softly glowing hallway. He didn't say a single word and, even if I do say so myself, with all the lights extinguished for the first time, I had truly excelled myself. It had taken me hours. Huge garlands of winter foliage entwined with twinkling white lights ran up and down the banisters. I had adorned all the interior plants in the same way and laid silver and glass baubles round their roots. Rick's mouth was open as he stared at the winter wonderland around him. 'Look in there,' I whispered, pointing at the sitting room. When he turned the corner, I knew exactly what he would see. An enormous Christmas tree, branches aching under the weight of all the lights and baubles.

There was one thing I hadn't yet done and I walked in to join Rick and handed him the final piece. 'I couldn't reach,' I said. Rick looked down at the star in my hand and said nothing. It was only when I saw the glow of his face in the half light that I realized he was having some trouble holding himself together.

'PLEASE DON'T DO THAT, William,' I said. You can imagine.

'Have you got an Xbox?' Josh demanded.

'Erm.' This was already coming unstuck. 'Afraid not.'

'PlayStation?'

'No,' I apologized. 'Sorry.'

'That's boring,' said the twins in unison.

'Yes, I know,' I said. 'Who wants to go out for a burger?'

The twins eyed me suspiciously. 'Mum says burgers give you mad-cow disease,' said William. 'That's why only stupid people eat them.'

I turned to Millie for a little moral support. She was clutching Teddy to her chest and peering around the flat with moon eyes. As I stood there, trying not to look like I'd never had to entertain a group of small children before in my life, I realized I was in serious need of reinforcements. 'Tell you what,' I said to the boys, 'I think I might know someone who can help.'

When Paul opened his door we must have looked like a small troupe of refugees. I smiled at him apologetically, unable to hide the desperation in my eyes. 'I don't suppose you've got a PlayStation up here, have you?'

Well, of course they did. And an Xbox. And virtually everything else that boys like to play with. Paul was his usual welcoming self and went to fetch Sally immediately. 'Hey, you with the fatherly hormones,' he shouted through to the bedroom. 'Now's your chance.' Sally was so cool with his expensive streetwear and Game Boy dexterity that the boys were completely bowled over. He knew all the finger-snapping handshakes and strange words that young people use, and when they had tired of the computer games, he showed them how to make origami waterbombs.

'So long as you have a piece of paper,' he drawled to them, 'you have a reliable weapon.' They spent the next hour or so throwing home-made bombs out of the window at the occasional passing car. You'd be surprised at the potential velocity of a few ounces of liquid in a Japanese paper bag. One driver stopped and shouted abuse to the invisible enemy above. The boys thought it was great. Even the grown-up ones.

Little Millie must have been tired. She curled up in my lap on the sofa in front of the Disney channel, had a glass of warm milk and some of Paul's home-made peanut-butter cookies, then fell fast asleep. The boys, on the other hand, appeared to need no sleep at all. They stayed up most of the night fighting and wrestling each other before crashing out long after I did.

The next morning, I was run ragged just trying to get them all washed, dressed and breakfasted. By the time we got out into the street, I was already at least half an hour behind schedule.

'You're late.' The man in the strange little shop pointed at the dusty grandfather clock in the corner. 'And there's a big rip in the Santa suit you brought back.' He opened a notebook. 'The repairs will have to be paid for.'

'Oh,' I said. 'Sorry about that. I had no idea.' He

looked at the children and acted out a very theatrical double-take.

'What do we have here?' he asked in wide-eyed fascination. 'Could these be – ' he squinted down at them and stroked his long, grey beard with a scrawny hand – 'cheeeldren?' He whipped the beard off his face and sang, 'Ta-raaaaa!' The twins frowned at each other, although I'm sure I did detect the merest hint of a smile on their faces. Milly, on the other hand, looked perplexed and held onto my hand tightly. 'So – ' he clapped his hands together and bent down towards Millie – 'what magic do you want to create today, little lady? Would you like me to make you into a fairy? A princess?' He held his arms out wide and flapped them up and down. 'Maybe a big, green dragonfly?'

'No, thank you,' said Millie in a small voice, shaking her head solemnly. 'I want to be a star.'

The next hour or so was enchanting. The crazy man in the costume shop went upstairs to fetch the wizened old lady who did the needlework. It turned out that she was his mother and that her family had been circus folk for as far back as her memory would take her. She had once harboured ambitions of mastering the flying trapeze, but her own mother had lost a cousin in a tragic accident when an elephant ran riot through the big top during a performance, collapsing the main braces and sending the structure crashing to the ground with two of them halfway through a mid-air fling. From that moment on, it was the costume department for her and she'd had to satisfy herself with sewing sequins instead. One thing had led to another, as is so often the way, and she had wound up making fantasy costumes for some of the big names of the day. Our very own late/great Diana Dors had thought the woman a marvel. They had the photographs and letters to prove it.

They made a strange pair, the two of them. There was something going on there that I couldn't quite put my finger on. One of those unusual bonds that sometimes develops between a mother and a son where they collude with each other's oddities and become entirely co-dependent. Wrapped up in this mothballed fantasy world of make-believe, they seem to have created a perfect mini-universe in which to live where nothing ever had to be real. The old lady measured the children from head to toe and told them they would be the toast of the cast. Then she gave them each a lollipop from an ancient jar and sent us on our way. Ushering the three of them outside ahead of me, I wondered if anyone looking at us would think that they were mine. Of course they would. I felt a bursting sense of pride.

Knowing my luck with the children's behaviour was bound to run out any second, we made our way home to Leoni's, but not before I bought them each a little something to secure their silence. The house seemed unusually quiet when we arrived. I knocked on the door but there was no answer. Oh dear. The last thing I wanted was to have to do an about-turn and drag them all back to my place. Maybe Marcus and Leoni had been rather the worse for wear last night and decided to check into a hotel instead of coming home. I stood there and wondered what to do.

'There's a key under the mat,' said William.

Josh pushed him roughly on the arm. 'You're not supposed to tell anyone that. Mum said.'

'Even burglars know there's always a key under the mat, stupid.' William stuck his tongue out.

I lifted the corner of the mat and, sure enough, there was the key. Slipping it into the latch, I pushed the door open and stepped inside. For a moment I thought I heard something. Then footsteps from upstairs. I glanced up and there on the landing was Marcus, wearing a bow tie and precious little else. I would have been treated to a full frontal of the crown jewels had it not been for the flashing Rudolph thong. Marcus stopped dead in his tracks when he spotted us, snatched a tiny towel that had been drying on the radiator beside him and held it defensively in front of his nethers.

Leoni's sing-song voice suggested they might have had a Buck's Fizz brunch earlier. 'Marcus!' she called out playfully. 'Come and adjust my decorations!' Marcus sprinted across the landing. The bedroom door slammed. I looked down at the children. They looked up at me.

'What's wrong with Daddy?' asked Millie. The sound of their parents thundering around the bedroom in a blind panic distracted them long enough to excuse me from having to find an immediate answer.

'Helen!' Leoni shrilled, emerging from the bedroom and trying to get her hair into some kind of order with her hands. Her dressing gown was on inside out. I smiled at her knowingly.

'Not disturbing you, are we?' I said mockingly.

'No! No! Not at all,' she flustered. 'We were just, just, erm . . .'

I turned and started to usher the children back out of the door. 'Who wants to go to the cinema?'

Vengeance Nut Puffs

Fill puff pastry squares with a
mixture of chopped lamb's testicles and
plenty of fresh thyme.

Seal the edges with beaten egg and glaze.

Bake for ten minutes in a hot oven,
then serve to your husband and his friends
when they get back from the pub.

Chapter Fourteen

STOCKING FILLER

I SOMETIMES WONDER if I'm ever going to have sex again. It's been such a long time. Yet as my body matures so unforgivingly, the prospect of taking my clothes off in front of some poor unsuspecting beau is no longer thrilling – more of a night-terrors phobia. If this is the way things are going to continue, it won't be long before the sight of an attractive man arouses memories rather than passion. Maybe I should have a word with Leoni about those swingers' clubs she mentioned. You never know, with a bit of detective work I might be able to locate one and start leading a lurid double-life.

It's not like Julia to be late. Rare is the time that I've

arrived at a rendezvous ahead of her, and I'm Miss Punctuality. It's our regular joint where the specials never change and Mario does his best to shatter glass with his famously spontaneous arias. Mario also gets himself into trouble regularly on account of his unfeasibly large salami. He suggests it to all the women, regardless of whether they are being escorted by their menfolk. Although most take it with good humour when he hauls it out of the kitchen to show them, his favourite joke has been known to backfire on him now and again, which explains why Tommaso was having to hold the fort all by himself today.

'It was terrible.' Tommaso was hanging around nearby, keeping me company with his gentle voice whenever he was free. 'They seemed like a nice couple. French.' He tipped a so-so with his hand. 'And when Mario finished his song the man just got up and punched him in the face. Pow – ' Tommaso swung his fist in the air – 'and he went down on the floor. Linguine everywhere. It was a shocking sight.'

I'll bet. He could have sold tickets. 'Poor Mario,' I said, when what I was actually thinking was that it had been bound to happen sooner or later. I've been on the receiving end of Mario's salami moods several times now and it's unnerving, to say the very least.

'He looks like he's been in the ring with Jake La-Motta. Oh. Excuse me.' Tommaso noticed some diners trying to get his attention and left my side. I read the menu again and tried not to look like I was being stood up. When Julia did eventually roll in forty minutes later, Tommaso and I had clean run out of conversation. He was visibly relieved when she made her way towards me looking flushed and radiant. I raised my eyebrows at her and tapped my watch.

'I know,' she said. 'I'm sorry. I lost track of the time.'

'You? Late? I was about to start making phone calls.'

'I said I was sorry.' Julia picked up her menu and Tommaso poured her a glass of wine from the bottle I had started half an hour ago. She ignored it and seemed uncomfortable and defensive. I couldn't help but wonder what had made her so late. Julia never takes her eye off the ball, never mind the clock. She didn't have a single carrier bag with her so I leapt to the brilliant conclusion that she had been doing something other than shopping.

'Meeting?' I ventured casually.

'Something like that,' she said.

My attempt to play it cool shrivelled less than two minutes into the game when the small talk became too tiresome to bear. 'Oh, come on, Julia.' I put my wine glass down with a thunk. 'I've been sitting here for three-quarters of an hour stewing over where you were and who you might be with. Do you think I'm the only one who's wondering what's got into you lately?'

Julia sighed. 'Oh, just leave it, will you?'

'No,' I said. 'You're being completely out of order.

If you don't want to talk to me about whatever it is that's making you act like this, that's fine, but I'm not going to stand by and watch you destroy everything you've worked so hard for all these years.' I was leaning across the table now, pressing my whispered words directly into her face. 'Leoni's convinced you're having an affair.' She didn't answer. Her eyes remained fixed on the table. 'Which means that she's bound to have told Marcus and half the world if her track record is anything to go by.'

Julia looked up, her eyes cold and dark. 'What about you?'

'What about me?' As soon as I said it, I realized I was stalling for time. What about me? The small pang I felt deep inside had an unpleasant smack of envy about it. That Julia had recently taken on a certain bloom had not escaped my notice. Her cheeks were rosy, her eyes shone. Was this not the familiar marker of a woman in love? And here was I, single as single can be, watching on as my sister turned her back on her high-scoring husband in pursuit of her inter-nationally aristocratic lover. Why does nothing like that ever happen to me?

Tommaso took one look at our faces and switched to discreet mode, barely making eye contact with either of us as he noted our order.

'It doesn't matter anyway,' Julia said. 'He's going away.'

'Oh,' I said. She seemed crushed and words failed me.

'He's asked me to go with him.'

There are certain secrets you cannot share with other people. Albert Einstein theorized that one of the three essential elements of happiness is knowing when to keep your mouth shut. I forget what the other two are, but have always felt this to be the most important. We all get so used to putting up fences and playing charades that it's easy to forget what lies beneath. So little of our talk remains real. Instead we prefer to communicate through a series of social semaphore messages wrapped up in polite chatter. I needed a walk after lunch. A long one. On my own. Julia and I held a lengthy hug outside the restaurant before she climbed into a taxi and headed off.

I didn't ask her the question. Whatever she was doing, it was her business and I thought it better that I didn't know any of the gory details. Besides, Julia would tell me herself if she wanted to. For the moment, she was keeping her secrets close to her chest. There was still an hour or so of daylight left. The cab dropped me off at a corner and I walked the rest of the way to the entrance.

London Zoo is lovely when it's chilly. Visitors are thinner on the ground and there are fewer snivelling children. So long as you're wrapped up warmly with comfortable shoes on your feet, there are few places in such a busy city where a stroll feels so surreal. I used to come here a lot when I was married, mainly when things at home were particularly bad and I needed to clear my head. Whether or not the attraction was anything to do with us all being so hopelessly caged in one way or another was not something I had ever given much thought to. Animals are nice creatures to share your inner feelings with. Either telepathically or with a satisfyingly one-sided conversation, depending on whether or not there are other people around. Animals always seem to know what you're thinking anyway. I took a seat beside the tiger's enclosure, not that there was much in the way of big cat action today, save a glimpse of a sleeping backside beneath its man-made hide, and thought of Julia. I wished I could be more like her. That I could know what to do and what to say to make things all right again. She'd been doing so well, her life mapped out, following the route she had so carefully set for it, and now everything had been turned on its head.

She wouldn't talk about Stan. She said she had a lot to think about and she didn't know what the future held. Only a fool would say that they did. I hoped with all my heart that she would find her way without breaking too many vases, then I closed my eyes and said a little prayer for her, not that I have that many credits to cash in. When I looked up the light had faded, forcing me to readjust my eyes. Right in front of me, behind the huge glass window in the white wall, the tiger had appeared. He was big and silent with burnished amber eyes. I smiled at him. 'Hello, handsome,' I said. 'I've been sitting here waiting for you to come and see me. Aren't you a beauty?'

'Thanks,' said a voice from behind me. 'I try to make the best of myself.' The keeper in the muddy boots smiled at me. His uniform was the same colour as the dusk, lending him a shadowy quality that was difficult to pick out in the twilight.

'I'm so sorry,' I said with a laugh. 'You must think I'm a crackpot.'

'Not at all, miss,' he said, wandering near to the glass where the tiger now lay regarding the pair of us with supercilious boredom. 'I always come back this way when I've finished me shift.' He introduced himself. 'I'm on penguins and otters,' he said, then nodded towards the tiger. 'But he's the man. Just look at 'im.' The keeper shook his head in admiration and sat down next to me at a courteous distance. 'I sits 'ere sometimes and watch 'im when all the punters have gone 'ome. I think about where he came from and wonder if he misses it, which is stupid really because he was born in Hertfordshire. But it makes you wonder, doesn't it?' He looked at me. 'Instinct and all that.' We both sat for a while admiring the cat. 'You've got it all in 'ere – ' he thumped his heart with his fist. 'No one can change what you're born with on the inside, can they? Doesn't matter if you're locked away for your whole lifetime, you'll still 'ave the same basic instincts. The same urges you'd 'ave in the wild.'

I smiled and agreed with him. Had he been younger I might have felt a few hairs rise at the mention of words like *basic instinct* and *urges* from a dishevelled man I've never met before, but his concentration remained on the tiger while he leaned on his broom handle, and I rose to take my leave. We said our goodbyes and I dawdled along the path that leads to the turnstile by the canal, thinking about what makes us the way we are. It's a quiet and pleasant place to walk, although I am also mindful that at this time of day it would be a perfect location for a spot of undisturbed murdering, if you were so inclined. My pace quickened and I hailed the first taxi that rumbled my way. Folding the zoo map to fit in my bag, I caught sight of an advertisement on the back cover. For some reason it made me think of Rick. Suddenly I knew exactly what to get him for Christmas.

SALLY AND ROSA were descending the steps to the street when I paid the taxi, her plum-velvet cape sweeping the black-and-white chequered tiles. Her trademark turban this evening was a delicious twist of scarlet raw silk, fastened at the front with a sparkling brooch set with a myriad coloured stones *en tremblant*.

Probably just an old lump of Fabergé she found knocking around the bottom of her handbag. Sally held her hand, looking rich and handsome in a sharply tailored tuxedo. There should have been bright lights and a movie camera nearby to capture their performance.

'Wow,' I said. 'You two planning on cutting a dash somewhere?'

'You can count on it,' Sally beamed, reaching to catch the door of my cab. Rosa was in fine fettle, her laugh tinkling with the remnants of long-flown girlishness.

'See?' she sang at Sally. 'I told you so!'

Sally held his hands beside his head and shook them around the way he does. 'She's a witch,' he said. 'We've been waiting in her apartment because she insisted we wouldn't be able to get a taxi outside. Then thirty seconds ago she changed her mind, and here you are . . .'

'With a car!' Rosa added. 'I'm never wrong.'

The pair of them got in and Sally pushed the window down. I waved them off.

'Have a wonderful time.' My curiosity then got the better of me, as usual. 'Where are you going?'

'The Dorchester,' said Rosa. 'The odious one is throwing his annual cocktail hoolie.' She squeezed Sally's hand. 'We're going to set a few tongues wagging. Aren't we, dear boy?'

'Fantastic!' My smile was wide and warm. 'I'll want to hear all about it when you get back.'

The taxi pulled away and I heard Sally calling, 'Don't wait up!'

The smell of Rosa's perfume hung on the air. The intoxicating scent wrapped itself round me. It was almost as though I could still hear their laughter as they rushed into the night like a pair of exotic bandits. I stood for a while breathing her in before coming into the warm. It's a colourful household I live in. On days like these, I wouldn't want to be any place else.

Settling in for the evening with the notion that I would at last sit down and write those cards, I was considering making a potato stamp when the buzzer snapped me to my senses. With the relative lateness of the hour I thought it best to take a peep over the balcony before answering. My heart sank. It was David. I shouted down my hello and let him in. He'd brought flowers.

'Hi,' he said, planting a kiss on my cheek. 'Mind if I come in?' As if I would.

'You've saved me from a fate worse than death.' I ushered him in. 'Christmas cards.' I pointed at the mound on the table. 'I've been wondering if anyone would notice if I just didn't bother.'

'We would,' he said. I made a pot of tea and asked David if he'd had anything to eat. He hadn't. Not since breakfast. So I knocked up a Spanish omelette and sat with him at the dining table while he ate.

'It's good to see you,' I told him. He seemed weary.

'I don't know what to do, Helen,' he said. We both knew what he was talking about so there was no use in my making any pretence. 'She's really distant. I catch her staring at the wall pretending to watch TV. I wish I knew what she was thinking.' David left some of the supper unfinished. 'If she wants me to go, I'll go.' I reached out and held his hand. 'Because I love her that much.' I squeezed his fingers in between mine.

'Don't do that,' I said. 'She's questioning everything in her life.' I voiced the thoughts that had been wandering through my mind for the past fortnight or more. 'Give her the space to work it out for herself.'

'Space?' David laughed bitterly. 'Since when did I have any say in what your sister does? You know Julia. She does what she bloody well likes and woe betide anyone who tries to stand in her way.'

I nodded. 'True.'

'Can I ask you a question?' His expression was earnest.

Oh, bloody hell. I did my best to keep an inscrutable face. 'Of course.'

'Do you think she's seeing someone else?' I couldn't help it. The blood rushed to my cheeks and my eyes widened no matter how I tried to freeze my features. 'I know it's a terrible thing to ask you, but there have been some unexplained gaps in her diary and my mind's starting to work overtime.'

David waited for me to respond. I let go of his hand. 'If she is,' I said with a clear conscience, 'then I certainly don't know anything about it.' I remembered to exhale. 'Of course, Julia sees lots of people. It's part of her job. She's bound to meet a few interesting characters but that doesn't mean she'd want to go running off with somebody else.' David looked down at his hands. 'Hey,' I nudged him gently. 'If she didn't want to be with you, you and I both know that she'd be somewhere else.'

'That's what I'm afraid of.'

'You mustn't think like that. This is a long-haul flight you took, remember?' David nodded. 'The two of you have been together for a long time. You can't expect not to get the occasional blip.'

'Blip?' David started laughing. 'You have no idea.'

'That's where you're wrong.' I stood up and took his plate. 'You think it's only men who have a mid-life crisis? Think again, David. And I reckon your wife's right in the middle of hers.' David followed me to the kitchen sink. 'Only we don't buy motorbikes and start wearing leather trousers. Women don't think like men. Remember that.'

'So, what, I just wait around until she decides to let me back into her life?'

Although I'm a big fan of David, I found this a pretty typical male response. He said it as though he shouldn't be made to wait any longer. That his wife's state of mind was an inconvenience beyond reason.

'That's exactly what you do,' I said. 'If you try anything else, I guarantee it will backfire on you.'

'Is that a threat?'

'No, David.' I wiped my hands on the tea-towel. 'It's a promise.'

Leoni's Fugu Vol-au-vents

Carefully remove the liver and ovaries
from the blowfish and set aside.

Poach the rest, cool and combine with lemon
mayonnaise before filling the vol-au-vents.

Traditionally served with a piquant dip,
squeezing in the contents of the liver is
optional and should yield enough poison
to kill about thirty tiresome guests.

Chapter Fifteen

SANTA, BABY

I HAD A CARD from Leoni in the post this morning. The cartoon on the front showed a woman smoking a postcoital fag in bed while Superman sits on the edge pulling his socks back on. In the caption she is saying, *Frankly, I expected much better*. Leoni had written inside, *Frankly, I must have been drunk*. When I'd finished laughing I picked up the phone and dialled her number. I'd not heard a peep out of her since catching her and Marcus in flagrante. This was obviously her ice-breaker.

'Funny card,' I said when she answered.

'Don't,' she groaned. 'I've never been so embarrassed in all my life.'

'Loved Marcus's outfit.' I decided to wring a bit of agony out of her blushes. 'Especially the flashing reindeer nose. Did he ask you to put the batteries in while he had it on?'

'He won it in the after-dinner raffle,' she said. 'They had an ice sculpture vodka luge.' Here comes the excuse. 'I got my lips stuck to it. Nobody believed me and they just kept slinging more vodka down the chute. It was either swallow or choke to death. Mind you, the frostbite left me with a real Scarlett Johansson pout. I looked bloody gorgeous.'

'I think it's lovely,' I said with a big smile. 'If the two of you can still get it together with a bit of fancy-dress thrown in, you know you can't be going too far wrong.'

'Yeah,' she said. 'Well, he'd better not go getting any big ideas. I'm not planning on making it a regular occurrence. He's suddenly decided that old scaredy-cats Relate woman is a genius and is busily researching a new activity for us to get involved in together.'

'That's great news!'

'Is it?' She spat her disapproval. 'The last thing I want is to end up being dragged off to ballroom dancing every Tuesday night with a load of creaking old people with clicking teeth.'

'Is that what he has in mind?'

'Christ, I don't bloody know, do I?' My questions were clearly testing her thin patience today. 'He's announced that he's going to surprise me.'

'Brilliant!' Might as well go the whole hog.

'What's up with you this morning?' she demanded. 'Sounding full of the joys of spring while my happiness hangs in the balance?'

'Nothing,' I said. Come to think of it, she was quite right. Today I was indeed feeling full of beans. The sun was out. The trees were bare (so you can peer in other people's houses more easily). It was a perfect wintry day. 'It's a nice day outside. That's all.'

'Yeah, well, why don't you go and annoy someone else with your unbearable cheerfulness. I've got massive PMT. Might go out in a minute and see how many arguments I can have with shop staff.'

'You do that,' I said and hung up.

THE BURST OF HEAT that hit me when I walked into Rick's place later that morning brought a rosy glow to my cheeks. I'm using a new moisturizer at the moment, with a big scientific word on the front, lopadopazomes or something. They're patented, in case I should lose any sleep over such things.

'Morning!' shouted Rick from the top of the first flight. 'Make us a coffee, would ya, Hell?' I've become used to being spoken to like a slave. With the hourly rate he pays me, he can call me whatever he likes. I rustled up a couple of frothy big ones and took them through to his study. He poked his face round the door. 'Not in there.' He tipped his head towards the sitting room. 'We can't see the tree from there, can we?' Since bringing the season indoors for Rick, his whole demeanour seemed to have changed. It was as though the sight of all the lights and baubles made him forget to be an ogre to everyone. I toddled in behind him and nestled on one of the sofas. Rick picked up his coffee and enjoyed the first inch or so with a couple of noisy slurps and satisfying 'aaahs'.

'Good?' I asked.

'You betcha.' Rick pulled a handkerchief from his pocket and wiped the froth from his top lip. 'So what's on the agenda today?'

'Don't ask me. I'm just the organ grinder's monkey.'

'Oh,' he said.

'Are you supposed to be anywhere?'

Rick thought about it for a minute. 'Nope.'

'No meetings? No one to shout at or take a contract out on?'

'Uh-uh.'

'So there's nothing you want me to do for you today?'

'I guess not.' Rick went back to his coffee. I looked at him blankly. He didn't seem to notice and continued to drink from his big round cup while gazing at the twinkling Christmas tree, so I did the same. Carried along by the soporific effect of the lights, I soon found my thoughts wandering pleasantly and my mind perfectly relaxed.

Rick finished his coffee and dumped his empty a couple of inches clear of the coaster. 'Wanna go out and do something fun?'

I didn't need to give the suggestion much thought. 'Yeah,' I said. I like using Rick's words now and again. 'Why not?'

Normally when I have a fancy to be spontaneous, I run into a wall of indecision. What shall I do today? Er, um. Come on! You live in the middle of the most exciting city in the world, surely there must be something fantastic you can go and enjoy? Erm, um. So I usually end up doing nothing and staying home freshening up the skirting board with a J-cloth. Not so with Rick. He didn't even ask me if I had any bright ideas, just said, 'Right. Get your coat on then.'

It wasn't until we were in the taxi heading towards Berkeley Square that I asked him where we were going. 'Shopping,' he said with a cheeky grin. 'For my new toy.' We pulled up on the corner and got out. Rick gave the cabbie a twenty for a six-pound trip and told him to keep the change. The bloke actually saluted Rick and told him he was a gentleman and a scholar. Obviously never met him before. Rick stuck a new cigar in his mouth, pulled open the heavy glass door of the showroom before the doorman could get to it, bent down and whispered in my ear, 'Wanna play a game?' The look of mild amusement I gave him said yes.

You know that thing about not being allowed to smoke anywhere any more? That doesn't apply to Rick. He sparks up wherever he likes. The ageing salesman virtually ran to his side to light the cigar for him. 'Good morning, sir,' he said, fully approving of his prospect's amazingly wise decision to smoke. 'May I be of any assistance?' Rick slipped me a sneaky wink from behind a Cohiba cloud.

'Yep,' he said. 'My girlfriend here wants one of those for Christmas.' Rick pointed past the man towards something behind him. We followed his finger and there, sleeping gracefully on the marble floor by the window, was the beast with perfect silver lines. The badge gleamed seductively. Oh, my word! My heart was racing so fast that for a moment I almost believed it was true. Just imagine. Rick's bark brought me down to earth with a thud. 'Waddya reckon, babe?'

'Oh!' I suddenly found myself centre-stage and going into full overblown actress mode. My speech came out strangled and much too loud. I punctuated it with a ridiculous high-pitched giggle and my arms started doing strange things. 'Yes!' I squealed, followed with a cringingly fake 'babe'. The man with the shiny shoes glided towards the car, taking us with him.

'Ah yes,' he said. 'An excellent choice, if I may say so.' He opened the door and offered his palm towards the driver's seat. Then I noticed everyone was looking at me.

Me? I mouthed to him silently.

'If you would like to step in, madam.' I crept in behind the steering wheel, conscious of my every move and trying desperately to remember The Correct Way to Get Into and Out Of a Posh Car, as drilled into me during my one bizarre term at the Lucie Clayton college. It was a while ago now and I didn't take too much notice during that particular module. Never thought in a million years I might need it. The obsequious salesman closed my door with the reassuring thunk of a piece of engineering that probably cost more than my flat. 'How does that feel?' he asked. My hands couldn't help but caress the soft hide.

How does it feel? Well, let me tell you exactly what's flashing through my mind right now. I'm thinking holy mother of Jesus this is the most fantastic car in the world. I'm not the kind of person who usually descends into a loathsome pit of self-indulgent desire but my mind is positively racing. I love this car. I want this car. I *need* this car.

'Mmm,' I mumbled. 'It's, erm, lovely.'

'Colour, babe!' Rick's shout echoed around the cavernous showroom. 'What colour you want? Red? Blue?

Something to match your eyes?' For a horrible instant I saw a picture of this classic beauty in a motley squirrel-turd brown.

'The black has a certain drama about it.' Shiny-shoes made a graceful wave towards the powerful shadow in the opposite window, then saw that I wasn't looking. 'Perhaps a little too masculine.'

'This one,' I said with a disgraceful longing in my heart. 'I like this one.' I began to open the door myself but Rick was there before me. I was completely over-whelmed and he knew it.

'Come on, babe.' Rick put his arm round my shoulders which, frankly, I thought was taking things a little further than absolutely necessary. Guiding me towards the door, I heard the shiny shoes quicken pace. The salesman tried to get to Rick's side before we made it to the exit. The doorman didn't know whether to open up for us or throw himself across the branded welcome mat. Rick flicked a business card out of his inside pocket and held it behind his shoulder. 'She'll take it,' he shouted as the doorman scrambled for the handle.

The salesman, staring at the name on the card, called after him, 'Yes, *sir*!'

I stood on the pavement outside next to Rick, totally bewildered. That had been like being air-dropped into a crazy Hollywood movie where you're Grace Kelly all of a sudden and everyone wants to marry you and give you massive diamond necklaces and pet leopard cubs. Blimey. What a trip. I blinked my eyes and tried to flip back into normal mode.

'Taxi or lunch?' said Rick, then squinted into my eyes with a wry smile. 'You all right, Hell?'

'Yes.' I didn't sound entirely sure. 'That was a bit mad, wasn't it?'

'Come on,' he said. 'I'll buy you a burger on the way back if you like.' He hailed a cab, opened the door for me and we got in.

Rick laughed as the taxi trundled along, took his BlackBerry out of his pocket and started reading emails. I looked out of the window as we passed Buckingham Palace and noticed that the Queen was in. I wondered if she was about to sit down to a tedious lunch with a herd of dignitaries from strange places. Then again, she might be channel-hopping daytime TV with a packet of custard creams wearing a crown. That's what I'd be doing, if I were her.

ROSA'S LIGHTS WERE ON. I could hear music playing behind her closed door but no voices. Rick's offer of lunch was soon forgotten when his BlackBerry almost exploded with new messages, so he dropped me off on the way and I found myself coming down fast from the morning's excitement. I didn't fancy sitting around on my own in front of the shopping channel. I'd much rather have a nice cup of tea with Rosa. I knocked gently on her door. An hour later I seemed to have settled myself in comfortably for the afternoon.

'We'll check it again at three.' Rosa came back to the sitting room and sat down beside me on the wide settee. She has been immersing herself in the rediscovered joys of having her own kitchen again. 'I don't think it matters about the pancetta. Do you think we should have put more wine in it?'

'It'll be fine.' I patted her hand. 'Worry spoils many a simple dish,' I added, as though it were an ancient Chinese proverb instead of a new Helenism.

'And what of your life?' she asked me in her direct manner.

'Good,' I said without much enthusiasm either way. Rosa seemed disappointed. 'Nothing new to report. Situation pretty much normal everywhere.' Sitting there sipping my tea I suddenly remembered my intention to be a good conversationalist for Rosa. 'Oh!' I said, as though I had let it slip my mind. 'You'll never guess what I did today.'

Her face brightened. 'Oh, do tell!'

And I recounted the whole story about me, Rick, the man with the shiny shoes and the car that was such a ridiculous extravagance that only someone like him would think of buying such a thing. I masked my shameful desire well.

'Rich men and their cars.' She nodded at a memory.

'Old Rex used to love that Rolls of his. It was the sister car of the one they made for John Lennon. The one with the flowers all over it? Surely you must remember.' A Pathé newsreel played in my head, the one with *that* car, and the Beatles, and free love. I nodded with a smile. 'They kept another one aside, exactly the same model, just in case something terrible happened with the paintwork. Rex bought it. There was a little plaque hidden inside the glove compartment with an inscription to say just that.'

So lost were we in Rosa's tales of being driven around Paris with the wind in her hair that we completely forgot about the lamb shanks (or lamb's knees, as Leoni calls them). She leapt from her chair and went into a panic until I sat her back down and reassured her that they would be all the better for it. When we ate supper together at five, they were tender and true to my word.

'Did you know that Julia stopped by to see me?' Rosa said over dinner without raising an eyebrow.

'Really?'

'Mmm. Wanted me to take another look at my cards for her.'

'She didn't!' I was aghast.

'You know I won't talk about it,' she said. 'But your sister's facing some very big changes in her life. She's going to need you around for support.' Rosa's face was poker straight. I felt no desire to doubt her word.

'Can you tell me if—'

Rosa cut off my sentence with a fierce shake of her head. 'No. That would go against my confidence,' she said. 'What Julia chooses to disclose is up to her. What I tell you is between you and me. We will just have to wait until this part of her destiny plays its hand. Then we'll see.' Noticing the concern on my face, she gave me a reassuring smile. 'You need to be there for her. The way that she's always been there for you. Now,' she said, changing the subject. 'Let me take a good look at your palm.' As if to lighten our moods, Rosa peered into my hand like a fairground attraction, tracing my life and love lines with her wrinkly fingers, uttering silly well-worn phrases like 'tall dark stranger' and 'going on a journey' until I laughed out loud. She returned my hand to my lap and patted it. 'Well,' she said, 'if I were to tell you the truth you wouldn't believe me anyway.'

Disposing of Your Tree

Forest fires are God's way of culling
all those trees that we don't really need.

Take a leaf out of nature's book and
you'll find that nothing goes up quite
like a two-week-old Christmas tree.

Feeding it into the open fire can prove
a little hazardous so you may prefer to
torch it in the street.

Chapter Sixteen

TWINKLE, TWINKLE

TONIGHT'S THE NIGHT. Creature of habit that I am, I like to put my decorations up precisely twelve days before Christmas. For fifteen years my only company for this annual ritual had been an illicit hot rum toddy. This year was different. I pounced on my upstairs neighbours the moment I heard Paul get back from work. 'Please say you're not busy,' I begged Paul when he opened the door. He still had his coat on. 'Please say you'll help me, no matter what it is that I am about to ask you to do.'

Sally heard my voice and appeared by the door. 'What does she want?' he drawled at his boyfriend with a fiendish glint in his eye.

'I have no idea,' Paul said. 'She appears to have gone mad. Maybe another dead animal in her kitchen?'

'I need two men. Right now.'

Paul and Sally looked at each other. 'Well, honey. You know we love you and all, but—'

'You don't understand.' I shook my head. 'It's your bodies I'm after.' I did a muscleman pose. 'It's twelve days to Christmas and I have to put up my tree.'

'Oh!' said Paul. 'Well, why didn't you say so? We can come down and do that for you, can't we, Sal?'

'Sure,' Sally said. 'Although I have to say—'

Paul elbowed Sally sharply in the ribs. 'That's quite enough of that from you, you man whore. You know that sleeping with women makes your wiener fall off. Don't be so disgusting. We'll be down in a couple of minutes.'

'Erm.' I swayed uncomfortably from side to side shaping my confession. 'That's the thing, you see.'

'The thing?' said Paul.

'Yeah.' Sally agreed with Paul and pretended to glare at me. 'What thing?'

'The tree. I haven't actually got it yet. I need to go out and buy one. And bring it home.' I sniffed and played with the doorknob. 'All on my own. Because I've got no one to help me.' I turned and started down the stairs with sunken shoulders. 'It's all right. I'll manage somehow. I expect I probably won't be run over trying to lug it back by myself.' Before I could say another word the pair of them came after me, catching me by the elbows to halt me in my sorrowful tracks. Sally dashed back inside for his coat and they led me off to the farmers' market in Chelsea to liberate (their word, not mine) the lushest Christmas tree that money could buy.

Getting it home was pure Laurel and Hardy. They took an end each and put me on duty in the middle section just for the comedy because I wasn't tall enough for the job. Sally insisted we stop at every pub we passed to buy the tree a drink. Mercifully there were only two, but the pair of gin and tonics lightened our heads, and Sally tried to teach us 'Jingle Bells' in Spanish for the last leg of the expedition.

The lonesome rum toddy was no more. Instead I held a glass of chilled Prosecco and had fits of giggles when Sally and Paul began arguing about who should put the fairy on the top of the tree. Sally brought down a new CD he'd ordered from his homeland and we danced while tracing the fairy lights around the branches that filled my home with the fresh zing of their fragrant needles. I got to do the honours with the lighting-up moment. We clapped, refilled our glasses with the last of the bottle and admired our joint effort.

My collection of festive greetings cards had grown to fill the mantelpiece. I rearranged a few and made sure that the one from Sally and Paul remained in pole position. 'You like that one?' Sally asked, watching me take particular care not to damage any of the tiny suspended snowflakes.

'It's the prettiest Christmas card I've ever seen,' I said in all honesty. 'I've been meaning to ask Paul where you got it from.'

Sally smiled. 'I made it for you.'

I'VE NOT SEEN much of Leoni recently. Neither has Julia, according to Sara's general gossip update. She had stopped on her way home to drop off a bunch of mistletoe. It's sold out everywhere I've tried and my life didn't feel complete without it. The man who sells flowers on the corner by the tube station shook his head at me and said, 'Hen's teeth, love,' when I asked him if he was getting any more in. So I rang Sara, cheeky as that may have been, knowing that she would have a secret supplier at her fingertips. Sure enough she fetched it for me that very afternoon.

'You might as well have all of it,' Sara said, putting the whole lot on the table. 'Dudley will only go and fix a piece to his head then chase me around the house for hours if I take any home.'

'So, let him!' I said. God, I wish someone would chase me around for a while. I doubt if I'd even break into a trot.

'You don't need to worry on that front,' she said.

'I'm shagging him senseless at the moment. Present time coming up, remember?' Sara tapped her temple knowingly. 'And it had better be something in a pale blue box from Tiffany or a red leather one from Cartier or there'll be trouble.'

'Have you dropped any hints?'

'Hints? To a man? Are you thick or something?' If forced to answer, I may have to give it some careful consideration. 'Hints, no. Written instructions in plain English, yes. I've warned him that lockjaw can come on very suddenly if a woman is distressed and we wouldn't want any nasty accidents over the holidays, would we?'

'Sara! You are a wicked, wicked girl.'

'Good,' she said. 'I'm refining a few new techniques.'

I put the mistletoe in a vase of water to preserve it until I decided where it should go. Above the front door? Perhaps not. You never know who's going to stand under it and demand a kiss. The pizza delivery boy, for instance. The one with the pepperoni face.

'So what do you think Leoni's up to?'

'Kids,' I said. 'They're breaking up for the holidays any day now and she doesn't know whether she's coming or going. Leoni hates Christmas. Says it's her worst time of year. We should go and kidnap her. Take her out and give her a break.' Since looking after Leoni's little bundles of joy for a straight twenty-four hour stretch I had gained a more realistic understanding of the tortures of parenthood. That woman deserved a purple heart.

'If you can get hold of her you're a better man than I am.' Sara glanced up at the clock on the kitchen wall. 'Shit! Is that the time?' She looked at her watch for confirmation and immediately started scrabbling for her hat and scarf. 'I'm supposed to be at home to let the television-repair man in. Buggeration. I've already forgotten about him twice and Dudley will be really disappointed if I let him down again. Not cross, you understand – ' she buttoned herself up and kissed me on the cheek – 'just disappointed.' Sara flashed her eyes at me and left. I closed the door softly behind her and smiled to myself. Sounds like those two are settling into welded bliss quite nicely.

The mistletoe and I had lunch together. The conversation wasn't up to much. I looked at it questioningly while it sat there in the vase and waited for something romantic to happen. I remembered that Julia had observed I was constantly hiding behind closed doors stupidly hoping that romance would come winging my way. I pulled a big sprig off the bunch and opened the front door, stood on a chair and pinned it to the door frame above. It wouldn't do my figure any harm to lay off ordering pizza for a month anyway, and I would be sure to double-check the spy hole before answering. Stepping back onto the landing to see how it looked, I was overshadowed immediately and caught in the heady rush of a full-on, lip-smacking kiss. It swept me clear off my feet. Literally. Before I knew it, my slippers were dangling in the air. Sally put me down before I could catch my breath.

'Nice.' He pointed casually at the mistletoe and fell back onto the staircase in an easy manner. 'Now I just wait here for you to come in and out.' He arranged himself gorgeously on the stair carpet and smiled at me in that bewitching way of his. 'Me? I could kiss you all day long.' The hairs stood up on the back of my neck.

I know Sally's gay, but so what? So is Tom Ford and, frankly, would that really be a deal-breaker? I don't think so. It's all about sex appeal. And Sally has it by the bucketful. I steadied myself against the wall. 'You,' I said, 'should be locked up. Better still, can't you bottle some of that, that, whatever it is you have.' I waved my hands around. 'You could sell it to ugly men and make a fortune.'

'I'm potent, aren't I?' He gave a little shiver.

'You're a bad influence on me, Sally Toledo Vargas.' (For that is his name, as I learned some time ago from the mail on the marble-topped console table by the front door.) 'Be away with you – ' I made a dramatic gesture towards their flat upstairs – 'before I tell your boyfriend you're a dirty, rotten straight guy who's heartlessly toying with his emotions.' Sally smiled and leaned back on his elbows, stretching his long legs out in front of himself and crossing his feet.

'Gay. Straight. I'm just a no-good sinner, baby.'

I wagged my finger at him playfully, left him where he was, then ran inside tearing my clothes off. I threw my perspiring body straight into a cold shower. Instead of feeling invigorated, I kept having steamy thoughts. The sort that you get sent to hell for.

'ARE YOU ABSOLUTELY SURE?' Leoni had finally broken cover and returned my call. 'They're completely crap, every year,' she said. 'I feel it's my duty to warn you that the school hall stinks of socks and wee. You have to sit on tiny chairs meant for small people. And some of the audience may smell.'

'I don't care,' I said. 'I have to bring the costumes along anyway. Besides, I promised the children I'd be there.'

'You're off your rocker.' She was eating something noisy. Crisps, maybe. Or a big bag of monkey nuts. 'But have it your way. Just don't come crying to me afterwards about what a terrible evening you've had.'

'I won't.'

'You'll need to come over beforehand. I have to take the children to the school an hour before kick-off and help them with their outfits.' Hmm. A glitch in my cunning plan.

'Why don't I do that for you?' I suggested. 'Then you can sit out front and grab some good seats.' Silence from her end. 'I really ought to anyway, what with me being responsible for their costumes.'

'Are you sure you're feeling all right?'

'Yes! It'll be a piece of cake.' My enthusiasm was starting to sound brittle. I'm not good with dishonesty. Even with the whitest of lies, it's still a lie. There was a part of me that wanted to tell Leoni that I had flunked out with her instructions, but the other part, the naughty side, was determined to keep a lid on the little secret I had hatched with her offspring.

The action was due to start at six o'clock. I booked myself a car from the same firm that Rick uses, packed in all the children's gear and picked them up from home on the stroke of five. They were as good as gold for a change, perhaps because my driver looked like the kind of man who ate naughty kids for supper. 'See you there in half an hour,' I called to Leoni as we pulled away. She gave us a thumbs-up and went back into the house.

I've not been inside a primary school for nearly thirty years. Thirty years. Can that be right? It must be. Goodness me. How time flies. The first thing I noticed was the smell. Disinfectant. The sort that goes cloudy in the water and is sloshed around classrooms with a filthy string mop from a metal bucket. The bossy lady who clapped her hands together to get people's attention and barked orders completely ignored the smile I gave her when I tried to introduce myself. 'Yes, yes,' she snapped. 'In there. And everyone must be ready IN PRECISELY SEVEN MINUTES.'

My children were beside themselves with excitement. As their costumes began to take shape the other mothers slowed and stared at us with open mouths. I made like nothing was out of the ordinary while dabbing the pad from Rosa's borrowed rouge on the boys' cheeks and noses. Josh looked at William and grinned. 'You look really stupid.'

'So do you, dog breath,' said William.

Millie's star was out of this world. I helped her into the yellow tights, pulled it over her head and guided her arms into the two hollows left for them inside. Her happy little face poked out of the front and her classmates gathered around and squeezed her points. A mother started making her way towards me from the back of the classroom. Josh padded to my side in his curly felt shoes, bells tinkling. 'That's Mrs Conway,' he nudged me quietly and half pointed at her. 'She's one of the classroom helpers. Her kids get special treatment. They're always showing off and trying to get us into trouble.' Josh looked up at me. It was hard for me to take his stern expression in earnest when he looked so cute in his jingling dwarf hat. 'She always makes the best costumes and goes on about it to our mum to make her feel bad.' It was the first time I had had any inkling the boys might actually care about their mother.

We both looked at the enemy approaching. I held Josh's hand and narrowed my eyes. 'Does she now?'

She stopped in front of us. 'Did you *make* that?' She stared down at Millie The Fabulous Human Star. Millie beamed up at the woman's crimson cheeks.

'Honestly?' I said. She waited impatiently for my reply. 'No,' I admitted.

Her face took on a satisfied sneer. 'I thought not,' she said.

Before I knew what I'd gone and done, my mouth was open again. 'Their mother did.'

Her shocked smile was fixed rigid as she walked away.

'EVERYTHING OK?' LEONI ASKED without much interest.

'Fine,' I said, almost exploding inside. 'Where's Marcus?'

'God knows.' The seats were starting to fill up and Leoni had to keep explaining that the chair beside her was reserved. The long version of this polite explanation soon bored her so she gave later arrivals an uppity, 'My husband's sitting there,' and kept her handbag on it. 'But if he's not here in the next three minutes I'm going to burn him at the stake. The children will be inconsolable. He's managed to cry off every single one of these and I swore to Millie he wouldn't miss this one. Not on his mother's life.' Leoni snuck a silver hip flask from her pocket, had a quick look round, then unscrewed the top and took a crafty nip. 'Medicinal,' she said. 'So now Millie thinks Granny Meatloaf will die if he doesn't come to the nativity. He's got no choice.' Leoni checked the door again then sighed and looked at her watch.

'Where have you been lately?' I changed the subject. 'Sara said she thought you must have fallen down a drain somewhere. Are you trying to avoid us?'

'I'm sorry, Helen – ' Leoni took another sneaky sip – 'but that's classified information. I suppose I could tell you. But I'd have to kill you afterwards.' Just then Headmistress Snooty Pants stamped into the room and clapped her hands together sharply.

'Good evening,' she said. Not satisfied with her effect on the audience, she cleared her throat and said much louder, much more rudely, 'I said, GOOD EVENING.' The parents sat to attention on the tiny chairs, looking ridiculous and trying not to gag on the fug of old socks and accidental urine.

'Good evening,' we mumbled back in unison, all of us transported to our early school days when all that mattered was not drawing attention to yourself or being made to stand in the corner facing the wall.

'The children have worked very hard this year,' she crowed. 'They've been busily learning their parts for weeks, so I hope you will all show your appreciation and give them lots of encouragement.' She fixed a steely gaze on one part of the school hall. 'So we won't be expecting any booing from the audience this time, and if any of the parents want to argue about whose performance was the best we'd be grateful if you would take it outside.' I noticed Leoni rummaging behind her coat and put my hand out for the hip flask when she had finished with it. 'The costumes have been particularly exciting this year.' All the mothers groaned. 'And I want to take this opportunity to let you know that there will be adult evening classes in needlework next spring, right here in the school hall. Some of you might like to think about joining.' Her beady eyes locked on my face for a moment, then flicked up and down disapprovingly. 'Although I suspect there may be one or two of you who think that adult education is beneath them.' I looked away. 'And now, without further ado . . .'

Leoni craned her neck looking for Marcus. 'I'll kill him,' she muttered. 'So help me God, I swear I'm gonna kill him.' I pressed my hand to her leg and told her to hush. Snooty Pants started the applause, a couple of the striplights were turned off and the youngest of the children filed into the school hall singing a hideous rendition of 'O, Come, All Ye Faithful', accompanied by a walnut pensioner playing an old, out-of-tune piano.

The door burst open. 'Sorry I'm late!' bellowed Marcus. The audience froze and all eyes turned. 'Haven't started already, have you?' The piano stopped. The children forgot their words. The headmistress glared at him.

'Sit down!' she commanded. Leoni indicated the seat she had saved by shaking a fist at him then pointing to it. He shuffled to the front and squashed his bulk into the wholly inadequate chair.

'You're late,' Leoni hissed through gritted teeth. 'Couldn't you make an effort and be somewhere on time for once in your miserable life?'

The audience went, 'Ssshhhh!' The rickety old piano struck up again. It didn't take long for the aroma to reach me and drown out the stench of the stinky hall. Marcus stifled a belch and the fumes intensified.

'You bastard!' Leoni whispered at him. 'You're drunk!'

Marcus looked at her through a lazy eye. 'Ssshhh,' he said.

And so it unfolded. The night of the caterwauling children. We were subjected to one snotty kid after another attempting to recite impossible words while being prompted loudly by a classroom assistant who obviously had her eye on a career in feature films. Every time she hurled an overcooked line to one of her charges, she turned to the audience with a big, gappy smile and winked. As the action moved on to the crux of the story, the crêpe-paper-clad door opened and in came the dwarves. All six of them, as Dopey was stuck at home with the galloping pyackers. Leoni dug her elbow into my ribs.

'Oh, my God!' – she was barely able to keep from yelling – 'look at the boys! How the hell did you manage that?' Josh and William caused quite a sensation and seemed genuinely tickled that their costumes should draw such delight from the gathered parents. Their identical looks and cheeky gestures stole the show. Leoni turned to the audience proudly, pointed at the boys and then to herself.

William's ASBO friend had misguidedly been given a key role narrating the main thread of the story, no doubt to head off a rerun of last year's controversy when he'd been dropped from the cast after setting fire to the scenery. The mother accused the school of discrimination just because his dad was in jail again and all hell broke loose. It made the local papers. The scowling kid stomped to the front of the stage. 'What are you doing 'ere?' he yelled aggressively into the face of the terrified Bashful.

'We followed a star,' said the shrinking dwarf, knees knocking together. ASBO kid forgot the next line and stood there flummoxed. Then he started getting agitated and looked like he might start nutting people. The prompting classroom assistant with the gappy teeth threw him a lifeline.

'Which star . . .' she whispered loudly, glancing back over her shoulder and grinning at us. The kid didn't get it. She tried again. 'Which star did you—'

'What fucking star?' shouted the ASBO kid. The audience gasped.

'Bloody hell,' laughed Marcus noisily. 'I thought this was supposed to be a nativity play! Brilliant!' Leoni landed a fist on his thigh and Marcus emitted a sharp yelp of pain.

There was some minor scuffling on stage while the classroom assistant tried to calm the players and the headmistress signalled wildly to the blind pianist. The walnut noticed the commotion and lurched into 'O, Little Star of Bethlehem'. The dwarves rustled along in a line and Josh stepped forward to save the day by taking the now crying Bashful's prompt.

'We followed the star from Bethlehem!' His words rang loud and true through the overheated hall and the door opened again. Out onto the stage, as proud as can be, shuffled little Miss Millie clad in a BBC-perfect yellow polyurethane star. She didn't have any lines to deliver. All she had to do was stand there and shine. I stole a glance at Leoni. She was speechless, hand over her mouth, tears filling her eyes. She put her other hand on my leg and squeezed it hard.

We skipped the invitation to suffer soggy mince pies and orange squash afterwards. The children didn't want to get changed back into their normal clothes. They were having far too much fun being admired by everyone and insisted on wearing their costumes home. 'I'll just dash back to the classroom and pick up their things,' I said to Leoni.

'I'll come and give you a hand,' she said automatically.

'Erm.'

'What?'

'There's something I need to tell you.' So I did.

We had to hunt around for William's other shoe, which one of his classmates had decided to hide. Leoni found it on a shelf with some dubious-looking pottery attempts. 'Very funny,' she mumbled to herself as she snatched the shoe and stuffed it in the carrier bag. 'Like I've got the time.' When she looked up, Mrs Conway was waiting to speak to her.

'Hello,' she said with a tight smile. 'I just wanted to congratulate you on making those amazing costumes.' There was a certain unpleasantness in her voice. 'Yes. We were all quite surprised.' She played with her string of simulated pearls and looked Leoni up and down. 'So we were wondering if you wanted to get involved with the costume design next year.' Leoni looked over at me. I kept my distance, as is wise if you suspect a grenade is about to go off.

'Afraid not,' she said tersely. 'I'm usually far too busy shagging my husband's brains out.' And with that, she linked her arm through mine and the pair of us turned and marched out, leaving Conway and her coven pale-faced and speechless. Leoni leaned towards me as we walked away. 'Stuck-up cow. No wonder her husband ran off with the local lollipop lady.'

We made our goodbyes outside the school gates. Just as I was about to step into my minicab, I felt something nudging my leg. One of Millie's foam points was pressing against my thigh. She smiled up at me with a wrinkled nose and tried to move her arms up, but all they did was bend her side points in my direction a little. 'Did you want another kiss?' I asked her. She nodded, so I bent down and planted one on her nose.

'I love you, Auntie Helen,' came her small voice. Then she shuffled off to her mother. She'd never called me that before. The pride that welled up inside me spilled over in a couple of big warm tears. What an old softie.

Helga's Prawns in Aspic

When making up the gelatine,
substitute vodka for the water.

Pass these cheeky little canapés around
whenever the party appears to be flagging.

Guaranteed to hit your guests like
an oncoming Siberian express.

Chapter Seventeen

THE SEASON
OF GIVING

'ARE YOU SURE that's everything?' I helped Julia pack
the last of her tropical essentials and stood by while she
closed the suitcase, hoping she wouldn't have to open
it up again in case she stumbled on the presents I had
quickly hidden among her beachwear while she wasn't
looking.

'I think so,' she said. 'If I've forgotten anything I'll
just have to buy it when we get there.'

'You'll be fine. What do you need except a couple
of sarongs and a big fat beach read?' The thought of

spending ten days on sun-drenched white coral sands warmed my cockles. 'Wish I was coming with you.'

'So do I,' she said. 'We could sit by the pool with eleven o'clock Piña Coladas and grade the talent from behind our sunglasses.' It was a nice thought, but I headed it off at the pass rather than letting my imagination run riot and setting my unserviced motors running again. David appeared.

'I was about to leave, if you wanted that lift to the station,' he said. 'Or I can come back and drop you later? It's no trouble.' I noticed with some relief that Julia actually smiled at him.

'It's OK,' I said. 'I'll come now. I think we're just about done here anyway.' Julia nodded and the three of us moved downstairs. I kissed Julia on the way out. 'See you again before you leave?'

'Sure,' she said. 'We're not going until Saturday. Don't ask me why I'm packing now. I've been feeling restless for weeks.'

David had already started the engine. I jumped in the passenger side, lowered the window and shouted bye as we drove off. 'Back in a few hours,' David yelled, holding his arm out of the window in a high wave.

'Thanks,' I said to him. 'For the lift, I mean.'

'I know what you meant.' He smiled straight ahead.

'How are things? With you and Julia?'

'Who knows?' he said. 'She's not been out of the house for three days. Last time that happened it was because she had the flu.' The car took a right at the end of the road. 'Don't get me wrong. I'm glad to have her around. At least I know where she is. It's just a bit weird, that's all. She's still acting mighty strange.'

'But that's good, isn't it? At least it's an improvement.' My immediate answer was nothing but a smokescreen. I knew very well that Stan was leaving this week, or was it last? Perhaps he had already gone. Julia hadn't said another word to me about him. Her silence spoke volumes. The subject was simply not up for discussion.

'I wouldn't like to say.' A cloud descended over his mood. 'She's been awfully quiet. If I didn't know her better, I might even say she's seemed a bit, well, *needy*.'

'Julia? Needy?' That can't be right. I let out an incredulous laugh. 'That'll be the day.'

'I know.' The station came into sight. 'She keeps hanging around me. My deepest fear is that she's building up for a big announcement. It feels like the calm before the storm.'

'Try not to worry,' I said. 'You'll be thousands of miles away from here in a few days strolling along a beach together holding hands.' To my surprise, David drove straight past the station and hung a left on the main road. 'David? Haven't you just missed the turning?'

'Oh, sorry,' he said. 'Forgot to mention you're being abducted. I'm coming to your neck of the woods anyway. Didn't want her indoors knowing what I was up to.'

'So you're not going to the office?'

'Are you kidding?' he said. 'I've been driving myself nuts trying to choose something for Julia. It's taken me a fortnight to narrow it down to two options. Want to come with? I could do with a woman's opinion.'

David buys Julia wonderful gifts. He had a very rude awakening when they were first together and she locked herself in the bathroom and cried over a red handbag he had bought for her during what I suspected was one of those last-minute commando rolls under a shuttered door on Christmas Eve. Or was it her birthday? I can't remember now. What I do remember is her having gone bananas at him and said that if he was the kind of man who couldn't be bothered to put some effort into her trinkets just twice a year then he could get on his bike and pedal in the opposite direction until he reached the county line. Everybody knows Julia detests red accessories, with the exception of rubies.

'I'd love to,' I said, not that I need have bothered. The antique sapphire and moonstone ring he'd picked out for her was every bit as fine as the amethyst necklace he had in reserve.

*

A SILVER ENVELOPE slid silently under my door as if by magic. I peeped through the spy hole. Nobody there. Taking it back to my comfortable sofa, I slit it open and slid out the deep-embossed vellum card. It was from Rosa, inviting me to a drinks party at her place on Friday evening, eight o'clock prompt. The day before Christmas Eve. Or, as we liked to call it as children, Christmas Eve Eve. How civilized. I was about to throw the envelope in the bin when I noticed another piece of her crested notepaper inside. It read: *I think it's about time we warmed my home, n'est-ce pas? Do try to come along.* And was signed off with her usual flourishing 'R'.

I took my tea and went back to the few Christmas cards lying on the dining table I had yet to write. The inconsequential ones to people I don't remember why I send cards to had all been taken care of. The remaining half dozen were to be distributed by hand between the friends I would see nearer the day and, of course, to Julia. These were the ones where I was likely to come unstuck, when the bog-standard *To so-and-so love from Helen* just won't do. I think it's verging on rude not to take the time to write something personal in the cards for one's inner circle. The one I had earmarked for Julia and David stared at me with its blank space. I chewed on the end of my pen. *To Julia and David, have a wonderful Christmas and try not to get divorced.* Perhaps not. *To Julia and David.* My pen hesitated. I drank some tea. Ate a biscuit. Picked up the pen and tapped it against my lips, struggled for several minutes, then wrote *Love from Helen*. Pathetic.

Present-wrapping was never one of my strong points either. I placed the latest inexpertly wrapped additions under the tree and brushed aside the pang from knowing there wasn't a single parcel among them with my name on it.

The Big Day falls on a Sunday this year. It seems fitting. I woke up on the Monday with a head full of must-do-before-Fridays. I got to Rick's place half an hour earlier than usual. It was all quiet downstairs, as I had hoped, so I crept into the sitting room and slid the shiny red gift box under the tree before shouting my arrival. I found Rick puffing away on a cigar while pulling strokes in his new exercise canoe upstairs. It's got a big clear plastic wheel at the front filled with water to give fat executives an authentic sloshing noise while they sit there and pretend to drag themselves along dry land. Not that anyone could reasonably call Rick fat any more.

'Don't you think you're pushing your luck?' I took the smouldering cigar out of his mouth and stubbed it out it in the ashtray.

'What? I'm only having a couple of sneaky puffs.' Rick stopped rowing and slumped himself across the oarless handles.

'I want you downstairs in ten minutes.' I tapped my

watch. 'I'm out of here from Thursday so if you want anything done before then, now's the time to tell me.' I left him to get his breath back and went to rustle up a couple of idiot-proof coffees.

Shaved and showered, Rick ambled into the study and relit his confiscated cigar. I'm well used to the smell of them now, not just in his home but clinging to my hair and clothes when I leave. He landed in his chair and gave me a big smile. 'So, Hell. What you doing for Crimbo?'

'Party on Friday, so I won't be here.' I thought I did rather well to sneak that in quickly. 'Recovering on Saturday until midnight mass. Christmas Day with Paul and Sally. I'm really looking forward to it. Paul's an incredible cook.'

'No family?'

'Not this year. Julia and David are going away and my parents have shunned me like the Amish.' I started to flick down my list. 'You know what, Rick? I think we've just about got everything covered according to this. I'll do your food shopping on Thursday. Is there anything special you wanted me to get in for you? I'll pop in and check everything one day next week, but other than that, you're on your own.' This was a thinly veiled hint that I wasn't expecting daily phone calls with his usual trivia.

'Nah,' he said, flicking his ash just short of the ashtray.

I put my notepad down and sighed patiently. 'What's the matter?'

'Nothing. I'll manage.'

'Oh, really, Rick. You're not even going to be here for most of the time.' According to my copy of his social calendar, he was flying to Gstaad on the twenty-fourth to join a snow-bound chalet party for the main event, then nipping across the pond to New York to see in the New Year at a bash hosted by the man who lends Donald Trump money. It must be nice to know exciting people all over the world. You need never feel like a plebby tourist again.

'Suppose so,' he said.

'Well, I know where I'd rather be,' I said, enviously eyeing the first-class British Airways tickets there on his desk.

'Yeah,' he said wistfully. 'Me too.'

THE NEXT COUPLE of days passed by in a flash. When Helga arrived on Thursday she had tinsel pinned in her hair and glittering baubles hanging from her ears. She insisted we have Russian snow-balls to mark the start of the holidays and pulled a half-bottle of cheap advocaat and a flask of home-brewed vodka from her bag. When Rick came home unexpectedly mid-morning, the loosening effect of our moonshine elevenses was more than a tad notice-able. We'd only had the two, but still I had let Helga decorate my head like hers and neither of us had done a stroke of work. We didn't even bother to pre-tend otherwise.

'I'm glad you're here,' said Rick with a big smile, pulling off his wet overcoat and dragging up a chair to join us. 'Got one of those for me?'

'Yah!' Helga cried, and made his double-strength. The stunned look on Rick's face when he tasted it reduced Helga and me to hysterics.

One of the most enjoyable perks of Christmas is that it's suddenly OK to drink in the mornings. Outside of the festive season it's only aristocrats and alcoholics who have that pleasure. Getting tipsy while the taste of toothpaste is still fresh on your tongue feels terribly naughty. But then again, most nice things do. When the clock struck midday, Rick insisted we knock off early. He helped Helga into her shabby coat and tipped me a wink.

'Oh!' I said. 'Of course!' I took Helga by the hand and led her into the sitting room. She admired the tree in gushing Russian. Rick picked up the biggest ribboned parcel under it and gave it to her.

'Happy Christmas, Helg.'

'Reek!' she cried. 'You make me present!' Helga opened her sagging Tesco bag-for-life, the one she's been carrying ever since I've known her. 'I make you present too! I have, with the bag, but I no think you make me present! So I keep! But now you have it!' Out of her bag, she produced two manky parcels wrapped in newspaper and tied with kitchen string. The names were written in felt pen directly onto the paper. To my amazement, she had spelled both correctly. One for Rick, and the larger of the two for me. Helga bent down and wedged Rick's under the tree.

Rick went to leave the room. 'There's something else I forgot.' Returning a few moments later with an envelope in his hand, he gave it to Helga. 'It's a special thank-you.' He stood back. She looked at it. 'Go on,' he said. 'Why don't you open it now?'

Helga tore the envelope wide open and gasped as she pulled out a pair of first-class airline tickets, just like the ones I'd seen on his desk.

Rick looked sheepish but pleased. 'I thought you might like to go home and see the folks.' Poor Helga tried and failed even to string the simplest English sentence together, then burst into tears. I was touched for her and, being just the wrong side of 'tired and emotional', I almost joined in.

Rick puffed away on a new stogie and insisted on calling his chauffeur-drive people to drive Helga and me home or to wherever we wanted to go. Seeing us out to the car, he wished us both a Merry Christmas. As the driver pulled away I slowly realized that I had been left out. For a moment I felt so upset I almost started to wail. But the fault was mine entirely. The one person I had left off Rick's Christmas list was, unsurprisingly, me.

Christmas Recycling

Go green: rewrap all those hideous
gifts from last year and foist them
off on someone else.

If one accidentally ends up back in
the hands of the person who perpetrated
the crime in the first place, so much
the better.

What goes around comes around.

Chapter Eighteen

WIDOW TWANKEY

WHEN FRIDAY ARRIVED, I treated myself to a shamelessly indolent lie-in. No more work, so hang the indulgence. By the time I managed to haul myself out of bed at half past twelve I was ready to eat a thirty-two-ounce T-bone. My winter appetite, which insists on trying to lay down extra fat deposits for the coming months of berry shortages, plays terrible tricks with my food cravings. I'm certain as a species we're supposed to hibernate. That's why I can't get up in the mornings after the autumn equinox and begin to yearn for big lumps of cheese and Battenburg cake. Still in my dressing gown when the afternoon movie started, I noticed a regular kerfuffle at the main door, with it banging open and closed with infuriating regularity.

I crept out on the landing and investigated with a cleverly angled handbag mirror tipped towards the entrance downstairs. A hive of activity was buzzing in Rosa's flat and it wasn't yet three o'clock. I slunk back inside and hung around near the closed French doors peering down at the street below. A steady stream of suppliers arrived one after the other, lugged boxes and crates up the steps, joined in the commotion for a while then left. Although the floors are well insulated, I could hear excitable movement and occasional bursts of loud laughter. By six thirty I was transfixed. It was like living in the middle of Piccadilly Circus. I popped down to see if there was anything I could do to help. (OK, to have a good old nose around and see what was going on.) Nobody knew where Rosa was. The uniformed catering manager refused to let me on the premises. Peering past her shoulder, it looked (and sounded) as though they were building a Hollywood film set. Scuttling back to my flat, I found Sally draped on the stairs in his lounging puma position. He gave me a depraved smile. With my self-control rations having already been depleted by his recent shenanigans, I wasn't certain that I could get through another tease-fest.

'What now?' I said. That man has no idea of the effect he has on me.

'Nothing.' Sally pulled a lazy loop of string from his pocket and wrapped a cat's cradle round his long, tanned fingers. He offered it towards me. 'You remember how to do this?' I smiled at his hands, threaded my fingers through the strings and confidently pulled it away. It landed just so. Sally laughed and made the next move.

'You like to play games,' he said.

'Only with you.'

'What are you wearing to Rosa's party?'

'I don't know yet. Maybe my blue dress.' Sally's eyes rose to mine in a manner that suggested disapproval. 'The red?' He shook his head. 'What then?' On the fourth pass I messed up the cradle and the finger-held trampoline instantly turned back into a plain old piece of string. Sally rolled it up and put it back in his pocket.

'I'm going upstairs to make a phone call,' he said. 'And you're going to go in there and rethink your outfit.' My mouth dropped open and I blushed. Sally rose to his full dizzying height and started up the stairs. 'Don't look at me like that.' He wagged a finger at me. 'You can do much, *much* better.'

Well, there's nothing like someone knocking the wind out of your sartorial sails at the last minute, is there? In a split second I had gone from feeling perfectly relaxed and rather looking forward to an informal evening with friends to suffering deep neurosis about everything in my wardrobe. I started pulling things out and trying them on but got all hot and bothered. In the resulting frenzy I became hopelessly entangled in an evening top with complicated sleeves. I'd not undone the side zip properly and the top rolled itself up in its lining and became impossibly wedged between my breasts and armpits. While trying to tear the thing over my back I started panicking at the all-too-likely prospect of having to hack myself free. Do dressmaking scissors go through sequins? Will I slip and accidentally snip through my own jugular? Christ. I can't possibly call for an ambulance with blood gushing down my neck and my bare gazongas hanging out. Oh for God's sake, what does it matter? She's only our bloody neighbour. It's not as though I want her to fancy me or anything.

Wait a minute. Oh yes. Now it all began to fall into place. Rosa's invited a blind date. She's gone through her little black book and invited not one, but two or three fantastically eligible bachelors she thinks will be just perfect for me. After all, this woman knows everybody who's anybody, and she of all people should know that the one thing I'd really like to find under my Christmas tree this year is a half-decent single man. That's why she's been so cagey. Well, glory, glory, hallelujah. Good old Sally. Giving me a sneaky heads-up and letting the cat out of the bag.

I rose to the challenge and went at my appearance

with a renewed sense of vigour. As Sara says, you only get one chance to make a first impression. I took a leaf out of Leoni's book and threw caution to the wind. At the back of the wardrobe in the section marked Things I Have Bought But Never Worn, lay a selection of outlandish impulse purchases that had never seen the light of day. I reached for the psychedelic silk kaftan, teamed it with some extra layers and wide silk palazzo pants. Looking in the mirror, I remembered why it had never made it out of my door. I completely disappeared behind all those bright colours and faded into thin air. There was an urgent knock at the door.

'Paul?'

He looked me up and down, breathed a sigh of relief and shoved me back inside. 'Thank God for that,' he said. 'Sally told me you were planning on going to the party of the year dressed like an optician.'

'What—'

Before I could voice my protest, Paul had hold of my arm and was turning me round to inspect my clothing. 'This is simply fabulous, darling.' He eyed me critically. 'But, oh my, I'd forget the *au naturel* make-up if I were you, and we've simply got to do something about that hair.'

My heart sank. 'That hair? You mean, *my* hair?'

'Whatever.' He shunted me towards my bedroom. 'Sit down here. Let's see what we can find.' Without a hint of inhibition, Paul started rummaging through my drawers, pulling out clips and scarves, admiring a few oddments and curling his lips at others. He set about my hair like Edward Scissorhands, then finished off my new look with a streak of catwoman eyeliner and sinfully painted lips. 'There,' he said, twisting my seat to face the mirror. 'What do you think?'

I couldn't believe what I was looking at. Paul busied himself adjusting the blue silk orchid he had pinned behind my left ear. I stared at my reflection, barely hearing Paul's voice. 'Do you have some dangly ear-rings? I really think we could use a little drama here.' A smile crept across my face. I tilted my head back a little and looked at my Egyptian eyes. Paul had teased and sprayed my hair into an unruly mop. Maybe I had come straight off the beach. Perhaps I had been driv-ing my throbbing open-top motorcar just a little too fast. My new look was utterly bohemian and just a little bit wicked. 'Well?' Paul stamped his foot.

I raised my hand to my unfamiliar face. 'I love it,' I whispered.

'Of course you do,' he sighed impatiently. 'I'm a genius. Earrings?' I pointed at the jewellery box on the dressing table. Paul wrenched it open and poked his finger around the scant contents. 'Is that it?' He looked at me, confusion in his eyes.

'Sorry,' I shrugged. 'With the kind of life I've led, baubles from lovers have been pretty few and far between.'

Paul gave me a sympathetic squeeze. 'Wait here,' he said. Hearing him leave, I got up and went to the full-length mirror. There was no doubt about it. I looked sensational. I went in closer to have a good look at Paul's make-up job. It was fabulous. Bold, peacock-blue eyeshadow flashed from behind the black liner with every blink. My lipstick was Morticia perfect. Skin flawless. The whole transformation had taken him less than fifteen minutes. By the time I heard him skip back into the room I was determined to pressure him into giving me lessons. He sat down on the bed and pulled a small red pouch from his pocket. 'Here,' he said, offering me a pair of miniature golden chandeliers. 'You can borrow mine.'

Even before we had descended the split staircase that ran from my floor to Rosa's below, it was evident that this was no ordinary party. Her entrance had taken on the form of a Bedouin tent, strewn with Persian rugs and silk cushions. Two mustachioed strongmen in old-fashioned fake leopardskins held back the gossamer drapes that concealed her door. We stepped inside to a heady scent of burning incense and delicious, spicy aromas. The interior had been transformed into a sumptuous Arabian Nights theatre, resplendent with pillars wound with red silk and tied with fresh palm leaves. Judging from the number of bodies languishing around, we were by no means the first to arrive.

'Wow!' Paul whispered in my ear. 'We are going

to have *such* a great time!' A lithe young thing, sprayed in gold from head to toe, floated up in a mini toga. The glass tray she offered to us without so much as a word of greeting held three long, narrow cocktails. Thick, white vapour overflowed from each of them, oozed across the tray's surface and dispersed in the air around her hands. I saw Sally looking at her legs.

'Nice,' he drawled at her, picking up one of the glasses. He put it to his lips. What? He's actually going to drink it? I thought it was some kind of *Top of the Pops* welcome joke.

'It's Rosa's love potion.' She purred her availability. Sally closed his eyes and took a long sip. I waited for the glass to slip from his grasp. For him to fall to the floor clutching his throat while hairs sprouted from the back of his hands, but he just stood there and returned her wanton expression. Paul snatched the remaining two drinks from the tray, thrust one into my hands, then fixed the waitress in his sights.

'Well?' He caught her attention and flipped the back of his hand at her. 'You've delivered the drinks, honey, so shoo.' She made no attempt to disguise her disappointment and wafted away.

'Helen! Boys!' Rosa sailed towards us, arms outstretched and trailing long ostrich-feather-trimmed kimono sleeves. 'Come in! Come in!' She kissed the air around us and linked her arms through Sally and

Paul's. 'You'll never guess who's come to see me,' she winked at Sally. 'The oily one from the Dorchester.' She lowered her voice conspiratorially. 'I think they want me back.'

I wondered if I should pull Rosa aside while I had the chance and quiz her about the gorgeous men she had invited along for my amusement. I could feel the blood pounding through my veins. My palms became clammy. Look, just calm down. All in good time. Knowing Rosa she would wait until the perfect moment to make her introductions and the whole evening would be precisely orchestrated. I took a deep breath and reminded myself that no matter who lay in wait in the rooms beyond, at least I looked the part. Eccentric, successful girl about town who doesn't mind being single at all because my life is *so-oo* interesting. Relationships? Me? Oh, if only one had the time! I suppose if the right person were to come along. (At this point I would emit a light-hearted laugh.) Not that I'm looking, of course, though I guess I wouldn't be completely averse to the idea! I would brush the entire conversation aside with a confident, alluring smile.

'Pssst!' Paul was tugging at my sleeve. 'Over there on the cushions. Isn't that the chap who used to be in *Star Trek*?' I stole a glimpse at the suspect in the corner. Sure looked like him to me. He appeared to be acting out one of the famous sick-bay scuffle scenes for the benefit of his tiny audience. As Rosa encouraged us into the sitting room, I overheard the American actor explaining that Klingon was now recognized as an official language. His entourage made a passable job of looking impressed.

'I can't believe what you've done to your flat,' I said to Rosa.

'Me? I didn't do a thing, dear. It's all smoke and mirrors.' I took a sip from my spooky cocktail. Rosa looked me up and down. 'I must say, you do look rather delicious this evening. Is this new?' She picked up the fabric of my sleeve and admired it.

'No,' I said. 'You'd be surprised at some of the spontaneous moments lurking in the back of my closet.'

'Well, well. Not quite the shrinking violet we pretend, are we? There's hope for you yet.' She patted my hand, let go of my kaftan and started scanning the cosily crowded room.

'Anyone interesting here tonight?' I tried to make it sound casual.

'Of course!' She laughed. 'What kind of party do you think I'd have! I know everybody in the whole world. All the fascinating ones, at least.' I nodded eagerly. 'Your little clan is in the master bedroom being entertained by my man from Sotheby's. Don't believe a word he tells you.'

'Oh,' I said, making no move to join them.

'Not keen?' Rosa had mischief in her eyes. 'Perhaps tonight is a night for making new acquaintances?'

'Perhaps it is,' I said shyly.

THE DIMINUTIVE COUPLE I got stuck with for the next half hour were so highly bred that I could barely understand a word they were saying. Something to do with the price of copper and nanny falling into a ha-ha. Each time I tried to break away, the chinless wife (although it could have been his sister for all I know) grabbed my arm and repeated their last sentence and waited for me to coo. I was stuck in social purgatory with no sign of rescue by my comrades. It would have been more fun had I decided to stay home and gnaw my own arm off.

'There you are!' Leoni yelled at me from a couple of people away. 'Bloody hell! I didn't recognize you! Want one of these?' She held up a couple of Rosa's cauldron refreshments.

'Do you think we really ought to be drinking that stuff?'

'Live fast, die young.' Leoni's face disappeared momentarily behind a cloud of horror fog while she took a generous slug. 'It's only a bit of dry ice, and you know what they say: what doesn't kill you makes you stronger.'

'Thanks.' I took the other glass from her hand.

'Have you seen Julia yet?'

'No. Is she here?'

'In the bathroom.' Leoni thumbed the air behind her. 'A whole group of us were in Rosa's bedroom getting a lecture from that fat bloke from Sotheby's. Michael? Michel? Mitchell?' She gave up trying to recall his name. 'She's only got a fucking Degas hanging above her bed. Have you any idea how much it's worth?'

'I wouldn't like to guess.'

'No?' Leoni's face crumpled with disappointment. 'Bollocks. He wouldn't say either. But I bet it's loads. Anyway, so he's standing there going blah, blah, blah, like anyone's actually interested.' She had another slurp. 'And all of a sudden Julia comes over all emotional and excuses herself to the bathroom.' Leoni pulled a face. 'So what's all that about then?'

'Search me. Is David with her?'

'In the kitchen with Marcus. The caterers have already thrown him out twice but you know what he's like when he's hungry. Have you seen some of the people Rosa's got here?' I nodded yes, although my mind was preoccupied with finding Julia. 'That bloody wossname, you know, the food critic, he's a bit of all right, isn't he?'

'Mmm,' I said, even though I have always thought the man a pompous arse who uses ridiculously abstruse words just for the sake of it. 'I bet Rosa would introduce you if you wanted her to.'

'Really?' Leoni gushed.

'Deffo,' I said, pushing her in Rosa's direction.

THE SECOND BEDROOM was in semi-darkness, having been set aside to hold the guests' coats and damp umbrellas. I pushed the door open. 'So, this is where you've been hiding, is it?'

Julia looked up at me. Her face was fatigued. 'Hi,' was all she managed.

'Everything all right?' I sat with her on the pretty cloverleaf conversation seat, Louis XVI no doubt, and held her hand.

'I was going to ask if I could stay with you tonight,' she said.

I responded without hesitation. 'Of course you can.'

'It's just that I've been feeling really drained and a little tearful.'

'Sure.' I thought for a moment. 'But aren't you supposed to be getting on a flight with your husband tomorrow?'

'Will you tell him?'

'Tell him what, exactly?' I didn't like the sound of this one little bit. 'Tell him you don't want to go home with him tonight, or tell him you're not getting on a plane with him tomorrow?'

'I just need to be certain,' she said.

'So it's just for tonight then?' I don't know why I was bothering to ask the question. She didn't even look capable of coming up with an answer. 'Oh, for heaven's sake.' I stood up and flapped my arms against my sides. 'I don't know why you have to drag me into it. Why don't you just run off like any other self-respecting woman and get it all out of your system?'

Julia smiled into her lap. 'Thanks, Helen. I knew you'd understand.'

Well, if she thought I was going to be understanding about it, she probably already guessed that David wasn't. On my way to find him I passed Leoni in the corridor shouting 'Beam me up, Spotty' to the ageing TV star. After breaking the news to my brother-in-law, I narrowly managed to avert a full-on domestic savaging by claiming that I was feeling insecure and really needed to have my sister with me before they both disappeared to Honolulu for a fortnight. It wasn't even mildly convincing, but my promise to have Julia in a taxi to Heathrow first thing in the morning to meet him and the luggage in plenty of time swayed the jury. Julia made her excuses shortly thereafter and took herself off upstairs alone. As she left, both David and I noticed that she had a small overnight case with her, the one that doubled neatly as a flight bag.

'Spur of the moment, was it?' David said with resigned sarcasm. 'I don't even know why I'm still here.' He left ten minutes later. I watched from Rosa's window as he braced himself against the drizzle and disappeared along the pavement.

'Helen!' Rosa had found her way to my side. 'I've been looking everywhere for you! There's somebody here you absolutely have to meet.' At last. The moment I had been waiting for. I wrenched my thoughts away from my sister's crumbling marriage and prepared to meet my destiny. Sure enough, Rosa presented to me a not-completely-repulsive-looking man who was probably closer to my age than hers. He smiled widely at her introduction, revealing murky teeth like a vandalized graveyard. My dream vanished in a whiff of halitosis. This time I didn't hesitate. He had barely finished his how-do-you-do when I said fine thank you, lovely, do please excuse me, and scurried away.

'This' – I butted into Paul and Sally's intimate conversation by throwing myself into the pile of floor cushions between them – 'is the worst party I've ever been to in my life.'

'Oooh! Who's stuck a pin in your balloon?' Paul adjusted my orchid.

'Nobody,' I said flatly. 'It's just that Sally led me to believe that there would be some attractive, eligible men here.'

'Did he?' Paul cast Sally an accusatory stare.

Sally directed one at me. 'Did I?'

'Yes,' I said. 'Well, not exactly.' I pulled at one of

the cushions. 'Why else would you tell me to get trussed up like a dog's dinner?'

'It's a party,' Sally chided, tracing the angular shape of a square with his fingers. 'You're supposed to look fabulous and have some fun.'

'But I thought you said . . .' I huffed indignantly and didn't bother with the rest of the sentence. Paul put his arm round me and gave me a playful hug.

'Honey. You really do need to get out more.'

The next thing I knew Leoni had me by the arm and was trying to pull me to my feet. 'Get up! Quick! Marcus is about to do his party piece!'

'What?' I jumped to attention. 'You have to stop him!' But Leoni had already raced back to the action. I turned to Paul. 'Please! Don't let him go through with it. He must have taken leave of his senses. Do something!' Although the legend precedes him, few humans have witnessed Marcus's performance art. From the smiles on their faces, I could see that Paul and Sally had absolutely no intention of interfering.

'Are you kidding?' said Paul. 'I wouldn't miss this for the world.'

We reached the sitting room to see Marcus with a big metal tea tray in his hand, having a quiet word with the balalaika players. He turned to his audience. 'Ready?' he shouted. A loud cheer went up. The lead musician nodded an intro to the two other players and they struck up a catchy cowboy rhythm. Marcus let it build for a few bars then began to stamp along to the music, grinning at his audience, urging everyone to clap, both arms waving the tea tray in the air above him. Then came the song, although I use the term loosely.

Girded by a deep breath, Marcus bellowed, 'Mule traaa-ain! Yeah, yeah.' And smashed the tea tray on his head. 'Clippety clopping over hill and plain.' The musicians gave it some oomph and the audience roared with approval. Marcus hunched his shoulders up and down in time to the beat. 'Seems as how they'll never stop.' Smash. 'Clippety-clop' – smash, smash – 'clippety-clop.' Crash, bang, this time on his leg.

Leoni yelled, 'Yeeeeee-hah!' and started slapping her behind.

Everyone was completely drawn into Marcus's astonishing performance. Jaws dropped wide open. People bent double with hysterics. I'm ashamed to say I egged him on just as much as the others through four verses of skull-fracturing tea-tray nonsense. The Americans in the room identified themselves with loud whoops and yelps of approval. Marcus began to feed off the adulation. 'Get along mule' – smash, smash. 'Mule traaaaaaaain!' Bam! The tray was now a mangled wreck. Marcus held it high for everyone to see. The balalaikas strummed a frenzied final chord with as much volume as they could muster and the crowd went nuts. Rosa said she'd never seen anything like it. Coming from her, I expect that was saying something.

MOST OF THE LIGHTS were out when I left the party behind and took myself off upstairs. I peeked into the darkened guest room, pushing the door wider to let some light in from the hallway. The bed was empty. It was only when I switched a lamp on in my room and began to undress that I noticed the shape under the duvet. I used the other bathroom to wash and brush my teeth without disturbing my sister then silently crept into bed beside her.

I had trouble nodding off. At first I put my tossing and turning down to having had one too many spicy canapés, then I noticed that the nagging sensation keeping me awake was actually a persistent knocking coming from my front door. I dragged myself out of the warmth of my shared bed and pulled a dressing gown round my shoulders. On reaching the door I could hear the muffled sound of giggling, punctuated by a regular command of 'Ssshhh!' The spy hole gave me a fish-eye view of Leoni and Sally making a poor job of propping up a very drunk Marcus. I opened the door with one finger in front of my lips.

'Keep it down,' I whispered.

'Don't suppose you've got a bin I can dump this in?

I'll never be able to get him home in this state.' Leoni didn't sound entirely compos mentis herself. I beckoned them in and pointed them towards the empty spare room.

'I'm going back to bed,' I said quietly. 'You should find everything you need in there, but I'm afraid I'm fresh out of Rudolph thongs.'

Giving Etiquette

A nice home-made gift shows
how much you care.

Chapter Nineteen

T MINUS 24 HOURS

THE FOLLOWING MORNING I must have either slept through the alarm or forgotten to set it. Blinking the sleep from my eyes, the clock beside the bed pitilessly stared ten thirty at me. I was awake immediately and spun around to shake Julia. She wasn't there. I leapt out of bed and went to the bathroom. Then the kitchen. There was no sign of her anywhere. Everything was gone. Her clothes, bag, coat – vanished. I instinctively reached for my handbag to find my phone and check where she was. Scrolling down to her name, I hesitated then changed my mind. Either she had gone to meet David or she hadn't, and nothing I said was going to make any difference. I made a cup of tea instead and turned the radio on quietly. The low winter sun streamed in through the windows, filling the flat with soft morning light. I took my cup through to the sitting room, lazed on one of the sofas and gazed at the Christmas tree.

Admiring my dazzlingly wrapped presents nestling on the carpet beneath it, I noticed that an interloper had infiltrated their midst, sitting proud of the others. All the parcels, except Helga's newspaper bombe, were uniformly silver and white to blend in with my chosen decorative theme. The impostor was bottle green with red ribbon and had a big sprig of holly tied to the bow. A swing tag dangled from one corner. I slid to the carpet for a closer look. It said, *To Helen, Love Julia*. I stared at it for a while. Tempted as I was to pick it up, I bent down instead and smelled the wrapping paper then pushed it back under the tree.

'Dear God.' Leoni came shuffling into the room wearing one of my old T-shirts and last night's make-up, which had declined into a near-perfect Alice Cooper. 'Please tell me there's a new-husband kit somewhere in that lot for me. I didn't get a wink of sleep last night. Did you hear Marcus snoring?'

'Morning, Mata Hari. Fancy a cup of tea?'

'Not half,' she said, following me to the kitchen. 'In fact, better make it a bucket. I've got super-dehydration and my tongue's turned into Velcro. Brilliant party.' I poured two big mugs for her. 'Makes a change from having a polite sherry with the vicar and pretending you're not a heavy drinker.' She picked one up and took it through to the bedroom, shouting, 'Oi, Gunga Din. Wake up, you snoring bastard. I've brought you some tea. Not that you deserve it.' Whether she put it by the bed or threw it in his face I'm not sure, but I did hear Marcus groan and tell her to bugger off.

Leoni and I lounged in the sitting room with tea and hot buttered toast. 'Thanks for the crash pad. It's so peaceful here.' It was too. Especially at the weekends when there's nobody rushing past in the mornings. 'In my house it's like waking up in the middle of the Somme every day. You need a tin hat and a rifle just to make it to the bathroom.'

'Who's got the kids?'

'The babysitter stayed over. No doubt she invited everybody she knew and had a party of her own.'

'You're not serious?'

'Dunno,' she said, pulling a good long stretch and ruffling her hair while she yawned. 'Don't care. I popped in on one of the neighbours before we left yesterday' – the ones she's still speaking to, I presume – 'and asked them to call the emergency services if they hear gunfire or see smoke pouring out of the roof.' Marcus appeared at the door looking very much the worse for wear and attempted a cheerful smile. 'Bloody hell,' said Leoni. 'It lives.'

Marcus braced himself for yet another long day of

marriage. 'Morning, dear. Isn't it a bit early for you to be out of your coffin?' Leoni flicked him the bird and looked the other way.

'Good morning,' I said. 'Shall I rustle up some bacon and eggs?'

Marcus raised his hand painfully and tried not to look as ill as he clearly felt. 'I don't suppose I could trouble you for an Alka-Seltzer?'

'Bathroom cabinet,' Leoni snapped without looking up.

'Leoni! Don't be so horrible. Can't you see the man's in pain?'

'Good,' she said. 'Guess what he's got me for Christmas?'

'Oh, here we bloody well go.' Marcus sighed at me. 'She's done this in front of everyone we've seen for the last week.'

'I don't know.' I resigned myself to playing piggy-in-the-middle. 'What has he got you?'

'NOTHING,' she shouted.

Marcus threw his arms up. 'She told me not to get her anything!' Then to his wife, 'Did you or did you not tell me not to get you a present?' Leoni sniffed at him and rustled the pages of a magazine. 'She says I always get it wrong and told me not to bother because I'll only choose something completely crap. I've asked her time and time again. But will she even give me a clue? No.' Marcus searched my face for sympathy. 'I give up. She's bloody impossible.'

'You're a useless, selfish bastard and I hate you,' Leoni said without looking up.

'Now, now.' I rose from my seat and attended to her sunken husband. 'I'm sure Marcus was going to put a nice cheque in a card for you.'

He looked relieved. 'Thank you, Helen. That's exactly what I was going to do. Although now of course the surprise has been completely ruined.'

'Yeah, yeah.' Leoni stifled a yawn. 'Push the boat out and stretch your imagination, why don't you. You needn't bother. I haven't got you anything either, arsehole.'

On closer inspection his head looked like it had been on the fast cycle in a washing machine. 'Oh dear,' I said, reaching towards his forehead. He pulled away before I could touch it.

'Don't,' he pleaded.

'Any blood?'

'Only a bit. I've pulled off the pillowcases and put them in the laundry basket.'

Leoni ruthlessly discarded her *Vogue*. 'I've no sympathy for you. You're old enough to know better.'

'Well, that's nice, isn't it?' Marcus looked at me for support.

'I thought you were magnificent,' I said.

Leoni relented and ran Marcus a nice hot bath while I found him a couple of the opiate-heavy painkillers Paul gets on prescription and deals to his friends. 'He's probably got concussion,' I fretted.

'Excellent,' she said. 'Serves him bloody well right.'

'He said he's feeling terribly sick.'

'I'm not surprised.' She gave me an evil smile. 'I saw him eating a bowl of pot-pourri last night. He was that pissed he thought they were vegetable crisps.'

I crawled around on the carpet and dug out all the parcels for Leoni's family so they would be sitting under her tree in the morning. A new teddy for Millie, a selection of the computer games the boys had gone crazy over at Sally's, a bottle of Rick's favourite Armagnac for Marcus. Leoni made a hopeless attempt to mask her excitement and checked that the biggest one had her name on it. 'Presents for us?' she said.

'No, Leoni. They're boxes of mouldy food-scrapings from my kitchen bin.'

She smiled and gave me a big hug. 'This is great,' she said, sounding happy as a sandboy. 'It's Christmas Eve and all I have to do between now and the New Year is relax and reheat. No more pretending to wrap up tons of leftovers in front of the mother-in-law while she drones on about her Turkey Thrift Pie. You'll never know how much this has meant to me.' She pulled away and started shouting at her husband. 'Marcus!' He winced and covered his head. 'Go down to the car and fetch Helen's present, would you?'

*

'Is Rosa here?' I asked the uniformed skivvy. There was as much commotion today as there had been yesterday afternoon. With all the dismantling going on, it looked as though the entire contents of her flat were being carted away.

'No,' she said matter-of-factly.

I offered her the heavy gift box I was carrying. 'I wonder if you would be so kind as to see she gets this,' I said. 'I would have put it under her tree myself, but she doesn't appear to have one.'

'I'm sorry,' she said. 'You've missed her.'

'I know. When she gets back. Just pop it on the table in the sitting room.'

'You don't understand.' The girl looked sorry for me. 'She's gone. Left. Moved out. We've been instructed to pack everything up and put it into storage, except those – ' she pointed at three black trunks – 'which were supposed to be on a flight an hour ago.'

'Oh,' I said, not quite following her for a moment. 'Do you know where she's gone?'

'Afraid not,' she said. 'And even if we did, we wouldn't be able to tell you. Data protection.'

'I see,' I said, and stood on the doorstep not knowing what to do.

'We could put it in the storage cases,' she suggested, pointing at the gift in my hands. 'But I don't know when she'll get it. We've had some of her stuff on ice for donkey's years.'

'It's OK,' I said. 'I'll hang on to it. She's bound to pop in and say goodbye at least.' Surely she wouldn't abandon me, just like that? We were barely getting warmed up. The girl must have been mistaken. I noticed that all the pictures were gone from the walls.

'Sure. Merry Christmas.' She smiled at me sympathetically and closed Rosa's door.

Much later, I buttoned up my overcoat, closed my door quietly and crept downstairs. All was quiet outside Rosa's. No wind-chime music. No fragrant waft of incense. Nothing at all. Stepping out onto the portico steps into the dark night, I noticed that the persistent drizzle of the afternoon had turned to a light flurry of snow. I popped up my umbrella, stood out on the street and watched it for a while cascading in soft helixes above the communal garden before settling in white shadows on the grass. The door behind me opened. Sally emerged and saw me on the pavement.

'Hello,' I whispered, not wanting to break the stillness. 'Where are you off to at this unearthly hour?'

'Midnight mass,' he whispered back.

I was warmed by the thought that my old friend had sent me some company for tonight's special worship. We shared my umbrella and walked to church together.

Task for the Day

Practise looking thrilled when
you open your gifts.

Chapter Twenty

THE MIRACLE
OF CHRISTMAS

I WAS GREETED on Christmas morning by a thick white blanket snuggling the world outside. A smattering of big fat flakes fluttered slowly earthwards. The window panes in the bedroom were heavy with the snow blown into their corners. I turned up the radio, ran a deep bath and treated myself to a festive schooner of Madeira. Today was going to be a wonderful day. The only decision I had to make was when to open my presents. If my self-control held out for long enough, I intended to wait until I was lying in bed alone that night to stretch the excitement to the last possible moment. I resisted the come-hither gaze of Julia's bottle-green parcel. There was no mystery attached to the appallingly wrapped table lamp from Marcus and Leoni, and Helga's fish and chip packet was far more fun unopened anyway.

Paul had banned me from bringing anything along to lunch except my company, so I was planning on earning my keep by amusing them with an even more outlandish outfit from the back of my wardrobe. The make-up took me three attempts before I got it anywhere near as good as Paul's masterpiece, but the cloud of emerald-green silk was every bit as audacious as the multi-coloured kaftan I had unleashed on Rosa's party. Checking the clock, I had a good half hour before my presence was required upstairs. I almost buckled and tore into Julia's gift, then decided I hadn't finished speculating about the promise of what might lie inside.

A swift bin-liner dash around the flat to straighten out some of the chaos from the previous few days kept my mind off the temptation under the tree. Leoni had left a scarf behind and I found Marcus's socks on the floor under the spare bed. I popped them in the laundry basket and wondered how long it had been since I had washed a man's smalls. I emptied the wastepaper baskets, hoovered up the stray pine needles in the sitting room and gave the bathrooms a quick once-over. Emptying the little chrome pedal bin in the guest room en-suite, something caught my eye at the bottom of all the spent tissues and cotton wool balls. On second glance I could see exactly what it was through the thin white liner. I'm not usually one to go trawling through the rubbish, but this time I made an exception, pushed the curiosity through the flimsy plastic and pulled it out.

I was still perched on the sofa staring at it in stunned silence when Sally knocked on the door forty minutes later. 'Merry Christmas!' He gathered me up in a bear hug and swung me around. 'You're late so I've been sent to come and get you before Paul's canapés collapse.'

I steeled myself, pushed the mystery of the evidence now sitting on the coffee table from my racing mind and threw myself into the spirit of the day. 'Here, you take these.' I passed Sally the last stack of parcels from under my tree, slammed the door shut and followed him upstairs where a jazzy melange of jingly music mingled with the warm scent of cinnamon.

'Merry Christmas!' Paul rushed me with an excitable embrace, saw the presents in Sally's arms and began to squeal.

'Is that mulled wine I can smell?'

'Urgh.' Paul brushed the suggestion aside. 'Why would anyone want to drink hot plonk that tastes of mothballs. It's a candle. We're having mimosas.' I accepted the glass from his hands. 'And you simply have to try one of these.' Paul waved a plate of artful canapés in front of me and watched my face intently while I did the honours and made appreciative noises. Clearing the third nibble away with a few sips, I wondered whether the news had spread yet.

'Have you heard from Rosa?'

They looked at each other in that way that smacks of a conspiracy. Paul began rearranging the nibbles. 'She came and said goodbye to us in the early hours of the morning once her last guests had left.' I tried not to look gutted. 'Don't take it the wrong way. She didn't want to disturb you.' Paul patted my hand. 'Our lights were on. We were up anyway.'

'Did she say when she'd be back? I didn't get to give her her present.'

'No.' Sally put his glass down and held my hand. 'She told us she needed to visit an old lover of hers in Cuba. Some guy called Rex. His wife passed away suddenly. She felt she couldn't wait and left almost as soon as she got the call.'

'Heart attack,' whispered Paul solemnly. 'At a party while doing the conga. Got dragged along the dance floor for a good few yards before anyone realized. Must have been awful.'

Sally nodded. 'From the look in her eyes it seems they have been waiting for each other for a very long time. I think maybe we will not see her again.'

'Oh,' I said. 'That's such a sad thought. We were only just getting to know each other.' I felt oddly bereft.

'Don't be so conventional.' Paul stirred his glass. 'People like that never stay in one place for very long. It's much too dull. We were lucky to have met her at all.' I couldn't help but feel just a little cheated. I had adored spending time in Rosa's company, but it was only now she had gone that I realized how much. 'She left us presents.' Paul flashed his eyes and smiled at me to cheer up. 'We got a Matisse drawing – ' a dramatic frown darkened his face – 'although she's written on the back of it that if we ever get divorced it's hers.' He pointed at a smug Sally. 'Why she should get special treatment I really don't know. Always the favourite, aren't you? Go on, tell Helen what you did.' Paul didn't give him a chance, barely pausing for breath. 'It was him, you know, at your dinner party, messing around with the candles and knocking on the table.' Sally started laughing. 'Oh yes, very funny,' snapped Paul. 'You have no idea what that did to my nerves.'

Sally stretched a lazy arm to the table behind the sofa, picked up a small ebony box and passed it to me. It was delicately inlaid with mother-of-pearl birds and intricate flowers of silver wire. 'She asked us to give you this.' I took it from him. From deep inside I could hear some objects rolling around. Examining the outside of the case, it appeared to have no joins at all. Each surface was as smooth and flush as the next.

'How do you open it?'

'That,' said Paul, 'she didn't say.' I passed it to him but he wouldn't take it. 'It's no good asking me. We were at it for hours last night. No joy.' Looking at it again, and it really was a beautiful thing, a clear picture of Rosa's smiling face appeared in my mind's eye. Why, the devil. She had done it on purpose. In a strange way, the mysterious box and everything about it seemed to make perfect sense. It might never reveal its secrets. I guessed that was the whole point. I put it down gently on the coffee table and raised my glass.

'To Rosa,' I said. 'Wherever she may be.' We drank to her health and happiness and held a comfortable moment's silence while my mind travelled to a place far away where she danced a slow tango with the man who had held her heart for all these years.

The three of us sat and exchanged gifts with much love and laughter before settling into a misfits' Christmas Day with far too much rich food and a stack of DVDs to digest after lunch. Nobody was interested in the Queen's speech anyway. 'I'm sorry,' said Paul with audible distaste, 'but the moment she started on about her anus horribilis she lost a fan.' He shielded his eyes against her offence. 'It just doesn't bear thinking about. Trust me. I should know.'

I fell into a coma during *Fiddler on the Roof* and woke

up with terrible indigestion and a rather attractive Mulberry throw draped across my legs. Paul and Sally were curled up together on the other sofa barely this side of conscious. I hauled myself up and kissed them both, gathered up Rosa's secret box and the gorgeous silk-lined bedroom set they had given me, wished them a final merry Christmas and stole silently out of the door.

Back home, the evening was drawing in, the dark Prussian blue of the winter sky outlining the chimney pots across the square. I left the curtains wide open to watch the heavy flakes of snow dancing beneath the street lamps, and switched on the tree lights. Sitting cross-legged on the carpet in front of my remaining gifts, I reached for Helga's and tore open the newspaper. Inside was a Russian doll. It looked old, as though it had passed through the hands of a thousand little girls. I opened her up and there inside was a sister, smaller, but the same. Then another. And another. I lined up all five on the mantelpiece and wondered how safe it would feel to be one of them. OK, I guessed, so long as you weren't the one on the outside. The eldest always takes the biggest knocks.

When the buzzer sounded I was expecting to find a group of carol singers rattling a charity bucket on the doorstep. It's that kind of neighbourhood. Instead of releasing the catch from the intercom, I went downstairs and answered the front door myself. I doubted any major criminals would be planning much in the way of pillaging tonight anyway. Opening the door to an empty space, my first thought was that it was a cherry door-knocking prankster who'd been at the brandy butter, then I noticed the familiar figure standing out on the pavement looking up at my balcony.

'Rick?' It was warmer outside than I imagined but I pulled the shawl closer round my shoulders anyway. 'Aren't you supposed to be in Switzerland?'

'Changed my mind,' he called back from where he stood. 'Besides, a certain somebody just put a tiger in my tank.'

I knew exactly what he was talking about and felt a smile warm my face. 'He's a beauty, isn't he?'

'That's the wildest thing anyone's ever given me.'

'Haven't got one already, have you?' At this we both laughed. 'They've put your name up on the adoption board and you can visit him whenever you're feeling gloomy.'

'I haven't been to the zoo since I was a nipper.'

'Look,' I rubbed my arms and glanced around at the open door. 'Did you want to come in for a drink or something?'

'Nah.' Rick waved his hand awkwardly. 'Just dropped by to deliver your Christmas present. He pulled a fat cigar from his inside pocket, clipped the end off with the cutter he keeps on his keyring and lit it with a match. The flame burned high in the motionless air. Rick ambled to the kerb and casually leaned against the side of a small white van and knocked on the roof. 'All right, lads. She's in.' Two men got out of the van and started unloading a large box from the rear and manhandling it up the stairs. Rick winked at me. 'You're gonna love this. Trust me.'

'What is it?' I asked.

'It's a secret.' He laughed. 'You'd better go and tell them where you want it.' He pointed his cigar towards the open door with a big smile, but made no move to join me.

'In here, love?' The older of the two delivery men was clearly keen to put the load down as soon as possible. I nodded them into the sitting room and watched as one inspected the ceiling while the other pulled a Stanley knife from his pocket and sliced through the outer packing tape. Out of the huge carton came bundle after bundle of bubble wrap. The sort that's nice to tread on with bare feet. I couldn't for the life of me imagine what might lie inside. How very exciting. The younger chap went back outside, returned with a set of stepladders and, to my surprise, started taking down the light fitting in the middle of the ceiling rose.

'Erm.' I tried not to get in their way. 'Can I ask what you think you're doing?' The bloke up the ladder took no notice and left his senior to carefully pull away the final layers of cotton wrapping to reveal a tissue-thin swirling glass sculpture in muted colours of every shade. The man handled it as though it were a rare bird and gently raised it towards his colleague.

'Viennese,' he said approvingly. 'About three hundred years old. It's an original Lobmeyr.' The name meant nothing to me, but the pedigree behind it was as crystal clear as the rubine flowers that clung to the trembling structure. It was so delicate I couldn't bear to watch them inching it into position. Then I remembered Rick and rushed to the window. He was still there, standing in the street looking up at the windows of my flat, the smoke from his cigar hanging on the air. I rushed down the stairs.

'Rick! I can't possibly! Wherever did you find such a beautiful thing?' My hands rushed to my cheeks. I was already feeling emotionally unbalanced since my bathroom discovery that morning and wasn't sure I could take any more big surprises.

'Like it?' He puffed on his cigar and smiled at me. 'I thought you would. Picked it up while I was in Vienna. Remember? There was something about it that reminded me of you.'

'I love it. But you really shouldn't have! I don't know what to say.'

'It's yours,' he said. 'From me.' Rick pulled the cigar from his teeth and came closer. 'With love.' His smile faded. Then he leaned down and kissed me. I mean, really kissed me. The whole world stood still.

Before I could regain my senses, he released me and was gone, walking briskly away with his coat collar pulled up. 'Rick!' I shouted after him. He turned and waved at me briefly, then picked up pace towards the traffic lights at the end of the street, raised his arm and let out one of his shrieking taxi whistles. 'Rick!' I yelled to the disappearing shadow. 'Don't you want to come in and see it?' He couldn't hear me, and after all those mince pies, there was no way I could have caught him up.

The two delivery men appeared on the portico steps with their ladders and the discarded packaging from my present. I thanked them for coming out on Christmas Day and asked them to hang on a moment while I got them a little something, but the older of the two assured me that they had already been generously rewarded, wished me a merry Christmas and got back into the van. I suspect the younger one would have waited around for the second tip and kept schtum about the double bonus.

Retreating in a daze to the warmth of my central heating, I just managed to get to the ringing telephone before the answering machine kicked in. Snatching up the handset, I prayed that it was Rick. My head was spinning and I could find no logical explanation for what he had just done. That kiss, still burning on my lips and churning my insides. It was unlike anything I had ever felt before.

'Helen?' The line was bad. Julia's voice crackled with emotion.

'Julia? Is that you?' I glanced at the carriage clock, tried to get my head around the time difference and guessed it was probably nearing lunchtime where she was, although why that should have mattered I don't know. 'Is everything all right?'

'Yes,' she managed. 'I just wanted to wish you a happy Christmas.' There was a pregnant pause. 'And I have something important to tell you. I hope you're sitting down.'

My heart turned over. I stared at the piece of evidence that I'd salvaged from the bin that morning still lying on the coffee table. I knew it wasn't mine. It couldn't possibly have been Leoni's either, seeing as she'd had Marcus neutered shortly after Millie was born. I closed my eyes, not daring to hope.

'I don't know how to tell you this.' Julia's voice began to tremble. 'But it would appear that I'm going to have a baby. I couldn't tell you before. Or David. I'm so sorry for all the worry I caused. I needed to be sure.'

I couldn't help it. Nor could she. The pair of us cried so hard that we were unable to utter another word. We stayed on the line together for the longest time, holding hands through the ether, sisters.

With red eyes and an overwhelmed heart, I sat on the edge of my bed with Julia's gift. It was heavy for its size. Solid. I rested it on my lap, undid the ribbon and pulled the paper off. Inside was a casket, shaped like a small pirate's chest with a brass escutcheon on the front. A tiny golden key was hidden in one of the folds of the wrapping paper. I unlocked it and lifted the lid. The gasp that rushed from my throat was understandable. Among the glistening riches that lay within, the first piece that jumped out at me was the jewelled tortoiseshell comb. I lifted it out and admired it. After that came the rare set of Chinese amber ornaments, then more jewellery of breathtaking splendour and finally a small box. Inside that I found the one item that I was sure she had returned many years before – the magnificent engagement ring that Stan had placed on her finger at the top of the Eiffel Tower some twenty years earlier. I opened the tiny envelope she had secreted at the bottom of the casket and read the short note. *Darling Helen. You were right about everything. Treasure these gifts as I once did and remember what it is to be loved. J.*

I wandered to the bedroom window and pressed my cheek against the cold glass, staring out into the night. It had stopped snowing and the world outside had taken on the stillness of a picture postcard. There were lights on in most of the houses across the garden square, casting a golden glow over the furthest tree-tops. I thought about those people in their homes, some young, others old, doing the things that people do. I wondered who they were and what their lives might be. My fingers rose to my lips, resting against their softness. Looking down into the street below, a big silver car slid silently along, its tyres pressing long dark tracks into the white blanket, before coming to rest beneath my balcony. The door opened, and a hazy cloud of blue cigar smoke curled high up into the starry sky.

extracts reading groups
competitions books new
discounts extracts
competitions
books
new
events books
extracts
new reading groups
interviews
events extracts events
discounts
new books events
events new
discounts extracts discounts

www.panmacmillan.com

extracts events reading groups
competitions books extracts new

www.ingramcontent.com/pod-product-compliance
Lightning Source LLC
Chambersburg PA
CBHW020420030726
47495CB00006B/1593